Natasha Narayan was born in India but emigrated to England at the age of five. She has had many jobs in journalism including working as a war correspondent in Bosnia. Like Kit Salter, Natasha loves exploring new places. She hopes to see the Great Wall of China one day, probably by plane and bus rather than steamship and horse. She lives in Oxford.

❧ The Kit Salter Adventures by Natasha Narayan ❧

The Mummy Snatcher of Memphis
The Maharajah's Monkey
The Book of Bones

A Kit Salter Adventure

The Book of Bones

Natasha Narayan

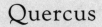
Quercus

First published in Great Britain in 2010 by

Quercus
21 Bloomsbury Square
London
WC1A 2NS

A CIP catalogue reference for this book is available
from the British Library

ISBN 978 1 84916 241 8

10 9 8 7 6 5 4 3 2 1

Designed and typeset by Rook Books, London
Printed and bound in Great Britain by Clays Ltd, St Ives plc

To Lulu, for all your kindness

UNITED KINGDOM
Oxford

EUROPE

ASIA

CHINA
Shanghai

Calcutta
INDIA

AFRICA

Malacca Straits

South China Sea

Atlantic Ocean

Indian Ocean

'The Mandalay'

N
W   E
S

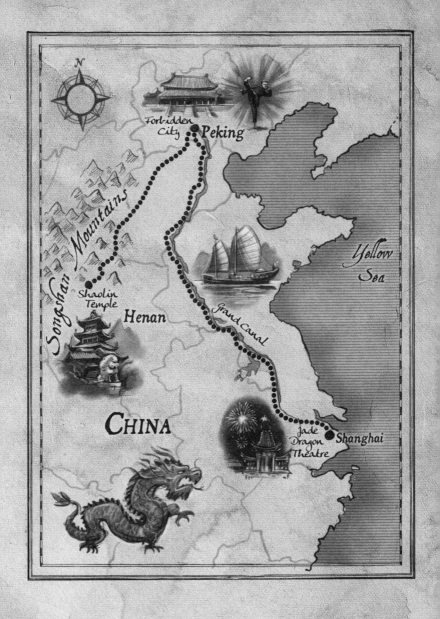

❧ Chapter One ❧

'Enemy advancing!' Waldo cried, leaning out of the window.

'Are you sure?'

'Carriage stopping. Lady in red hat getting out and approaching house. Ringing doorbell.'

As if on cue, the doorbell chimed.

'Right. Troops on standby.'

The front door slammed. We heard the faint murmur of conversation. My father's bleating voice mingled with that of a shrill female. Any moment now our new governess would walk into the classroom and demand to take over. We couldn't let this happen. As every schoolchild knows, teachers are a lot like puppies. They must be taught who is in charge, or all hell breaks loose.

Instead of 'puppy training' we had planned a spot of 'teacher training' for our new governess. All right, we were going to play some practical jokes on her. These tricks would show Mrs Glee who she was dealing with. First, we had balanced a bucket of water on top of the door. It was just waiting to topple down and splatter the woman as she entered the schoolroom. Second, a gold coin glittered on the floor. When Mrs Glee tried to pick it up, she would find it mysteriously stuck! Hopefully, she would become all flustered, not realising we had glued it to the floor. Best of all was the 'hat trick': a raw duck egg sewn into the lining of the new bonnet we had bought her as a present.

When our Mrs Glee put on the hat she would literally have egg all over her face.

Your friend Kit Salter had thought up the plan, but my allies Waldo and Isaac had taken it up enthusiastically. Indeed the egg was Isaac's idea. Everyone was behind the escapade, as we waited for my father and Mrs Glee to appear. Everyone but goody-two-shoes Rachel.

'Every time you do something like this it blows up in your face!' Rachel snapped, glaring at me. 'Why are you always so *childish*?'

'Perhaps because, *technically*, I am a child,' I snapped back, while Isaac and Waldo grinned sympathetically at me.

Rachel was playing her familiar role of wet blanket, her face as sour as an old lemon. She was overreacting, as usual. The tricks we'd planned to welcome Mrs Glee to 8 Park Town, Oxford, were harmless enough. Just a few jolly jokes.

I don't want you to think we were being cruel. Hard

experience has taught me that I 'learn' better without a governess. Our last teacher, a Miss Minchin, had left us to become engaged to the younger son of a baronet. My heart had leaped at the news. I thought I would be rid of all those boring attempts to turn me into a nice young lady. Plus lessons. I have never been all that keen on lessons.

I would be free. Gloriously free! At liberty to gallop about on my mare Jesse, have adventures and generally 'educate' myself. Instead disaster struck. My father, Professor Theodore Salter, insisted we have a new governess. Luckily, I had been able to sit in on the interviews and dismiss all the candidates so far, for one reason or another. Finally, he had lost his patience. He proclaimed that if we didn't accept this Mrs Glee, who was due to arrive any moment now, we would all be packed off to boarding school.

Boarding school was impossible. For a start you had to get up before dawn – and the food was said to be worse than prison.

So I had to think on my feet. Of course, Rachel warned, we would be punished, but I wasn't worried. Usually poor Father threatens us with various horrible punishments – and then he is so absent-minded he simply forgets.

We heard a footfall on the landing. The dreaded governess-to-be had arrived.

'Enter the dragon.' I muttered. 'Everyone ready?'

'Aye, aye, sir,' said Waldo, with a mock salute.

'Then let the games begin.'

Our tormentor appeared on the threshold. The sight gave me pause. Anyone less like a dragon than the grey-haired person chattering to Papa I could not imagine. Mrs Glee was a tiny old thing, at least forty years old, dressed in widow's weeds, who was drifting towards us like a wisp of thistledown. Everything, from the faded red bonnet she carried, to the monocle she wore dangling around her neck, suggested genteel poverty. Her watery blue eyes exuded meekness. She was probably the relict of a vicar, I decided. I am a good judge of people, and there and then I decided she was a gentle, dreamy poppet.

'How lovely to meet you,' the lady trilled out as she glimpsed the four of us sitting at our desks. 'I'm Vera Glee. But you can call me Vera, dears, for I don't like to stand on ceremony.'

'Call her Vera?' Who'd ever heard of calling a teacher by their first name?

As she advanced to the half-open door, I had an awful vision of the bucket crashing down on her head. We had made a dreadful mistake. This old lady looked too frail for jokes. We might knock her out. She might need a doctor, or to be rushed to hospital. Even *my* father would remember to punish us if we actually *killed* our new governess.

'STOP!' I yelled, rising from my seat.

Too late. Father pushed open the door for Mrs Glee and, forgetting that it is 'ladies first', advanced into our schoolroom. I froze as the bucket fell from its perch, just missing the side of his head. A stream of water poured over his hair.

'Kit!' he bleated, looking up at the ceiling. 'It's raining indoors.'

'It's . . . er . . . the leak in the roof,' I said, desperately running to them, while Waldo and Isaac jumped up and tried to hide the bucket.

'But it's not raining outside,' he replied, glancing out of the window. Father is one of the cleverest men in England, if you want an opinion about the Petrarchan sonnet. Sometimes he's also reasonably sharp.

'Drains must be blocked,' Waldo jumped in.

'Must get that old oak chopped down,' Father muttered, while Rachel, who had grabbed a towel from the basin, dabbed at his sodden jacket.

Mrs Glee had walked into the schoolroom and was peering dreamily at the gold sovereign glittering in the middle of the floor. She looked as if she had spotted a rainbow. Really the coin looked very inviting, gleaming on the bare boards.

'Professor Salter,' she said, 'someone seems to have dropped a great deal of money.'

Father wandered over to join her and peered down. 'Must be one of mine,' he said. Then he bent over and picked it up.

Or rather he didn't.

'Kit,' he bleated again. 'This coin is very strange.'

Exchanging glances with Waldo I strode over to help him. 'It seems to be stuck,' I said.

'Sovereigns aren't sticky.'

'There must be some . . .'

'I dropped some glue earlier,' Isaac interrupted. 'All a bit of a mix-up I'm afraid.'

Father straightened up, suddenly wincing with pain. 'Oh no, I've put my back out again.'

Meanwhile Mrs Glee had wandered over to the desk and spotted the large paper box, decorated with a red bow, which we had placed on her desk. She read the card attached to it and smiled with delight.

'A present for me!' she fluted. 'I do declare, you are the kindest, most thoughtful children I've ever met.'

Beaming, she untied the ribbons and opened the box. I had a sinking feeling in the pit of my stomach as Mrs Glee unwrapped the layers of tissue paper. How could I explain it away to Father, when Mrs Glee had egg running down her face? Even he would smell a rat.

The sheer awfulness of my behaviour struck me, like a blow to the head. If I were someone else, I wouldn't think much of Kit Salter. I would judge her to be headstrong, childish, thoughtless and sometimes, yes, even a bit of a bully.

Why do I never consider the consequences of my actions? I was filled with shame as my eyes locked on the new straw bonnet. It was decorated with artificial silk pansies and violets and skewered with a jewelled hatpin. Really pretty, if you like that sort of thing.

Mrs Glee clearly did, for her face glowed with happiness.

'My angels,' she gasped, overcome with emotion. 'I don't know what to say. You've made me very –'

'May I take a look?' I barged in and held my hand out for the hat. I had to take it away and somehow remove the egg. But Father had already picked it up, while Mrs Glee tenderly lofted the jewelled hatpin.

'This is very generous of you children,' he proclaimed, lifting it up in the air. 'Thoroughly decent.'

'Professor! No!' Waldo blurted.

For a moment Father looked as if he was about to absent-mindedly try on the hat. Oh heavens, I thought, visions of egg yolk running down Papa's sodden and dirt-streaked face. (The water in the bucket had not been entirely clean.) But luckily he handed the bonnet back to

Mrs Glee who tried it on, placing it well forward on her forehead, poking the hatpin through the straw.

Rachel screamed.

I watched in fascinated horror as the egg cracked and a dark dribble ran down her forehead. Isaac and Waldo were gazing at her open-mouthed. We had plotted for this moment, but somehow it was awful, not funny, as we'd expected.

Rachel continued to scream, a shrill note in her voice. 'Blood . . . It's blood!'

'Pull yourself together,' I hissed in her ear. 'It's egg.'

'Hard boiled.' Rachel said. 'I changed it for a hard boiled egg.'

Rachel's screams had finally attracted attention. Mrs Glee blinked at Rachel. Her hand flew up to her forehead and dabbed. Drawing her fingers away, she held them up to the light. They were dripping wet. She looked at them as if they belonged to someone else, as if she had never seen her own fingers before.

'Heavens!' she said in surprise. 'My hands are quite bloody.'

An invisible claw reached out and grabbed my throat, causing me to choke. I felt awful. Now I could see what had happened, but it was still truly puzzling. Mrs Glee had pushed the new jewelled hatpin right *through* the straw bonnet. She had literally pushed it *into* her head. I could see the wound where the pin had entered the side of her forehead.

There was something terribly wrong here, for it should have hurt like the blazes. Mrs Glee should have been screaming. But clearly she didn't feel a thing.

Either our new governess was the strongest, bravest person I've ever met. Or something very odd was going on here.

'Mrs Glee,' I said, 'I think you'd better lie down. I'll show you to your room.'

My handkerchief was scarlet by the time we reached the room where Mrs Glee was to live. It was a charming chamber, light and airy, furnished with a lace bedspread, a chest of drawers and a rosewood desk. Our governess twittered her appreciation and then suddenly announcing that she was feeling a little breathless, sank onto the bed.

'Do you mind finding my medicine, dear? It's in the valise.' She pointed to a small leather case, which the maid had brought up. I rummaged around and found several bottles, which I drew out. Each time, however, Mrs Glee shook her head. Finally, I found a small, glass-stoppered vial, full of a reddish-brown tincture. I could see the relief in my governess's eyes as I handed it to her.

'A little water, my dear. I am absolutely parched.'

I poured her a glass and handed it to her. Taking the vial with eager hands, she put a few drops from the stopper into the water and then, as it went muddy, gulped the liquid down. She had sunk back against the fluffy white pillows piled on her bed, gazing blankly at the ceiling. Her pupils had contracted to tiny black pinpoints. She seemed to have forgotten that I was there.

'Mrs Glee?'

There was no answer. As she'd collapsed she'd placed her dirty boots on the bedspread. It shocked me, to see the smear of mud on the clean white lace.

'Please, um, Vera. Can I go now?'

With an effort, Mrs Glee switched her eyes away from whatever was happening on the ceiling. She smiled at me, her expression full of sweet sadness.

'You mustn't be frightened of me, Kitty dear,' she said. 'I suffer from stomach pains and my medicine gives me a bit of a turn, is all. You run along now. I'll be there in a few minutes.'

Something was gnawing at me as I rushed back to the schoolroom. Remorse, you might think. Well, yes. The practical jokes seemed very foolish now. But it was another emotion altogether, something more frightening.

I hadn't liked the way Mrs Glee's gaze slid out of focus. The way she sprawled on the bed, like a broken puppet. Worst of all were her eyes. The memory of her vanishing pupils made me turn cold.

Her eyes were somehow not human; they were like marbles, not windows to a soul. In the few seconds after she'd downed that liquid, something had grabbed our new teacher and spirited her away from us.

❧ Chapter Two ❧

'I agree with Rachel,' Waldo said as we talked things over a few days later. 'You're wasting your time worrying about Mrs Glee. Who ever heard of worrying about a *teacher*, anyway?'

'There's something broken about her,' I mumbled. 'I think she needs our help.'

I had been trying to explain my fears about Mrs Glee, but none of my friends shared my anxiety.

'You're a mystery, Kit,' Rachel said, with a withering look. 'You're terribly silly most of the time. Then, out of the blue, you get all het up about the most bizarre things. I'd thought you might have grown up a bit, after what happened in India. But it seems –' she stopped mid-sentence her eyes lingering on my scar.

There was an awkward silence. I hadn't told anyone what really took place in the icy mountains of the Himalayas, when I'd become separated from my friends and stumbled like a sleepwalker on the legendary paradise of Shambala. The whole journey seemed so long ago, so dreamlike. Sometimes I would wake up in the night feeling sad, but not quite knowing why. Then I would remember our friend Gaston Champlon, the legendary French explorer, who had been buried by an avalanche. He was infuriating and charming in equal measure, the only man alive who could make my Aunt Hilda blush. We owed him our lives. We would never see him again. All that remained of our ill-fated voyage to India was the scar on my cheek. Thankfully, it had faded quickly. Much faster in fact than seemed possible. Our doctor had expressed surprise. Still the marks of a tiger's claw could still be faintly seen in the scar.

'Mrs Glee's in some sort of trouble. I just know it,' I said, changing the subject back to our governess.

'If she is, it's down to you,' Rachel snapped. 'Practical jokes are hardly the way to make someone feel welcome.'

I hung my head. Our failures with the bucket and sovereign had dented my spirit. It was the end, I had decided, of my life as a practical joker. In case you are wondering, I *did* manage to remove the (hard-boiled) duck egg from the bonnet, and our lessons had proceeded without mishap. Well, there had been a few hiccups. The second day with Mrs Glee, I had been dismayed to see our new timetable chalked up on the blackboard:

6 a.m. Prep

7–7.30 Breakfast

8–9 Copy Books

9–10.15 Arithmetic

10.15–10.30 Break

10.30–11.30 History (with special emphasis
on important dates)

11.30–11.45 Break

11.45–12.45 p.m. Latin

12.45–1 Poems

1–1.45 Dinner

1.45–2.45 Rest (walking using backboard
for the girls. Bible study and reading
aloud from Sir Walter Scott for the boys)

2–3.15 Mental arithmetic test

'Not a backboard!' Rachel gasped, sounding horrified.

Mrs Glee smiled gently. 'I can't abide slouching.'

'What *is* a backboard?' I asked.

Mrs Glee had produced a piece of wood with hooks
at the side for arms. I recalled, dimly, what it was. Back-
boards were invented to make girls stand up straight –

but truly they were instruments of torture.

'You really will find it most useful,' she beamed. 'It will do such a lot of good for your chances.'

I didn't need to ask what Mrs Glee meant by 'chances' – marriage was clearly what she had in mind for us girls. She meant to be kind, as really she was a good-natured lady. It was just that she had rather old-fashioned ideas about things. A black gloom descended on me.

'You've rather the wrong idea, Mrs Glee,' I said, gently. 'We're used to a bit more time for . . . general education. My father – the professor – believes –'

'Does he, Kitty?' she said vaguely. 'I must ask him about it. In the meantime, kindly turn to page forty-two in your Pliny. Now, do sit up straight, dear.'

Even Waldo had been anxious that our lives would become, well, more difficult. It didn't turn out that way though. Although Mrs Glee's intentions were strict, she tended to be rather erratic. She would often disappear to 'the powder room' or 'have a funny turn'. Sometimes I thought it was even easier to pull the wool over Mrs Glee's eyes than my own father's. Which is why today, as she had disappeared for a good three-quarters of an hour, I was fretting. There was an oddness, now and then, in Mrs Glee's green eyes. A look almost of despair. Sometimes her face was so strained that the wrinkles on it stood out like raised veins. I had tried gently to ask her if anything was wrong. But she had just smiled and talked of her stomach.

I thought it was more serious than that. I feared that she was dying.

'I've remembered what the bottle was – you know, that I saw her swig,' I said. 'It had Sydenham's printed on it.'

'I know that tincture,' said Waldo. 'It's perfectly harmless, Kit. Soothes pain or something like that.'

Isaac had burst out laughing. 'Did it say Tinctura Opii on it?' he asked.

'Something like that.' I nodded.

'You really are a silly goose,' he said. 'Mrs Glee is taking laudanum is all.'

'What is laudanum?'

'Opium mixed with alcohol. Perfectly harmless, I believe. Used to relieve indigestion and stomach pains and aches of all sorts. I believe they even give it to babies.'

'But isn't opium a vile drug?' I asked. Vague images flashed through my mind: smoky opium dens, Chinamen with long clay pipes, emaciated artists. I had heard of many artists and writers who took it, and tales of those who became slaves to the drug and even died from it. Fear took hold.

'Opium is terrible,' Isaac said, trying to sound knowing. 'But laudanum is a sort of medicine.'

Rachel wasn't listening. She had pulled out her pocket

mirror and was studying herself in the glass. I noticed she had curled her hair in a new way, so glossy ringlets cascaded over her ears. Pretty, I suppose, but hadn't she anything better to do than gaze so lovingly at her own reflection? She may accuse me of being childish, but my best friend had changed. She was always mooning about over dresses and ribbons. Yesterday I caught her applying beetroot to her lips to make them redder! The final straw was when I saw her drooling over a pair of peach satin dancing slippers. Shoes, for pity's sake! The infatuated look on her face made me think I was really losing my friend.

Sometimes, I thought that as we grew up Rachel and I were becoming strangers. She was turning into one of *them*. If you don't know what I mean, you're probably one of *them* too!

'Rachel,' I barked, just to make her start.

'Sorry.' She instantly slipped the mirror back under the desk. 'I'm just wondering how to arrange my hair for Miss Minchin's wedding.'

The boys and I exchanged gloomy looks. Rachel might be excited about our former governess's wedding to the Hon. Charles Prinsep, but the rest of us were dreading it. I was looking forward to the ceremony, in the baronet's ancestral castle on Dartmoor, about as much as having a tooth pulled out with a pair of pliers. I would have to wear a flouncy peach gown for the ball, which Waldo said made me look like a 'turnip in frills'.

Of course Rachel looked lovely in her gown.

The door opened and Mrs Glee appeared. Her cheeks were flushed, little red spots standing high on the wrinkled white skin. Her eyes had a hectic glitter.

'Good news, my dears,' she announced with a smile. 'No lessons today!'

'Fantastic!' I blurted, with visions of taking Jesse for a canter on Port Meadow.

'Instead we're going to brush up our etiquette for Miss Minchin's wedding. I want you *all* to be a credit to me.'

A deep sigh went around the room. Lessons might be bad, but learning manners was worse. Far worse.

❧ Chapter Three ❧

'Would you do me the honour of the first waltz?' A young man stood on the edge of the dance floor and made me a courtly bow. He was quite handsome, I suppose, in his bow tie and tails. But there was something rather too intense about him, with his flushed face and shining eyes. We were at Miss Minchin's engagement ball at her fiancée's castle. Merriford, set on the bleak sweep of Dartmoor, was more used to the whistle of gales than this sparkling society throng.

'No, thank you,' I said firmly, moving my peach taffeta skirts back against the wall. 'We're only here to watch.'

But the young man seemed not to hear. He held out his hand towards me, with another bow.

'Look, I don't mean to be rude, sir,' I snapped. 'It's just we're not interested in dancing.'

The young man was clearly an idiot. He was gazing at me, a dazzled expression on his face. Strange, for I didn't look *that* wonderful. Then I glanced at him and realised that *I* was invisible. He was actually looking past me, towards Rachel. And she was gazing, or do I mean *swooning*, back at him.

'Stop,' I said stepping between them. 'This won't do.'

He held out his hand for Rachel's dance book, an elaborate gold one with ruby tassels, and I saw the page was already full of appointments. Rachel was glowing, her lovely face peeping out above her white lace collar. The ball had scarcely started before her first admirer had crawled out of the woodwork. I didn't like it at all. There was something odd about the young man. Besides, Mrs Glee had been quite clear, Father had said we weren't meant to dance – only to observe.

'I'm afraid *she* can't dance either,' I said firmly.

'Can't or won't?' the young man asked, gazing at her. Rachel flushed, pink flaming up her neck till it reached her ears. Annoyingly she looked even more beautiful.

'Oh, Kit, be reasonable. I'm sure Mrs Glee won't mind if I dance this waltz. You know I love waltzes.' With that Rachel let the young man take her hand and sweep her away onto the dance floor. It was a pretty sight, the gas lamps flaring and the women blazing in gowns as vivid as a thousand tulips. Hot, though. I was already sweating under my corset. An ice would cool me down. I turned, intending to skirt past the dancers into the refreshment room, and bumped smack into Waldo.

Isaac and Waldo were standing together, grinning. With a sinking heart I realised they must have witnessed the whole scene.

'I suppose I had better dance with you, Kit,' Waldo smirked. 'Before you go making a fool of yourself again.'

'As a special favour, I'll dance with you too, Kit. Though I'd rather be home with my chemistry equipment,' Isaac said. 'We've all got to do our bit to save you from more embarrassment.'

'I'm not dancing with anyone,' I snarled. 'Certainly not with one of you clowns. Anyway, Isaac, shouldn't you be looking after Rachel? She *is* your sister.'

Isaac glanced at Rachel. 'I think she can look after herself,' he grinned.

Sighing, I sidled away from my friends. Give me an ice before a boy any day. The daintier treats were always popular at parties. It was wise to get in quick before the rush, else you could end up disappointed. I had no love of Cornish pasties or the bony ends of fowl. But with a rough tug, Waldo had taken my hand and pulled me into the crush of dancers.

'Waldo, what are you doing?' I gasped, when I could get a word in. It was hard for there was such a press of bodies.

'Keeping you out of mischief,' Waldo smiled, looking down at me.

My heart was beating disturbingly. Waldo steered me firmly through the crush. I pulled away, but found that he was stronger than me. I glared at him but he smiled straight back at me, his blue eyes infuriatingly smug. Nice eyes – though I would never let Waldo know I thought so.

What could I do? I didn't want to make a scene, so I had no choice but to submit and let Waldo trundle me around the dance floor. After a few minutes I found, to my surprise, that it was actually quite pleasant. Waldo was a better dancer than I'd imagined, his guidance strong and firm. He didn't tread on my feet or breathe on my face. My thoughts slid above the throng as my feet broke free.

'Kit,' Waldo was grinning down at me. I realised with a start that my feet were still moving, though everyone else seemed to have stopped. 'The dance is over.'

'Oh.'

'That wasn't so bad, was it?'

I shrugged. 'Better than Mademoiselle Blanche's dancing school, I suppose.'

'Oh, come on, Kit, you loved it.'

'What girl wouldn't be honoured to dance with *you*?'

Frowning, Waldo steered me back to my place, where the girls were huddled by the wall waiting for young men to ask them to dance. Well, *I* wouldn't be a wallflower.

If I had to go to this ball I might as well do something. I was just about to suggest to Waldo that we take another turn around the dance floor, this time to a lively polka, when I noticed someone was desperately trying to catch his eye. She was a blonde girl, with perfect ringlets, pale blue eyes and a little rosebud mouth. Quite pretty, I suppose, but I have to confess I took an instant dislike to her. There was something so sugar-*sweet* about her.

'I see you have an admirer,' I snapped.

'Hardly an admirer.' Waldo laughed. 'Just Emily.'

'*Who* is Emily?'

But Waldo did not answer my question. Instead he said abruptly, 'Look, Kit, you don't mind if I skip this dance, do you?' Then he was off, scurrying over to Emily, whose face was alight with pleasure.

I turned away. I wasn't going to stand about watching as Waldo trampled Emily all over the dance floor. Anyway Mrs Glee had just arrived, and I was sure she would forbid us all to dance. After all, my father had said we had to 'be a credit to him'. But to my dismay she took one look at Rachel and the wavy-haired young man, another look at Waldo and Emily and promptly vanished.

Feeling a little sulky, I brushed off Isaac's suggestion that we do the polka together. Isaac, I am sure, would murder my toes, for his mind would be full of his current experiment – making a bomb out of cake ingredients. He seemed delighted with my suggestion that we locate the ices instead, so we left the ballroom.

I was a little upset with Waldo, for we were meant to be friends and yet he had deserted me at the first sight of a simpering Emily. But the ices cooled me down. I had three helpings. One a delicious melting pink concoction flavoured with rosewater, another vanilla-ish, and a third which was a mystery. Isaac swore it was rum, but I have never drunk the sailor's tipple and I'm pretty sure he hasn't either.

I returned to the ballroom alone, for Isaac could not be torn away from the refreshments. My mood soured when I saw that Waldo was dancing with Emily again, this time a slower waltz. They were quite making exhibitions of themselves, for Emily seemed to be whispering in his ear. Anyway, I leaned against the wall frowning and a moment later Miss Minchin – soon to be Mrs or even Lady Prinsep – stopped.

This beaming person was such a different creature to the thin-lipped governess who had come to our house all those years ago.

'Dear Kit.' She beamed. 'Let life into your heart.'

'Pardon?' I asked, taken aback.

'You're not a boy,' she said. 'I know you want to be one. But, Kit, you're a girl. Be lovely.'

'Being lovely is hardly an occupation.'

'Oh, it is,' she beamed. 'It's jolly hard work.'

I backed away, for there was a gooeyness about her that made me uneasy. For one ghastly moment I even thought she was going to embrace me. Luckily her groom-to-be called to her and she was lost in the ball gowns. The next thing I knew, Waldo was standing next to me, frowning.

'Something is up, Kit,' he said.

'I beg your pardon?' I replied, a little coldly.

'It's Emily. She says Mrs Glee is not what she seems.'

'What on earth does she mean?'

'It's odd, Kit. I don't like it.'

'Spit it out.'

'Emily claims that Mrs Glee is not Mrs Glee at all. She says she recognised her at once. She's a Mrs Dougal and she was their housekeeper till she disappeared last summer. There was some mystery about it, but Emily never found out what really happened.'

'So?'

'Thing is, some valuable cufflinks vanished at the same time.'

I was perturbed, for it was an odd tale. But then I thought of the blinking, simpering Emily and felt doubtful. Who did I trust? Mrs Glee, who was thoughtful and had our best interests at heart, despite her illness. Or the conniving Emily?

'I'm surprised you believe what Emily tells you,' I shrugged. 'She has obviously forgotten her spectacles.'

'Emily doesn't wear spectacles,' he replied.

'Of course not.'

'What do you mean?'

'Sheer vanity. Emily is so short-sighted she can't see beyond the end of her nose. If she had her spectacles on she would know she'd never met Mrs Glee before. Instead she makes up a story to try to impress—'

Without waiting for me to finish my sentence Waldo flashed me a disgusted look and walked away.

❧ Chapter Four ❧

It was a cheerless day to travel, the wind howling off
Dartmoor, buffeting the coach that was taking us back
to Oxford. A storm was blowing up and soon a few fat
droplets began to splatter against the windows. The track
leading off the moor past the small country villages was
rough, full of potholes that jerked us about till our bones
ached. I pitied Hodges, our genial coach driver, sitting on
his perch high above the horses. He was exposed to the
full fury of the elements. Even more, though, did I pity
the four poor beasts. Already their bridles were lathered
in froth.

Mrs Glee had decided we would travel from Merriford
House back to Oxford by coach, even though the train
was so much more convenient. I had tried to argue but
she had made up her mind. I suspected, frail as she was,
she was frightened of train travel. So here we all were,
cold, crushed together and jolted. Huddled between
Rachel and Isaac I recalled the old legends that told of
great beasts that roamed the moor, of highwaymen

who preyed on unguarded travellers. I shivered a little. But I got no sympathy from my friends. Indeed the atmosphere inside the coach was as thick as fog. I could have choked on the dark looks, misunderstandings and ill humour wafting around. Both Waldo and Rachel were furious with your friend Kit Salter, and had declared they would never speak to me again. Rachel had been especially hurtful.

'You know what your problem is, Kit?' she had spat. 'Apart from being downright domineering, of course. Jealousy. Don't look so surprised. J.E.A.L.O.U.S.Y. You don't like your friends having other friends. You want to be number one the whole time.'

The silence in the coach left me plenty of time to reflect on Rachel's words. Uncomfortably, I had to admit that there might be some small element of truth in what she was saying. But minuscule. Really very small. Truly!

As neither Waldo nor Rachel was talking to me, and Isaac was lost in his own (possibly explosive) thoughts, I turned to Mrs Glee, who was crocheting a hideous pink bonnet.

'Merriford House was splendid,' I said. 'So gloomy. All that wind whistling down the chimneys.'

'Lovely,' she agreed, with a vacant smile. 'I'm so happy for Miss Minchin. Marrying a baronet's son. Usually sweet fortune does not smile upon poor governesses.'

There was a wistful look in her green eyes as she said this. I wanted to take her hand and squeeze it to give her a little courage. Life, I guessed, had not been kind to Mrs Glee. You could see her own misfortunes in the lines on her face and in the anxiety with which she greeted everything. She did try, our poor new governess, but she just wasn't strong enough for this world.

I had never found out about Mr Glee. I was tempted to try a little probing.

'Do you miss Mr Glee very much?' I asked.

To my surprise she went rigid.

'Why?'

'Sorry?'

'Why do you ask?'

'I just wondered. I thought –'

Mrs Glee was biting her lip 'He was a brute, Kitty, a brute.'

I didn't know what to say. This conversation wasn't going as I'd imagined. She sounded so fierce.

'I didn't know,' I muttered lamely.

'Not a day goes by, not a single day, when I don't give thanks that I am rid of him.'

There was silence after this. The four horses pulling our coach laboured in front of us. All that could be heard was their panting and snorting and the fierce whoosh of the wind outside. I was wearing a thick navy travelling cloak over my serge dress, but I was still chilled. Inside and out. There were so many mysteries about our new governess – her anger as well as her suffering. Everything seemed to make her fearful. Why had Mrs Glee turned down the quick and modern train? Dark shapes loomed against the grey darkness of the moor. Wind-blasted trees, the occasional wretched cottage. I wondered that the horses were able to canter so fast, avoiding potholes in the dusk.

The coach stopped with a jolt. Rachel was thrown against Waldo and screeched. Isaac's glasses fell off as the horses began to neigh, a high terrifying sound. Odd noises were louder in the silence of the moor: the driver Hodges shouting, the crack of a whip and then another deep voice intermingled with scuffling. I peered through the window but could see only dark shapes through the smudgy pane.

'What's up?' I yelped, leaping into action. 'Hodges?'

'Stand back.' Waldo pushed me down.

'Highwaymen!' Isaac shrieked.

'It's nothing, you booby!' Waldo snapped. 'Probably just some drunk on the track.'

Mrs Glee was the only one not caught up in the commotion. She had retreated from everything into her crocheting, ignoring the horses' frenzied neighing and the lurching of the coach. Waldo was struggling now with the door handle but quite unable to open it.

'Let me have a go.' I said. 'You have to twist it this way.'

Sighing, Mrs Glee put down her crochet. 'I doubt that will do any good.'

'What?' We stopped and stared at her.

'I am sorry, children. The door is locked.'

Both Waldo and I were frantically tugging at the door. It was certain now that there was something more than an ale-sodden peasant on the track out there. A sharp crack outside brought us to a stop. A second bang rent the air, followed by a moment's deep silence.

Gunshots.

'I locked the carriage door for your own safety, Kit and Waldo. I really don't want you to get hurt,' Mrs Glee murmured.

'Open it at once.' I exploded. 'There's a highwayman out there.'

'I'm so, so sorry about this.'

'She's raving, Waldo. Smash the windowpane.'

But Waldo had already taken off his shoe and was thwacking hard at the glass with the wooden heel. Once. No effect. Twice. The glass still held.

'Hurry,' I yelled, for the noises outside were disturbing. 'Look, I'll smash it.'

Waldo shoved me away and bashed with all his might. A thin crack split the pane and at the fourth blow it shattered. Waldo was about to put his head through the jagged hole when something appeared at the window. A face. It was of perfect plump roundness, framed by a fringe of blond hair at top and bottom. At first glance friendly. Except for the malice in the piggy eyes and something nasty in the way the glistening rosebud lips were pouting.

''Allo, Vera,' the man said.

Mrs Glee put her crochet on her lap and looked at the man. 'So you're here, Bert.'

'Always on time,' Bert said. 'You know me.'

'Go easy on them, Bert.' Her hands, those wrinkled hands holding the crochet, were trembling. Her face, though, was calm.

'Orders is orders,' Bert shrugged. 'No loose ends.'

The rest of us watched this strange conversation in confusion, for things were happening too fast. Rachel screeched suddenly and Mrs Glee frowned.

'Quiet, please,' she said. 'For your own good, be quiet.'

'What's happening?' Rachel gasped. 'Who are you?'

'It doesn't matter. I'm nobody.'

'Mrs Glee?!'

'I beg you to listen to Bert. It will be better for *all* of us if you do.'

I had never been so bewildered in my life. Mrs Glee was clearly frightened, I could see that in the trembling of her hands and the tautness of her face. But other things were wrong. She knew this thug, Bert. Were they trying to kidnap us? Waldo's Emily had been right. There was something twisted out of shape about Mrs Glee. Never mind that now, I had to act.

'I'm sorry too,' I said, bunching my hand into a fist.

I thwacked Mrs Glee with all my might as Waldo picked up a piece of glass and held it to her throat.

'Call off your men,' I snapped, pinioning her arms. 'Or Waldo will cut your throat.'

Mrs Glee was shivering uncontrollably. 'Stop it, stop it! Please. Someone will get hurt.'

'Put the glass down, Waldo,' I hissed.

'No chance.' Waldo barked, his hand quivering at Mrs Glee's throat.

'He has a gun.' I said quietly.

Waldo turned and saw Bert's pistol, pointed straight at Rachel's head. In a flash it was all over. Mrs Glee stood up and handed something through the window to Bert. He took the key and unlocked the carriage door and then was inside, bringing a rank stench of sweat, grease and gin with him.

'Room for one more?' he grunted as he heaved his lumbering body into the carriage. Squashed up as we were, we had no choice. The villain sat massive on the bench. The gun lay limp in a fat paw. I saw Waldo eyeing it, but signalled him no. It wasn't worth taking a chance now, for this was a desperate game.

'The driver?' Mrs Glee asked the thug.

'He's out.'

'We bringing him along?'

'Don't you worry your soft little head about that. Your business is done.'

'Please be—!'

'Shut up.' Bert closed his eyes. I could see him looking at us through his sandy lashes.

Were they talking about our coach driver, Hodges? The gentlest of men with horses, or indeed anything on four legs. Was he even now struggling, bound, in a ditch, bleeding? Or worse, surely they wouldn't have murdered him?

'You'd better not have hurt him,' I burst out. 'My father will kill you if you've harmed Hodges.'

The carriage rumbled off. The horses whimpered and neighed, accompanied by the brutal crack of the whip.

'What is this?' Waldo spat, his eyes red in a furious white face. 'Who are you? What are you doing with us?'

'Questions, questions.' Bert smiled, while Mrs Glee sat whey-faced.

'If you're hoping for a ransom, forget it. Our parents aren't rich.'

Bert grinned as though this was a huge joke. 'Bit of a

long day,' he murmured. 'If any one of you pesky brats opens your mouth again, I'll cuff you.' A set of handcuffs had appeared in his hands, along with the pistol.

I hoped that something, anything, would happen to save us from this gang. Perhaps the horses would stumble and overturn the carriage, perhaps someone would stop us and prevent whatever dark business was afoot. I glanced over the faces of my friends, shadowy in the gloom of the coach. Rachel, sucking her lower lip. Isaac, pale as chalk. Waldo, eyes glittering with fury. We had to wait, watch, be patient, and when it came, seize our chance.

Bert seemed to read my mind. He turned to me, his eyeballs barely visible between two rolls of fat. Plump lips opened and a blob of spittle just missed my feet. Shuddering, I sank back in my seat and felt Waldo's hand gripping my arm. Stay strong, he seemed to be signalling. If we could only be alert, surely our chance to escape would come?

❧ Chapter Five ❧

Rough hands shook my shoulders. Despite my best intentions, I must have dozed off because a lantern was dazzling me. Someone trod on my foot. Hands pulled me up and we were led out of the coach. I looked around wildly, but could see little as it was a night for nothing but owls and wolves. Underfoot was wet sand. Dimly I spied the outlines of three men.

One of them raised the lantern and a pool of oily light spread out about us. We were on a beach stretching for miles. Above us loomed ebony shapes, a denser black against the moonless night. I could not tell if they were cliffs or hills. The distant shriek of a gull and the lap of water was all that could be heard apart from the muffled commands of the men.

'Get in,' one of them snapped. A small but sturdy rowing boat was moored on the sand. Mrs Glee was already comfortably seated in the prow and now Rachel and Isaac were herded in. I felt Bert prodding me in the back with the gun and I hastily clambered over the side with Waldo scrambling after me.

'Where are we going?' Rachel asked. With a pang I remembered that this wasn't the first time she had been kidnapped.

'Boating,' Bert replied.

'Good one, Lips,' a thug hollered.

The men laughed, as if he had made a witty remark. But Mrs Glee looked upset. I stared at Bert with loathing. His nickname was quite apt. I could see his pouting lips, moist enough to make one shudder.

The thugs began to row. Vigorous strokes, moving us quickly through the water. Thoughts of hurling myself overboard flitted through my mind. But I dismissed them quickly. No doubt the men would shoot. Even if it was difficult to hit me in the darkness, my travelling cloak and heavy dress would weigh me down. I am a good swimmer, but I would surely drown.

Who had captured us in this violent fashion? Of course it could have been a random act. The action of a kidnapper hungry for some bounty he imagined our parents would pay. But there had been such organisation in the whole trap. First Mrs Glee had wormed her way into our home as a governess, then she had organised it so we would travel the lonely moors with only a driver for protection. Yes, there was something deeper, more sinister, in this web of violence.

I could think of only two men who would wish us such harm. We had tangled twice with those reclusive millionaires the Baker Brothers. The first time, in the Egyptian adventure, I had thwarted the Brothers' plan to steal a manuscript of immense age and wisdom – thought to be the oldest book in the world. As a result of their wickedness, ancient forces had cursed them with a mysterious and disfiguring skin illness – 'the mummy bite'.

More recently we had come across the Brothers in India. They had been involved in theft, kidnapping and the murder of a Maharajah, as well as the quest for the fabled elixir of immortality. I had kept quiet about my meeting with the Brothers in the very highest mountains on earth. I intended to keep it that way. But the Brothers had vowed to take their revenge on me. Might their withered hands be behind this?

I thought of everything I knew about the Brothers. Their immense wealth, their worthy donations to charities including orphanages and hospitals. Their horror of appearing in the newspapers or attracting any publicity at all. Why were they so wary of any attention from the world? There were said to be no paintings of the Brothers in existence. Though they shunned the public, the Bakers moved in aristocratic circles – indeed they were said to be intimate friends of the Prince of Wales.

Our Queen's son was rumoured to be a playboy, fond of actresses and 'fast society'. Not much in common then with the Brothers, except that they too coveted beautiful things.

Waldo had clearly been thinking along the same lines. He leaned over to me and murmured below the splash of oars, 'The Baker Brothers.'

One of the men looked up. Casually he flicked Waldo across the face, catching him on the cheek and bridge of the nose. My friend clenched his teeth but didn't utter a sound or a word of protest. The others laughed, pausing a moment in their work of rowing the boat. I wanted to get up and kick the man in his shin, but with an effort I kept my temper in check.

Waldo might be pig-headed and obstinate. But he was brave, no one could doubt that.

Now that we were away from land, surrounded by nothing but black water, the men didn't bother to keep their voices down. The boat sliced through the heaving sea; the wind howled about us, heavy with the tang of salt and fish. Now and then a spray of water from the oars would land in the boat, close to my gown. I was bone-weary, chilled and damp. I guessed we were being taken to some ship, and my spirits sank for it would be even harder to get away.

My guesses were wrong for we had been rowing for

not more than an hour when I spotted a beam of light playing over the water, directing us through the sea. I realised it was a lighthouse clearing a safe way through the rocks. The men seemed confident, as if they had made this journey many times before. The waves were bigger, sending the boat scudding this way and that, as we neared an island. But the men brought the boat smoothly into a rocky little bay.

More lanterns were lit, illuminating an empty cove scooped smoothly out of crumbling white cliffs. Just one blue and grey shack, which looked to be newly painted and in good order. Probably a boathouse.

Having helped Mrs Glee out of the boat, handling her like a sack of potatoes, Lips leaned over and gestured to us with his gun. We were going to get even rougher treatment. I took Rachel's hand, which was feverishly hot, and tried to pull her to land. She was limp, unresisting. Her brown eyes were glazed, hair hanging damp and tangled over her cheeks. She looked at me and forced a grin.

'I'm not a china doll,' she said, scrambling out of the boat.

The men assembled us into a single file. Mrs Glee went first, followed by Lips. We followed, two thugs panting in our wake. It was a steep climb up the cliffs and by the end my breath was coming in gasps. Rachel looked truly alarming, her cheeks bright pink. At the end of the climb the path struck left and there was a splendid carriage, decorated with a golden crest. Sleek Arabian mares were pawing the ground, their breath steaming in the night air. We were led into this carriage, and sank onto soft leather seats. Behind us, the headrests were upholstered in velvet. I was thoroughly bewildered. Where were we heading in this magnificent fashion?

'Bit more like it,' said Mrs Glee, sinking into the cushions. She glanced at me, her eyes appealing for sympathy. 'You'll see, Kitty, it won't be all bad once we get to the castle.'

'The castle?' I wondered. 'What castle?'

'It's amazing. You've never seen anything like it,' she replied.

'Who lives there?'

Instantly Mrs Glee clammed up and would say no more.

The horses were off, at a brisk pace. Lips squatted in one corner, like an enormous mouthy toad, his pistol covering us all. We galloped through whispering darkness – down below was the wash of the sea. We were lost, far from help, from civilisation even. This island did not seem to be inhabited for we did not pass a single village. But I had scarcely a glimpse through the windows. Before long we came to a stop and were prodded from the carriage. As I stumbled out, I could not help but catch my breath in wonder.

Gaslights? On this remote, forsaken island? It made no sense. The most powerful lights I had ever seen glowed, turning the skies golden. Arising like some fairy-tale dwelling in their enchanted arc was the castle. Thick granite walls bristled with battlements, turrets and watchtowers. One could imagine archers loosing their arrows on the enemy, soldiers pouring boiling oil on marauding invaders. The castle should have been green with moss and age but confusingly the stones gleamed with newness. A drawbridge cranked down over the moat and as if by magic the thick oak doors swung open.

The merry sounds of a polka came drifting out towards us. Lips and his thugs urged us forward and I caught a glimpse of a merry throng – of gay ball gowns and dancers clutching champagne glasses on a green lawn.

'Hop it!' Lips grunted, poking me in the back.

My heart heavy with a sense of evil, I took a stumbling step. Every nerve and fibre in my body was screaming: Stay away, Kit. Fly! But there was nowhere to run, for even now the pistol in my back was urging me forward.

❧ Chapter Six ❧

The first person I saw as we were harried past the fringes of the party was a tall woman in flowing white. She wore her toga-like gown with a regal air, her blonde hair topped by a helmet, and she was carrying a trident and sceptre. A hairy man, covered in yellow fur, hovered at her elbow. They looked very foolish. What were they supposed to be? Then the solution struck me – Britannia and her famous lion, symbols of England's mighty Empire.

Britannia was chatting to a Fearsome Turk, his head swathed in turbans above his coal-stained face. Alongside her was Titania, queen of the fairies, her dress of a silver gauze. Diana, the ancient Greek goddess of the hunt, was chatting to Napoleon Bonaparte, stout in his red breeches.

'What *is* this?' whispered Rachel, looking upon the revellers as if they were mad people.

'A fancy-dress ball,' I whispered back.

I could sympathise with her confusion – the orchestra, the revellers drifting in clumps over the lawn. How utterly strange to find all this here on this windswept island. I wished I could run to the party folk and throw myself on Britannia's mercy. But there was no hope for us; the thugs were quite openly waving their pistols and had surrounded us on all sides as we were led to the huge entrance. Nobody took much notice of us at all, though I heard a rather hearty Robin Hood say to his friend, 'Jolly original wheeze, what!' as we paraded by. If I ran and they fired it would be dismissed by the guests as just another masquerade, an original game to tickle their jaded fancy.

The musicians had just struck up Chopin's last waltz as we entered the castle , leaving behind the warmth of the summer's night. The waltz's haunting melody lingered a little and then vanished. We were chivvied up a circular staircase, along a corridor and then through a door into a carpeted room.

A thug lit a brass lamp and then retreated, locking the door. We were alone. I looked around and marvelled for we were surrounded on three sides by gleaming gilt frames. I am no expert in the arts but I could tell that here was something special. Mostly, I think, they were Old Masters. Those sketches were perhaps by Rembrandt or Raphael – a pair of gnarled hands, rheumy eyes in a peasant's head. Here, gorgeous in tones of flesh and crimson, a glistening oil painting. Voluptuous red-haired women, reclining on velvet pillows, their heaving bosoms painted in frightening, fleshy detail.

'Ouch,' said Isaac, catching sight of them, but Rachel shushed him, 'It must be a Titian,' she whispered. 'Priceless.'

The fourth wall was covered by a maroon velvet curtain. Isaac pulled a cord and the curtains began to swish apart. I was expecting more treasures but they revealed a window, so huge it covered the entire wall. Behind it was a great ballroom, more exotically dressed dancers and shimmering crystal chandeliers. Through the glass I could dimly hear the strains of a polka. In front of us, but tantalisingly out of reach, was a table collapsing under the weight of a mountain of mouth-watering treats.

Fowl, venison and oysters. Roast goose, oozing grease in a heap of browned potatoes. A whole swan pickled in aspic, its noble white neck decorated with strings of berries. Little tartlets, pastries and flans, but it was the puddings that made my saliva run. Nothing had passed my lips since lunch, an eternity ago. Oh, how I longed to pick up a cool pistachio ice. To lick a spoon full of creamy trifle. To feast on great heaps of meringues and strawberries until I was sick. To gorge on blancmange, jelly and chocolate cake.

'Stop dribbling,' Rachel snapped. 'We're kidnapped by maniacs and all you can think of is sherry trifle!'

'How do you know it's sherry?' I asked.

'Isn't it?' said Rachel.

'Could be Marsala-flavoured or even vanilla.'

'No one makes vanilla trifle.' Rachel's eyes were glued to the pudding, as if she could gobble it up with her gaze.

'Think about something other than your bellies, girls,' Waldo interrupted. 'Look over there.'

A line of guests were heaping their plates with food; a red-faced perspiring man had more on his plate than I would have thought it was physically possible to eat. Boar, quails eggs and flan, with a large slice of swan. It was the middle-aged lady next to him who had caught Waldo's attention. She had a serene face with drooping eyebrows, and severe brown hair topped with a lace cap. The woman had a dignity about her that set her apart from the other guests, but maybe that was partly because she hadn't bothered with a ridiculous costume.

'Who is it?' I asked. 'I think I've seen her somewhere before.'

'Don't you know?' Waldo teased. 'I'd have thought you'd have her image engraved on your womanly heart.'

'What?'

'The Lady with the Lamp.'

'Florence Nightingale,' I gasped and it was true I did

admire her deeply. She had treated the sick in Crimea, fought for the rights of women to go to the battlefield, to be useful and not just stay home knitting socks for the soldiers. She was a great heroine – but what on earth was she doing here?

'Over there!' Rachel murmured. 'It can't be.'

She was pointing to a portly man wearing feathers and carrying a tomahawk decorated with black ribbons. A Red Indian clearly, but who was the owner of the chubby face so crudely daubed with red and yellow war paint. Could it be?

'Tum-Tum,' Waldo blurted. 'It's old Tum-Tum.'

'Don't talk of the Prince of Wales like that,' Rachel said. 'He *is* going to be king one day.'

'I'm an American, remember,' Waldo said. 'I'm not impressed by all that royal nonsense.'

'You could show a little respect,' Rachel said.

'Anyway, hope he goes easy on the cakes before that. Otherwise he'll keel over stomach first,' Waldo retorted rudely.

'It's not Tum-Tum I'm worried about,' I interrupted. 'LOOK!'

Partly hidden by the portly Red Indian was a woman, dressed as a squaw. She had clearly buttonholed the Prince and was bending his ear about something. My friends stared at the comical figure – stout, determined, looking most alarming in her leather fringed dress, boots, feather and paint-covered face.

'Don't you know who it is?' I asked.

'No idea!' Waldo shook his head. Then he peered more closely. 'It can't be.'

'It is,' I murmured.

Now all my friends were staring at the small figure, who was gesturing forcefully to the Prince as she spoke.

It was Hilda Salter, lady explorer, patriotic spy, sharpshooter and the terror of native tribes from the Amazon to the Kalahari. The smooth talker who could part a Maharajah from his crown, a Khan from his camels and a prospector from his gold. She could even, I believed, have relieved a sheikh of his harem.

'*Your aunt!*' Rachel spluttered. 'What is *she* doing here?'

I shook my head. 'Playing some deep game, no doubt. She won't leave this castle empty handed.'

'But Kit, these people – whoever they are – they're kidnappers! They've—'

'Clearly rich kidnappers!' I interrupted. 'Kidnappers with royal friends.' I didn't say so to Rachel, but I was becoming increasingly sure it was the Baker Brothers behind all this. But what was my aunt doing in the home of our sworn enemy?

'It doesn't matter what she's doing here,' Isaac interrupted. 'We have to get a message to her.'

'Hammer on the glass!' Waldo bellowed. He rushed

up to the pane and beat on it. 'Oi! Oi!' he yelled as we all followed his lead.

We banged on the window as hard as we could, screaming to attract the attention of the revellers standing just inches away from us. To no avail. We might as well have been invisible.

'It's a game,' I said, as exhausted we fell back. 'Our kidnappers are taunting us with that scene. The Prince, my aunt, Florence Nightingale.'

We were interrupted by a knock at the door and two white uniformed waiters pushed a trolley into the room. A most delicious smell wafted from a silver tureen. One of the waiters proceeded to set the table, which stood in the corner of the room, with four plates, knives, forks and glasses, while the other unpacked the trolley. Mrs Glee had appeared and watched in silence, a frail figure hovering uncertainly by the doorway. Behind her were two burly guards.

'I told you they would treat you well,' she murmured. 'I apologise for Lips on the way here – but—'

'No more excuses,' Waldo cut in.

'Vera,' I said, 'if you are really sorry, can you just tell us – what on earth is going on?'

Mrs Glee blanched and backed out of the door without speaking. In an instant she was gone.

'No use looking for answers in that quarter,' Isaac said.

It seems odd in the light of our serious situation, but my eyes were on the trolley. We hadn't eaten for hours – the coach ride, the gruelling journey across the sea. I was famished, that's my excuse. Scrumptious dishes were on display, including many of the dainties we had spied through the window. My stomach was rumbling.

Isaac and Waldo were already at the trolley, scooping food onto their plates. Isaac had forgotten his plan to contact my aunt. I followed their example. There was a choice between ginger ale and lemonade. I filled my goblet with lemonade and it slid cool and tangy down my parched throat. Heaven! Then I took a small selection of flan, boar and guinea fowl in honey sauce. Well, fairly small. I didn't leave much room on that plate.

I intended to save myself for the trifle. Someone had to investigate if it was sherry flavoured!

With a troubled look Rachel followed our lead and was soon wallowing in chicken pie. Yes, maybe this feast had been provided by an enemy. Did it matter? With my spoon heaped with boar and potato, I was able to take a more mellow view of out captors. Was it just possible that I had been wrong to sense evil in the castle? Perhaps our kidnappers were not the Baker Brothers? Perhaps this was all some sort of extravagant jest.

Certainly whoever had snatched us off the moors had a good cook.

✎ Chapter Seven ✎

'Definitely sherry.' I licked my lips of the last spoonful of creamy, spongy trifle and sank back in my chair. Eating, especially in large quantities, *can* be exhausting.

'I feel bad,' murmured Rachel. 'My mother always used to say, "You should know a man before you sup at his table."'

'It hardly matters what your mother thinks,' I blurted, then immediately felt guilty. Rachel's mother was dead, like my own poor mama. We never talked of it.

Isaac glared at me and put a comforting hand on his sister's arm.

'I didn't really mean . . .' I muttered. 'I just meant, it's too late for second thoughts now that we've filled our bellies.'

'Hear, hear,' someone murmured. In unison we turned to the door. But the man wasn't there; he had materialised, ghostlike, in our midst, though no one had heard the sound of the key turning or the door opening.

'Your mother was an uncharitable woman, Rachel.

She should have heeded the Jewish proverb: "If your enemy be hungry, give him food to eat."'

It was a Baker Brother, standing so close I could feel the chill. He put his hand, which was encased in a white glove, on my shoulder and I flinched as if I'd been struck. A stray ribbon – black, I noticed – tickled my cheek.

He was handsome, this man, with golden skin, fair wavy hair and the palest of pale blue eyes. Walking down a street, he would have drawn admiring glances, with his youth and air of well-being. I knew this beauty was a mask – I'd seen the real man in the Himalayas. His voice was reedy and he gave off an unwholesome smell. Something of the grave, of decomposing bodies. And when I looked at him more closely, I saw a peculiarity about the skin on his face. Too taut, too stretched – all wrinkles and marks of character had been blanked, like an alabaster statue of a Greek god.

'Which one are you?' Waldo asked coldly.

'A strange question, though fair, I suppose,' he replied. 'After all, we've never been properly introduced.'

The Baker Brother removed his hand from my shoulder and extended it to Waldo. I could see my friend struggling with the question of what to do: shake the loathsome glove or spit on it.

'Pity.' The man recalled his hand with a sour smile. 'I am Cecil Baker, precisely thirteen and a half minutes older than my brother Cyril, whom you've already met. If you look through the window you will see him in the ballroom, playing the gracious host to our future king.'

We all stared through the window and saw a strange sight. Another pale handsome man, with the same rubbed out and remodelled look as his brother, was standing in a group around Albert, Prince of Wales, uncomfortably close to Aunt Hilda. He was laughing, sharing a joke with our future king. As if he knew we were talking about him, Cyril Baker turned his head towards us and a look passed between the two men.

Or seemed to.

'You need not be afraid that any of our distinguished guests will see you.' Cecil Baker strode up to the window and tapped it playfully. 'This is a one-way mirror. We can see through it, but all our guests can see is a shiny mirror reflecting their pretty costumes back at them. I assure you, Cyril and I find this jolly useful, not to say amusing.'

'Spying on your guests,' Waldo said. 'Hardly the behaviour of gentlemen.'

Ignoring him, Cecil pulled out a chair and sat down.

'Is this your new business plan?' I asked. 'Are you adding kidnapping to murder and thievery?'

'That's a vulgar way of looking at it,' Cecil Baker gave me a wintry smile. 'I prefer to see it as inviting you on a luxurious and mutually profitable visit. If you do as you're told, that is. Going by your history, I cannot say I'm confident.'

He looked me over, from head to toe. I felt like a slave being sized up at a flesh market. I recalled the last time I had seen this man, in that magical glade in the Himalayas. The shrunken, wizened being lapping greedily at the waters of immortality. For the time being, at least, his gamble with fate appeared to have paid off. He was much changed from the wheezing ghost we had first spotted leaving the steamship at Bombay. Now, in appearance at least, he was young and handsome.

'I have a job for you,' Cecil Baker continued. 'An exciting opportunity.'

'Bet it's an opportunity to get ourselves killed,' Waldo said.

'We won't go into the details tonight. You will eat, drink and sleep. Cyril and I will meet you again tomorrow. We will have a little chat and then I believe you will see sense.'

Cecil Baker stood up. 'I wish you a good night. Things always look rosier after a decent sleep.'

'I won't do a thing for you and nor will my friends,' Waldo spat. 'We're not for hire.'

'We shall see.' The man smiled, to reveal perfect white teeth. With that Cecil Baker was gone.

We looked at each other after he vanished, not knowing

what to say. We were all very scared, but unwilling to admit it to each other. The silence hung heavy in the air.

Finally Waldo said, 'It's not as if we have any choice, is it?'

'We could run? Fight?' I said. 'Maybe we could climb out of the windows.' But though I tried to sound brave I was despairing inside. I couldn't see how we could escape from this castle fortress.

'He *has* us. Don't you see it, Kit?' Waldo shook his head. 'The Bakers are famous collectors, aren't they?'

"So?"

'*We* are their latest exhibits.'

❧ Chapter Eight ❧

That night we were given an elegant chamber furnished with twin beds, the sheets silk, the pillows filled with the softest feathers. Two starched cotton nightgowns were laid out. There were even hot-water bottles. Rachel curled up in an eiderdown, looking over the marble washstand, the velvet curtains, the Turkey rugs on the gleaming floorboards. It was everything we could have wished for.

But we were not on some luxurious holiday. We were prisoners – high up in the castle's guest quarters. There were guards on the door. Through the night drifted sounds of revelry that excluded us. The strains of a mazurka from the lawns below, then some jolly peasant dance. The faintest chink of champagne glasses. And beyond, the sounds of the other orchestra, more plaintive. Neither Rachel nor I was in the mood for conversation and we lay in our soft beds in silence. I finally drifted off to sleep with the sounds of the violins in my ears – their sadness echoing my own mood.

I woke up with a jolt, my limbs stiff and aching, despite my feather bed. At first I thought it was the orchestra – still fiddling away. No. It was a human voice I heard. Someone wailing in the spaces over our heads. It was a heart-rending cry, grief-stricken. It sounded high, like a child's. It made me want to weep; at the same time I was desperate to jump out of bed, charge out into the night and stop whatever was causing this sadness. No use. Armed guards on the door and, besides, this castle was a pit, full of horrors I did not yet know.

Uneasily I dropped back into an aching, dreamless sleep.

I was woken again by the door opening. Two different waiters in white livery, their faces as expressionless as the others, were pushing another trolley. Breakfast. What a breakfast! Fried eggs, quail, bacon, sausages, toast – a feast. I wasn't hungry. Still, you know Kit Salter. I managed a few mouthfuls.

We had scarcely finished breakfast when the guards came. We were marched through endless corridors, down twisting staircases, over a bridge, till we came to an elaborate teak door. I was struck by the carving. The beautiful figures on it looked foreign to me. There was a female in the centre, with a globular head, a panther squatting at her legs. I sensed she had been imported from some distant, scorching land. The door swung open, revealing an enormous room.

'Butterflies,' Rachel whispered.

There were hundreds, thousands of butterflies, crawling, sleeping and fluttering in the glass cases, which towered to the ceiling. One section of the wall shimmered an iridescent blue. Another glowed a coppery orange. Still another, whiter than snow. I marvelled at the extravagance of a nature which could create such joyful patterns. One of the turquoise butterflies had white splodges marching up her wings, as if someone had dipped their finger in paint and anointed her with tribal marks. The guards pushed us onward, leaving us only moments to feel for these beautiful creatures trapped in their glass prisons. Then we were in another chamber, similar to the last but full this time of dead treasures. Like the butterflies they glowed, though this time in more restrained colours. Yellows, blues, subtle shades of white. The most delicate Chinese porcelain you could imagine – from the Qing and Ming and other dynasties, a quick glance at the labels told us. All this wealth was illuminated by the light that poured in from a large, arched window. Looted, judging from the stained glass at the top, from some abbey or cathedral.

The Baker Brothers were sitting under the window, two misers in the midst of their wealth. In the middle of the circular table there was a large square shape, covered by a checked tablecloth. Cyril was reading *The Times*, Cecil the *Illustrated London News*. Both of them were wearing spotless white cotton gloves. They looked up as we approached and Cecil greeted us with a pallid smile.

'Up with the worm, I see,' he wheezed.

He gestured us to sit, waving a white paw. All four of us did as we were bid. Cyril was staring at us with glassy eyes and I was struck again by the Brothers' oddness. Their faces didn't really have *expressions*. When they smiled their faces scarcely moved, as if some doctor had drained the humanity out of them. No doubt about it, drinking of the waters of immortality had turned them into freaks of nature. They were fine, yes, almost beautiful, but only as a statue is beautiful. They were blond, clean, free of the marks of age, but it had somehow robbed them of life itself.

'My brother has convinced me of the wisdom of inviting you children to Hadden Castle. I took some persuading, I can tell you!' Cyril said, his voice even more papery than his brother's.

'You're very fortunate,' Cecil smirked. 'My brother *does* have an unfortunate tendency to bear grudges.' In the look he gave his twin, I saw for the first time, some fondness.

'Thanks very much for the "invitation" – but none of us *asked* to come to Hades Castle,' Waldo said boldly.

'Hadden Castle,' Cyril snapped, then to his brother he murmured, 'I believe some of the workmen took to calling it Hades.'

'Impudent beasts,' said Cecil, and then he turned his blue gaze on me. 'You were invited here, dear children, for a reason. I have in mind a task for you. A very special mission – which will test your intelligence, your nerve and, how shall I put it, your survival instinct – in equal proportion. I am convinced you have these qualities in some measure. You see, it is a rare person that can best *me* in a challenge.'

Cecil was staring at me with something like admiration and I felt a glow of pride.

'Kit Salter, you reached Shambala. You made it to the temple of the oracle in Siwa. You are a very unusual girl.'

My glowing feeling spread. Then abruptly I remembered who was flattering me and I felt hollow.

'I'm not interested in your compliments,' I spat.

Cyril eyed me like a cobra sizing up a mouse while Cecil shrugged. 'I offer them freely. It is your qualities that made me choose you, Kit Salter – and your er . . . seconds . . . Waldo, Isaac and Rachel of course.'

'What is this task?' Waldo asked wincing at the description of himself as a second. 'Not that—'

'We take it for granted that you will protest,' Cyril interrupted – and Cecil flashed him a look of amusement. 'We don't expect you to do anything for us freely.'

That word, 'freely', hung ominously in the air.

Cecil pushed a gloved hand through his hair and then, leaning forward, steepled his hands on the table. I caught a merest glimpse of the wrist under the glove. It was a repulsive sight. The skin was wrinkled and browned, like that of a rotten apple. It reminded me of a monkey, or a very aged man. Somehow to see it side-by-side with smooth flesh was particularly revolting.

'What's wrong with your hands?' I blurted. 'Is that why you wear those gloves?'

The amiable expression on Cecil's face was replaced in an instant by pure malice.

'Just this once,' he said very, very slowly, 'I will overlook your appalling manners.'

'Get to the meat,' his twin murmured, who seemed a man of fewer words.

Waldo said, 'Give it to us straight. Why did you kidnap us?'

'Cards on the table.' Cecil leaned back in his chair and spread out his gloved hands. 'We are sending you to China, in the care of our best captain and crew. There is something I need you to – how shall I put this – retrieve from a secret monastery in the Songshan mountains.'

'You want us to steal? From monks?'

'Exactly!' Cyril grinned briefly. He glanced at his brother, who bowed his head. 'Let's call a spade a spade.

61

There is a book in that monastery that we want. You will bring it to us.'

'Why do you want this book?' Rachel asked.

'Is it their business?' Cyril asked his brother.

'I suppose they have a right to wonder,' Cecil replied.

'Very well,' Cyril said. 'I am talking of the legendary Book of Bones. It contains the finest of Kung Fu wisdom.'

'What is Kung Fu?' Rachel whispered.

'An ancient Chinese system of fighting. Usually there are no weapons involved, just the skill of the fighter. It's what they call martial arts . . . a bit like boxing but more sophisticated, in a way.' Isaac replied. He can rarely resist an opportunity to show off.

'This doesn't ring true,' I said. 'I would have thought guns and bombs were more your style than bare hands.'

Cyril turned his chill gaze on me. Inside I felt very, very cold. 'I would have thought *you* would understand, Kathleen. In Shambala we conquered mortality. The Book of Bones will enable us to – how shall I put it – perfect our perfection!'

'Perfect our perfection!' Cecil murmured. 'That's good, brother, very good.'

'What the Hades are these guys talking about?' Waldo whispered to me. 'They're about as perfect as a pair of gargoyles.'

'Look here,' Isaac interrupted. 'I'm not being rude, just trying to understand. Are you saying you want this Book of Bones as a sort of health manual?'

Cyril inclined his head. 'Precisely.'

Something was wrong with the Bakers, despite their seeming good looks. Something that was making them desperate for this Book of Bones. The withered hands, the rotten smell that they gave off when one came too close.

I remembered the words of Maya, the guardian of Shambala. She had predicted that their beauty was a curse. It would quickly wither in the outside world. Did they believe this thing was a talisman, which would help them in some way? What was this Book of Bones?

'I don't understand,' I said. 'Why me? I mean, if you want this Book of Bones so much, why don't you just go and get it. Or if you don't want to risk your um . . . good looks, send one of your minions.'

'Sharp as ever, Miss Salter,' Cecil murmured. 'The reason is simple. It is said that only one who is "pure of heart" will be able to remove the Book from the monastery. Our experiences in Shambala convinced us that, although you are an infuriating nuisance, you have some valuable virtues. So we have entrusted you and your friends with this little commission.'

For the first time, I knew I had some power. 'No,' I

said firmly. 'I will not play your game.'

'You're quite sure about that?'

'Bully and bribe all you like! We're not going anywhere!'

'You know I'm almost glad to hear you protest,' Cecil said. 'You see we cooked up a little insurance policy. Tell them, Cyril.'

Cyril's rubber lips pulled back over his perfect teeth. 'We thought of torture, pulling your fingernails out one by one, that sort of thing. But it was so messy. Then we came up with something a little more subtle.'

'A plan sprung fully formed from Cyril's fertile mind,' Cecil interjected.

'A little something was added to your food yesterday,' Cyril said, slowly drawling the words for maximum effect. 'One of you has been poisoned.'

'What?' Waldo asked dully.

'I repeat. One of you has been given a deadly poison.'

'Just . . . one of us?' I asked.

His pale blue eyes scanned us, looking over each of us in turn. Was it my imagination that they lingered a little longer on me? They were openly amused. My heart beat faster and my hands began to tremble. Was I the ill-omened one? Somehow I just *knew* it was me.

Cyril held up his gloved hand to silence our uproar. 'This is a fatal poison, deadly and subtle. The "chosen one" won't feel anything yet. But be assured. Our chemist is a *very* talented man. If you are not back from Peking with the Book of Bones, in precisely five months you will go off to meet your maker; I promise you that. One of you will die. You will die a very horrible death if you do not take the antidote.'

'Why not all of us?' Rachel burst out. 'I would have thought it was more your style to kill us all.'

'Certainly not,' Cyril snapped. 'That isn't how we operate. We aren't heartless. It wasn't *necessary* to poison you all.' He paused a moment, smiling. 'We don't believe in taking a sledgehammer to a nut. As I said, just one of you has been given the fatal dose.'

'Who?' I asked. 'Which one of us have you poisoned?'

'That would be telling!' Cecil said.

'Our cruelty is strictly scientific,' Cyril added.

'What does that mean?'

'It means we want to keep each and every one of you on tenterhooks, guessing, worrying, fearing. You'll pass sleepless nights, check each other for signs of illness. It will all be tremendously frightening,' Cecil replied.

'You're sick,' Waldo spat. 'Twisted.'

'Perhaps,' Cecil shrugged. 'It doesn't bother me.'

He got up and stretched his arms, as if rather bored. Then he leaned over the table and whipped off the checked cloth that hid the mound in the centre, revealing a wire cage. Lying at the bottom was a golden Labrador. Its coat was still glossy but everything else about the hound was badly wrong. Its eyes were open, blank and staring, covered with a film of white mucus. Poor beast, its jaw was badly contorted, teeth protruding. A pool of dribble lay under its muzzle. Everything about the creature spoke of a death in screaming agony.

'A nasty death,' Cecil said, looking down with something like regret. 'Rather a shame, really. Still, Pippin *was* getting rather old.'

'Unless you want to die very unpleasantly,' Cyril said, 'I suggest you follow our orders.'

'It's a trick,' Waldo replied faintly.

But I scarcely heard. I couldn't look at the animal. I was going to be sick.

'You are trying to trick us into doing your dirty work,' Waldo continued.

But his voice lacked conviction. I knew the Baker Brothers – they would have no qualms about a mere poisoning.

Cecil smiled and rang a bell. Another liveried minion appeared, carrying a silver platter. On it was a leather folder. Cecil took the folder and opening it drew out four slips of paper. The words Peninsular and Oriental were emblazoned on them. I knew instantly what they were – steamer tickets.

'Here are your tickets. You hardly need them, dear children, for of course my brother and I will be hiring the entire steamer. Still, we thought you'd appreciate the gesture.'

'Take a word of advice,' Cyril added. 'I'd make damn sure *one of you* doesn't end up as dead as poor Pippin.'

I rose from the table and walked out, the others following my lead. I saw Waldo had taken the tickets, and although I wished he hadn't, I couldn't blame him. At the door I heard one of the Brothers call out to us:

'You'll need a guide, of course!'

'Don't worry Cy,' the other drawled. 'They'll have plenty of time to work it out.'

❧ Chapter Nine ❧

We sailed to China on a ghost ship. The *Mandalay* was a modern and elegant steamer, but lifeless nonetheless. This was hardly surprising. Anything touched by the withered hand of the Baker Brothers lost its pulse. Rachel and I shared a cabin, the boys were next door. The rooms were large, luxurious. Ours was panelled in walnut, fitted with a thick maroon carpet and decked with wardrobes, leather armchairs, bookshelves and mirrors. One could have fancied oneself in a gentleman's club stuffed with old men smoking cigars – rather than aboard a floating prison.

The dining saloon where we had our meals was also lavish, with crystal chandeliers, steaming tea urns and the finest Chinese porcelain. It could have fitted a hundred or more people, but we were the only passengers, eating our lonely dinners in the midst of a vast empty space. I had detested the Memsahibs on our voyage to India, who were always criticising my manners. Now I would have positively welcomed their company, our solitude was so sinister. True, there were the mute Chinese waiters who brought us our food. I had spied Lascar sailors scrubbing down the decks. But no one would answer us if we said a friendly hello. Sometimes at night I would imagine that I heard the same haunting cry that had disturbed my sleep at Hadden Castle. A high-pitched wail, like a trapped fox, but so ghostly I put it down to bad dreams.

We had been sailing on like this, seeing hardly a soul except Mrs Glee, who dropped in on us every day to continue our education. Mrs Glee was positively shrinking, becoming more frail and breathless as each day passed. Sometimes she seemed on the brink of a confession, but then she would pull back. I realised that she felt guilty about the harm she was doing us, for she often left little treats on our pillows. Packets of candied peel or butterscotch. Jars of salted almonds. We ate the treats, of course. But they didn't make us like her, certainly not respect her. Luckily Mrs Glee was often called away by a bell to some other mysterious task and we were left with free time.

Not that there was anything to do. True there were books, but we had soon read them all. We played games – hangman, noughts and crosses, cards, jacks with small stones. Mostly we just brooded. Little wonder that we all, individually, thought we were the one who had been poisoned. I was convinced my heart was burning, while

Isaac suffered from nausea and Rachel from headaches. Only Waldo seemed relatively unaffected, though he had nervous tremors in his hand. He'd lost a finger in the Himalayas to frostbite – now he claimed 'the poison' was making his whole hand tremble.

I am making light of it now, but it was no easy thing that voyage. The aches, the foulness – each one of us certain we were going to die. I was the most downcast. At night I could barely sleep for the nausea in my throat. I woke up each morning weary to the bone, my neck stiff, and dreading the day ahead.

We had been sailing on like this past Italy, through the Indian Ocean and the Malacca Straits on to the South China Seas when one day at dinner Waldo threw down his spoon.

'This is hell,' he announced. 'I can't stand it any more! Mrs Glee's lessons! This disgusting food! We should make a raft and just jump overboard.'

'We'd make good shark bait,' I murmured.

'Waldo!' Rachel snapped. Her dark eyes had filled with tears and her voice had an edge of hysteria. 'If you can't talk sense just keep your mouth closed.' With that she threw down her napkin and slammed out of the saloon.

'What did I do?' Waldo asked, bewildered.

Isaac shrugged. '*Girls*,' he explained, lifting an eyebrow. 'They have these vapours. Nerves, they call them.'

'She's not the only one who is on edge,' I snapped. 'It's hardly pleasant being a prisoner of this crew.'

'You can't call those two a crew,' Isaac said, gesturing to the captain, who was outside by the railings talking to Mrs Glee. 'They're more like characters from Frankenstein.'

The captain was our old friend Bert, aka 'Lips', who seemed to combine running a ship with a little kidnapping on the side. Whenever he was around, Mrs Glee became even more timorous, like a spaniel beaten so many times that it cringes at the sight of its master. We saw her now, a nervous smile on her lips, positively shrinking while Lips puffed and preened. We saw them turn and watch Rachel. Since he had hijacked our coach, Bert had somehow acquired a scar which ran down the left side of his face and made his rosebud lips even more repulsive.

Watching him, I could only shudder. No wonder Mrs Glee was so terrified.

Why, you might be wondering, did we agree to undertake the voyage to China at all? The answer is simple, we could see no other choice. Somehow it might have been easier if we had *all* been poisoned. But with a sword hanging over just *one* of our heads, we miserably gave in to their demands. Oh, it was a very ingenious plan those two Brothers came up with – inspired both in its nastiness and in the ease with which it threw a noose around our necks. The Brothers had assured us, in the most honeyed tones, that there was no use trying to escape. There was no use consulting doctors. The poison was absolutely untraceable. It would not show up in tests at all, until it killed one of us as stone dead as Pippin.

All these threats didn't prevent us trying to find a way out. I was especially concerned to get news of our plight to the outside world. My father, Waldo's mother, Rachel and Isaac's guardians – so many people must have been frantic with worry. They probably believed us dead, murdered on that lonely Dartmoor road by highwaymen. I thought that if only I could somehow contact Aunt Hilda, she might have a plan. My aunt, as you know, is an intrepid explorer and spy. She had contacts at the highest level in her Majesty's Secret Intelligence Service. She was actually present at that party in the castle, talking to the Prince of Wales. If she could whisper in the right ear, might she have the Baker Brothers investigated?

I could only hope.

Meanwhile, we were helpless. Lying in our bunks that night, staring at the oak-panelled ceiling which seemed to hang oppressively close, Rachel and I chatted.

'Have you thought how odd this steamer is?' she asked.

'Sinister, more like,' I replied.

'I mean, all we see is the captain and Mrs Glee, but there must be others. Seamen who run the engines and stoke the boiler things.'

I nodded. 'We're imprisoned up on the top deck. There's stuff going on in the ship that we know nothing about. For a start, what do you suppose our cargo is? We're clearly not a passenger ship.'

'Opium?' Rachel asked, the horror in her voice drifting up to me in the top bunk.

'No,' I replied quickly. I had thought of that possibility but did not want my sensitive friend to dwell on it. 'There's no reason to think of opium.'

I was not telling the truth. There was every reason to think we might be on a steamer involved in the opium smuggling business. British merchants directed the trade, which was said to have infected the Chinese people with the evils of addiction to the poppy – but made merchants like Jardine Matheson very wealthy. Shanghai, Canton, these were ports grown fat on the profits of opium. Indeed, to the shame of many reformers, Britain had even recently fought two 'opium wars' to demand access from the Imperial Chinese government to the drug. Critics of the war, such as our current Prime Minister, William Gladstone, who was then a young reformer, had roundly condemned the trade and the war. But it was a slippery business. Opium was not smuggled from England, but from British India. Just a few days ago we had stopped in the Indian port of Calcutta. Had we picked up supplies of opium to sell for many taels of silver to Chinese drug smugglers?

I turned over irritably in the bunk; my sheets were sticky with sweat despite the cool air blowing in through the porthole. These were unprofitable thoughts.

'Kit . . . why don't we go and investigate?'

'It's the middle of the night.'

'We're not likely to get very far in daylight. Please.'

I was reluctant. Usually it was the other way round, me urging on a doubtful Rachel to adventure. Maybe it was the stiffness in my neck and back. The poison slowly working its evil magic on me. Perhaps it was because I was filled with dread, scared of what we would find aboard this steamship. Nevertheless I changed out of my nightgown and pulled on some clothes. Then we knocked on the next-door cabin. Waldo stuck his head out. It seemed that our friends were also kept awake by the muggy heat. They agreed to join us and soon we were creeping stealthily down the first-class deck.

There were no lights on anywhere. But the moon was bright, hanging low over the Indian Ocean. A thousand, a million, stars guided us. We had candles; we could light them in an emergency.

'Wait!' I suddenly stopped short and hissed. 'How are

we going to get through the doors to the lower decks? You know Bert always keeps them locked.'

'I've thought of that.' Isaac grinned, his teeth glimmering white in the moonlight. He held something up, which looked like a scrap of wire.

'What is it?' I asked.

'I've not been idle, you know, cooped up on this hell-ship,' Isaac replied. 'I call it my all-purpose lock-pick.'

'You really think it will work?' Rachel asked. The hope in her voice made me feel weak. Whatever we found at the bottom of this ship, it wasn't going to set us free.

Isaac shrugged. 'Let's give it a try.'

We went as softly as we could down the deck. Past the cabins, where we knew the captain and Mrs Glee slept. But where were the others? Where were the first mate, the stewards and all the other sailors needed to run a great steamship? Isaac reached the door before the rest of us and scratched away frantically with his lock-pick. We held our breath. Then with a loud creak the door swung open and Isaac stepped back with a triumphant air.

'Enter!' he proclaimed, holding the door open for us. As the smell hit him his expression changed. 'What is that?' he blurted

It was hot and rancid, the stench of faeces and decay. The kind of smell that instantly makes one run in the other direction. But even though inside we probably all felt the same – desperate to turn tail and run – none of us wanted to look a coward in front of our friends.

So we made our way down the stairs. This was a different world to the gleaming, varnished one we inhabited above. The stairs were of rusting steel, the walls unpainted. The sudden heat was almost worse than the stink. It was muggy in our cabins, hot even on the deck outside. But here it was roasting.

'Kit?' Rachel whispered.

Silently I squeezed her hand.

Not one of us wanted to walk down those steps.

❧ Chapter Ten ❧

We climbed down the steps into the bowels of the great ship. At the bottom was a corridor running between iron walls as tall as houses. With mounting trepidation we entered the hold, past the deserted second- and third-class lounges. Every now and then came a great rattling thump, which Isaac said was made by the engines. It was noisy down here and steaming hot, with great hissing, banging crashes. So far we had clung to the shadows and not seen a soul. In front of us was a massive iron door painted with a white L. I heard a faint whine from within and looked at Waldo, who was just behind me, seeking reassurance that we should go in. He nodded, so cautiously I pushed down the handle and the door creaked open.

A clinging white thing swung out at me, enveloping me. A slimy, faceless thing. A ghost!

Screaming, I took a step back and collapsed into Waldo's arms. My heart was pumping like a steam engine and I was trembling uncontrollably. I couldn't get the thing off me, it was damp and limp, sucking at my face.

'Help me.'

'You're a goose,' Waldo murmured, holding me tight. 'A silly goose!'

More ghostly shapes were fluttering in the dark, careering towards me out of the shadows.

'It's attacking,' I wailed, trying to shake off the damp, clinging poltergeist.

'You're the first person ever to have been overpowered by a sheet.'

'What!?'

'This is the laundry room, Kit!' Isaac stepped forward and held his candle high, illuminating a mass of bed linen drying on clothes lines.

Something *was* thrumming in the darkness, but it was only a mechanical engine. I saw my friends' faces – they were all grinning delightedly. Even Rachel's eyes were sparkling. Embarrassed, I released myself from Waldo and thrust off the wet sheet.

'Come on,' I said briskly, turning away. 'We can't stand about chatting. We've only got a little time before Mrs Glee comes to wake us.'

I heard the others giggling behind me as I led the way down the passage. Frankly, I was not in the mood to see the funny side, for the overpowering heat, the oppressive rattle of the steam engines and the towering iron walls were all working on my nerves. I was scared, down here in the belly of the Baker Brothers' beast. Every shadow struck me as sinister, and I knew the others felt the same, which was why they'd welcomed the chance for a laugh at my expense. Without another word I continued down the corridor, the others following. They may make light of my bravery, but I noticed no one, not even Waldo, seized the chance to take the lead.

Turning a bend, we came to a giant space. Above us reared an iron monster choking with pistons and valves pounding away in regular rhythm. Funnels and tubes stretched to the roof, different counters and dials whirred. I could make out four pistons, and cylinders spiralling away to the ends of the room, but frankly could make no sense of it all. Isaac, however, burst into enthusiastic explanation of how we were in the engine room and over there was the screw propeller, which along with its twin on the other side bore the great steamer forward. He was embarking on further explanations about cylinders and drive shafts, though we were rather bewildered, when Waldo put a stop to it.

'Come on, there must be more down here.'

It was infernally hot. Though we all wore the lightest clothes, we were perspiring and red with heat. My cheeks were on fire; sweat trickled down my back till my blouse was damp and sticky. Unbelievably it was becoming even hotter as we moved deeper into the hold, and now a great roaring noise engulfed us and here was a red, ravenous beast.

'The stokehold,' Isaac murmured.

Young men, begrimed with dirt, stripped to their vests, were feeding the stokehold with great shovels of coal, and the beast responded by dancing red and hot. More and more black dust disappeared down the maw of the furnace. In an exhausting waltz the men fed her, scuttling crablike between huge bunkers and the two roaring fires. They were Chinese coolies for the most part, though the head stoker who was bawling orders was a Lascar. They took no notice of us, though we were practically among them. There was something hypnotic about the way they worked. As though they had worked for a long time and would continue to do so till they dropped with fatigue. Nothing else mattered down here, but the coal and the billowing flames – or so I thought.

One of the men turned. The way he looked at us, we could have been ghosts. His eyes swivelled over us, one by one, bulging with some emotion I could not understand. His teammates were working in unison, shovelling and filling, but he stood stock still, frozen to the spot. It was Rachel who sensed what was wrong.

'He's scared. The poor man's terrified.'

'Of *us*?' I said. 'Why?'

'I don't know, but it's obvious he's frightened.'

'Come on, Kit! Let's get out of here.' Waldo tugged at me, and we all stumbled away, turning right and climbing up the stairs to the first floor. Here there was an iron door, which we'd ignored on our way down. Now I had to pass through, and so I seized the bolt and turned it. Isaac's candle flame showed us nothing, just empty rooms, barred and bolted with mortice and tenon locks. The smell was dank, disgusting – of ordure and something fleshily decaying.

'Probably the pens where they keep livestock,' Waldo said.

There were an awful lot of these empty pens. We walked past one after another, iron cages with wire-mesh walls and doors. Some of them had iron hooks embedded in the walls, which I guessed were for tethering cattle. The floors had been hosed clean, but here and there was still a bit of straw or a dark spot – dried blood, I guessed. They were gruesome things, these cages. I felt sick that I could have eaten animals kept in these conditions.

'I'm definitely off meat for now,' Rachel murmured. 'What do you call those people who only eat carrots and things?'

'Vegetarians,' said Isaac, his voice sounding sick and muffled.

'I'm turning vegetarian.'

'Me too,' I said, hurriedly pushing onward. Finally, thank goodness, we were past the cages and into something else. This was a huge cargo hold full of cases and boxes stacked in careful order. Here was something far more cheerful. Bottles of Champagne marked 'Oudinot' and over there dozens upon dozens of boxes of potted meats – mustard, calves-foot jelly and pale ale. Every dainty that the homesick imperialist could crave. In another section were stout oak boxes, banded and locked with bronze clasps.

'Can you open one of those?' I asked Isaac. 'They look important.'

He had already bent down and was fiddling away with his bits of wire. The lock clicked open. I seized it and Waldo yanked open the container. Not easy, as it was heavy. Inside was a puzzling sight: the chest was subdivided into numerous partitions, each of which contained a ball the size of an apple, wrapped in fine material. The balls gave off a pungent, sickly sweet smell.

'Mothballs?' Rachel burst out. 'Why do they lock up their mothballs? They aren't made of gold.'

I didn't answer, although I already knew. Judging from Waldo and Isaac's sudden silence, they too had guessed what the chests contained.

'Come on. Nothing important,' I said, backing away

from the chest. 'Lock it back up, Isaac. Let's get out of here.'

But Rachel let out a little gasp and I knew she had guessed. 'I know what it is,' she said, her voice steady. 'You don't have to protect me. It's opium from India – smuggled for all those poor Chinese who are addicted to it.'

Waldo had put his hands in his pockets and stood slouching. 'Girls,' he said, adopting a lordly tone, 'you have to understand something.'

'What?' I snapped.

'This is business. Pure business. Opium is sold to the Chinese because they want it. We do nothing wrong in trading freely in it, for we receive tea in return. Opium is a huge business worth millions of pounds a year. Some say it is the biggest contributor to the Empire's coffers. Many of our merchant princes made their fortunes in it.'

'It brings such misery,' Rachel said quietly. 'I've heard people sicken on it. Lose interest in all work and suchlike – and can die within a few years.'

'It is the Chinaman's choice after all. If a fool chooses to take poison, you cannot blame the man who sold it to him,' Waldo declared.

This was true enough. But somehow I didn't feel easy as we left that place, walking back through the great empty pens. Waldo may have talked with such confidence about the benefits to trade of opium, but

I don't think he had made the full connection. Now I finally understood the purpose of this steamer. It wasn't merely to ship luxuries for the gentleman of the Orient. It wasn't just to provide the great merchants of Dent and Son and Jardine Matheson with duck liver pâté and foie gras. It was a ship that traded in flesh. In Bombay the *Mandalay* had picked up opium; now we were sailing through the Malacca Straits with it. We would take this cargo to Shanghai, exchange it for silver – and then fill those great pens with bonded labourers for the factories and railroads of the New World.

I had made a mistake. The cages were not used to transport animals. The iron rings in the walls weren't to hook cattle, but to punish disobedient slaves. Those dark patches on the walls could well be dried blood.

Human blood.

✺ Chapter Eleven ✺

Up on the quarter-deck I heard it again. The wailing had first woken me back in the Bakers' fortress, Hadden Castle. Those cries of distress had punctuated my dreams on the long weeks of this voyage. I heard it again now as we silently returned to our quarters. I didn't know about the others, but I was desperate to get back to our cabin. I longed for clean white sheets and a chance to close my eyes and rid my mind of the disturbing images we'd seen down below.

That awful crying.

I had thought I had dreamed it up, that it was a figment of my imagination. I had thought the wailing was made by a ghost. But now I heard it quite clearly, coming from behind an iron door.

'Someone's crying!' I said, halting. 'Over there.'

The others had frozen too. For some reason, I had never mentioned the wailing. No one had. But now from my friends' faces I realised that I wasn't the only one to have heard it. Isaac got out his lock-pick and went to work. The Chubb lock clicked loose and the door opened a fraction.

The cabin was dark, an apish shape looming in the corner. The wailing stopped for a second as we entered, then resumed, as high pitched as the whine of a boiling kettle. I could sense shuffling. Something was looking at us.

'Hurry!' I snapped to Isaac, who was fumbling with the damp matches to light a new candle.

There was a smell of sulphur but no light. Isaac finally managed to strike a match, a weak flame. Our wavering candlelight illuminated the scene.

A Chinese child propped on pillows. A waif, no more than seven or eight or nine years old. Its shrunken limbs were shrouded by a white sheet. The face was wide with delicate lips and slanting, almond-shaped eyes. Sick eyes, full of a milky pus in which magnified pupils hung dark. I was reminded of Pippin, the Baker Brothers' poisoned Labrador.

Awful as that had been, this was far worse. Repelled, but consumed by curiosity, I moved closer.

The child's skull had been shaved bald as an egg. Black lines had been painted on the scalp, dividing it into wavy, irregular sections, each of which was numbered. Some of the sections were filled with spidery writing. MORALITY fitted into 21, TIME into 31, PERCEPTION into 27. It was hard to make out the writing for a contraption had been fitted over the head. It was a cage, made of wide copper bands, held together by thick bolts. Probes went down to the head and curly wires connected the *thing* to another contraption, which stood on a tripod near the bed. There were batteries gleaming on the tripod – and it was making a hissing sound as needles moved.

'What abomination is this?' Rachel asked in an agonised whisper.

No one replied. We were all silenced by horror.

The child was looking at us, but without *seeing*. That awful wailing whistle had halted when we came with our candle into the room. But now it started again, redoubled. A chill entered us, which blew away the tropical heat and enfolded our bones in ice.

'I think I can guess,' Isaac said at last, staring at the conscious sleeper.

'What is it?'

'Phrenology.'

'What?'

'You know, bumpology. They call themselves scientists, those quacks who believe they can read people's minds by the bumps on their heads.'

'I've heard of it,' said Waldo. 'I think my mother is keen on it—'

'She would be,' Isaac interrupted scornfully. He

pointed to a pair of cruel-looking metal tongs that had a measuring scale along one axis. 'That's a craniometer. Spiritualists and phrenologists often work together. They think they're uncovering the secrets of the mind.'

'How?' Rachel asked.

'I don't know,' Isaac shrugged. 'They think one bump on the head means you are good at words, another that you're a vicious criminal. It's all nonsense.'

'They're treating this child like a lab rat!' hissed Waldo. 'They're experimenting on a living *human*, in the name of this phrenology thing!'

I didn't care what it was called. I wanted it to stop. It was awful, the child's cry. Despairing, but at the same time automatic, like a whistle. Punctuated all along by the busy chit-chattering of the needle in that bed of wires and batteries attached to the dummy-shaped tripod. Call it science or progress or what you will, this smelt of evil. I sat down on the bed. As I came closer I saw it was a girl, who continued to gaze forward, immobile, unknowing. Gently I drew down the sheet and took her hand, which was lying limp, crossed over her chest. Her hand was frozen, a lump of ice. She didn't resist or show any sign that she felt me pressing her fingers, willing her to life.

Suddenly, the girl sat forward on her pillows, struggling for air. Like someone drowning who, gasping, breaks the surface of the water. Every muscle, every nerve in her body was tense. I could feel her fingers rigid as metal. Her eyes were drilling into mine – *seeing*. I backed away because her eyes were disconcerting. I noticed one was grey, the other green.

She spoke rapidly, her mouth moving in a gabble of Mandarin Chinese. At least that is what I believe it was, for we understood not a single word. Even Isaac, who is brilliant with languages, shook his head.

'No,' I said, my voice breaking. 'I can't speak your tongue.'

'I spik English.'

The girl took her hand away from mine, then raising both hands she clasped my cheeks, forcing me close to her face. Her breath was sour, her eyes poking hot into mine.

'Help me.'

✎ Chapter Twelve ✎

'What is your name?' Rachel asked gently.

The girl had let go of my face and collapsed back into her pillows. Her eyes were filming over again. I took her hand, pressing it, willing her on.

'Please?' Rachel whispered. 'Please tell us your name.'

'Yin Hua.'

'Why are you here?'

'I prisoner.' The child turned her ill-matched eyes to Rachel and a hand rose from the bed to graze Rachel's face.

'We mean no harm.'

'Take me away.'

'I will,' Rachel promised. 'If . . .' she relapsed into silence.

What could we do? Rachel's clenched jaw told me she didn't care how powerless we were. The others were sagging, their shoulders slumped. How could we break this child out of her prison? We were prisoners ourselves. Caught in the Bakers' butterfly nets. We could flutter and struggle – but what had they said? 'There is no way out.'

'What is this?' Waldo asked, gesturing to the wires and tubes and machines. 'Why are they doing this to you?'

'*I see.*'

'What do you see?'

'I see the –'

Abruptly, in the middle of her sentence, Yin switched her gaze away from Waldo and looked at the door.

'Go. Fast.'

'Nothing there, Yin,' Waldo said, looking at the closed door. It had an opaque panel at the top through which we could see the water. 'Nothing but starshine – no one out there.'

'Go,' she insisted. 'Tomorrow come.'

'It's all right,' he soothed.

'GO! GO! GO!' she yelped. The whistle came again from between Yin's lips and the needle began to chitter-chatter on the machine by her side. 'Go way.'

'Come on,' said Isaac, sounding frightened.

'NO,' Rachel said. 'We stay. We want to help you, Yin. Please be calm.'

Yin wasn't listening. The eerie whistling scream came from her lips, striking dread into my heart. I stood up and began to back towards the door.

'Maybe we should listen to her,' I said.

'No.' Suddenly Yin ceased whistling. 'Too Late! Hide!'

She was pointing at the large white cupboard in the corner of the room. 'Now.'

'We can't all squeeze in there!' I exclaimed.

'GO!'

As one we dived towards the cupboard, opening the door and herding inside. It made no sense for there was no one about, no one outside as far as we could tell. I wouldn't have obeyed Yin's orders, but there was something so panicked in her voice I felt we had no choice. The cupboard was dusty and uncomfortably full of things we couldn't see in the dark. But we could glimpse through the shutters back into the room. My heart almost stopped as a shadow appeared at the door. It swung open and a man carrying a powerful lamp was silhouetted against the stars.

'I believe I'm becoming sloppy,' he drawled to himself. 'I could've sworn I locked the door.'

The well-bred voice belonged to a man wearing a white coat, which he'd hastily thrown over some striped pyjamas.

'What seems to be the problem, Yin? You're whistling fit to bring the house down.'

He stepped into the room, haloed by the lamp, and we saw him clearly, a stranger never before glimpsed in all our weeks of tedious voyage. He had blue eyes, sparse blond hair and lips so thin they almost disappeared into his skin, along with a very weak chin. An Englishman to the core. He was chattering to himself, a sound oddly like that of his dummy-like machine. Yin was slumped back against the pillows, lifeless as a marble statue.

'Naughty girl, waking the doctor in the middle of the night.' He stood by the bed and gently smoothed her hairless scalp. 'You know I'm preparing my paper, little Yin. It's hard work, not like lounging about in bed all the time. I'm very angry with you. Better pull your socks up or else we're not going to have much of a show in Shanghai!'

As he talked to himself, he was preparing a syringe, filling it from a bottle he'd pulled out of a bureau. He tested the syringe by squirting some of the white liquid into the air, and then, satisfied, he plunged it into Yin's arm. She moaned but lay still.

'That should keep you quiet for a bit!' the doctor muttered. He picked up the callipers and began to measure Yin's head, kneading and probing. He got out a pen and began to scribble something on her skull. All the while he kept up the steady stream of talk – drivel really.

'You'll do me proud, little Yinny,' he said. 'No more nonsense about phrenology being a fake. Cooper will eat his hat and so will Portland. Lord Portland indeed. I'll lord it over him when I'm done. It takes rare skill, it does, a case as complex as this. Perhaps they'll "Lord" me. No more doctor, I'll be Lord Billings of Shanghai, fellow of the Royal College of Science, renowned from the banks of the Thames to the Soochow flats. Ha!'

I had a powerful desire to burst out of the cupboard, to swat the doctor, if that was what he really was, with one of his own machines. Most probably, rather than a real doctor given to the healing of the sick, he was one of those quacks who haunt fairgrounds but are known sometimes to stalk the corridors of universities and hospitals. Still muttering, he opened a notebook and jotted down some of his readings. Flipping it shut, he reached out again and stroked Yin's head, as if smoothing down imaginary hair. It made my flesh crawl. But there was a tenderness in the man's gesture – so would a father pat his daughter's head.

I thought with a sudden pang of my own father, back in Oxford. He must be frantic, poor Father. Had he managed to pick up our trail at all?

We all held our breath, scared to move a muscle though it was hot and cramped in the cupboard. The doctor straightened up and wished Yin goodnight. My heart stopped as he moved towards us. He was going to open the door. But at the last minute he veered off and my breathing returned to normal. His lamp cast a pool of bobbing light as he walked out of the laboratory.

We stumbled out of the cupboard. I took Yin's hand

and tried to wake her. The injection had obviously dulled her for she was frighteningly unresponsive. Though her eyes briefly fluttered open, they quickly closed again. The brief glimpse I'd had of her eyeballs, swimming in a yellowish pus, chilled me.

'We'd better go,' Rachel whispered.

Through the tiny porthole window we could see the sea blushing pink, the first signs of the approaching dawn. The crew would be up and about soon. If we were found here, it would be all the worse for Yin.

The machines were still as we left the girl. No more chattering, no more whining shrill. Only an underlying hum, like the breathing of a great mechanical beast, which I'd not noticed before. I was the last to leave the laboratory and the only one to hear Yin's parting words. I turned round sharply to gaze upon her. But she was still mute and immobile – quite impossible that she'd spoken. Perhaps I had imagined the girl's words. Or perhaps in some fantastical way she was speaking to me direct, thought to thought.

'*I'll meet you in the belly of the dragon,*' said the high voice, echoing in my mind as we tramped the silent steamer back to our cabins. Her words haunted me. Try as I might to unravel their meaning, I could make no sense of them.

'*I'll meet you in the belly of the dragon.*'

∽ Chapter Thirteen ∾

From dawn till dusk on the day following our discovery of Yin and the opium, we were kept busy with our Mandarin lessons. I am ashamed to say I was not a good student. Indeed I barely learned a word of that odd language. It was sundown before the four of us found the chance to grab a moment. The sea was choppy, making the *Mandalay* roll and tumble. Her sails had been furled as a precaution against the weather, but the gale still whistled through the rigging. The oily smoke pouring through her red funnels was whipped by the wind into fantastical shapes like ragged washing in the sky. Though we were all seasoned sailors by now, even I felt a little queasy. We talked in hushed, rapid voices, our words half swallowed by the swoosh of the propellers churning below us, making good time towards Shanghai harbour.

'Enough,' hissed Rachel. 'We have to take a stand.'

'They'll murder us,' Isaac murmured.

Rachel persisted. 'We can't leave Yin to their mercy.'

She was right, of course. We had to do something. But what?

'What's your bright idea then?' Isaac asked in a choking voice. I glanced at him. His face was yellowish and I realised he was very frightened.

'This whole thing stinks,' Rachel said. 'It's evil. I want to get out.'

'Jump overboard if you like!' Isaac snapped.

'Oh, keep quiet, Isaac. It's all very well for you geniuses. You live in a fantasy world full of wires and engines. But this isn't about science. It is real life. That poor child is *suffering*.'

'Truce,' I said, walking up to the rail between them. When brother and sister squabbled like this, amazingly enough it was up to me to play peacemaker. 'We know the Bakers are evil. The question is what to do about it? We're not free agents, they've snared us in their coils. We've only a couple of cards up our sleeve.'

'Such as?' the others chorused.

'One: the Baker Brothers need us. Without us they can't get this Book of Bones thing.'

'Maybe,' Rachel murmured. 'What else?'

'Look! We're nearly at Shanghai – our first chance to escape from these thugs. We need to do something really important before we try to save Yin.'

'What?'

'Find a doctor. We must find medical help in Shanghai or else one of us will die.'

'How will we get away from Lips and his gang?' asked Rachel.

'The hand of God?' I shrugged. 'Look here, it is impossible to escape at sea – but once we're on dry land, who knows?'

Through the mist, the boulevards of Shanghai were beckoning us. This city was a legendary blend of East and West and I was desperate to reach it. But we couldn't travel fast up Soochow Creek as we were stuck in a mess of waterborne traffic. What a lot of boats! Dutch traders, Imperial warships, Japanese junks and Chinese sampans. Ships of wood and others of iron, painted and unpainted, bearing scarlet sails or drab white masts. There were even craft decked in gorgeous flowers, like floating roof gardens. Among this motley assortment were the sleek shapes of the opium smugglers – the Fast Crabs and Scrambling Dragons.

The iron flanks of our majestic steamer were pushing aside the wooden junks and sampans. I spied a lorcha with a dragon painted on her bow. Suddenly the boom of our klaxon cut our discussion short. We had finally arrived in Shanghai! Our trunks and valises were already laid out on deck, and as the gangway went down three Chinese porters appeared from nowhere to carry our loads. I was not surprised to see Mrs Glee and Lips, the captain, in his full uniform, waiting for us on deck.

'Goodbye,' Mrs Glee said, extending a hand towards me.

'What do you mean?!' I exclaimed, totally thrown. My friends were equally bewildered. Were we now on our own? Suddenly all my fantasies of escape were pointless.

'Our instructions are to leave you in Shanghai,' Mrs Glee said. Her eyes rested on me briefly. 'Oh . . . I'm so sorry.'

'Don't be,' I said coldly. 'You made your choices.'

'Kit . . . Waldo . . . I never meant you any harm.'

'You're soft as a sponge, Vera,' Lips sneered. 'They'll be right as rain. Good riddance, say I.' He turned disgustedly away from us and leaning over the rail spat a wodge of chewing tobacco into the sea.

Mrs Glee was holding something out to me – a leather case. I opened it and saw that it was packed with documents and heavy silver coins.

'What is this?' I asked stupidly.

'Papers you need. Money. Imperial silver taels,' Mrs Glee answered, not looking me in the eye. 'We were told to leave you in Shanghai with plenty of money and, well, you would take care of the rest.'

'But –' Waldo spluttered, indignantly. 'The Baker Brothers –'

'I know as little as you do,' she said, though she was still refusing to meet our eyes. 'I'm a servant. I do as the Brothers instruct me. I know they've set you a task. "Those children will find their way to do it," they said. "They're stubborn little devils."'

'But where will we stay?' Waldo spluttered. 'What are we meant to—'

'I can't help. I really can't . . . I'm . . . I'm so—'

'Don't say you're sorry again,' I interrupted. 'Hot air doesn't mean a thing.'

Mrs Glee flashed me a hurt look, but at least it cut off another string of excuses. She turned her back on us and clipped away, her sharp heels clacking down the deck. For a moment I repressed a pang of pity; she looked so frail in her sea green blouse and jade beads. Even her walk was trembling. Then I thrust those feelings away.

'Well –' Waldo whistled – 'I expect that's the last we'll see of her.'

'I shan't regret it!' Rachel snapped.

My mind was already on something far more important than Mrs Glee. 'I'll meet you in the belly of the dragon,' Yin had said. China was a huge country; we couldn't scour it looking for dragons' bellies. Where was this odd-sounding place? In Shanghai? Peking? Or the wilds of the countryside?

✐ Chapter Fourteen ✐

We had scarcely landed at Shanghai before we were attacked. At least that's what it felt like. 'Ouch!' I growled at the coolie in the straw hat who was tugging me away from my friends towards his rickshaw. 'I don't need a haircut!'

'Wha?' The coolie grinned.

'That's my hair you're pulling.'

I realised I had snapped at the wrong man – another coolie was tugging my hair. Such a mob of drivers, touts and most probably pickpockets had surrounded us as we disembarked that I felt I was losing my wits. All of them seemed to be clawing at me, jabbering, 'Missy, Missy.' Rachel was lost from view in a jumble of plaits and hats, Isaac was flailing. It was so hot even the stones on the quay seemed to be steaming, covering everything in dense perspiration.

Thankfully Waldo took charge, shoving people out of the way and barking commands. He had grown so much lately he towered over the sea of conical straw hats.

Somehow we managed to select a rickshaw pulled by two strong but stick-thin coolies, who took us to a boarding house on Bubbling Well Road. Our rooms were clean, our beds dressed with heavily embroidered Chinese silks. Exhausted, we collapsed into sleep. But I woke in the night disoriented at missing the gentle motion of the steamship. I was deeply uneasy, with a sour taste in my mouth and a sickness in the pit of my stomach. The Bakers' poison working its way through my veins? We must find Yin. But how? What chance did we have in this huge, teeming land where we had the advantage of neither language nor friends.

I almost wished Aunt Hilda was with us.

The next morning we breakfasted early on porridge laced with treacle and got directions to an English doctor from the Welsh lady who ran the boarding house. Rather puzzlingly Shanghai is divided into many 'concessions', with the English, Americans and French all owning portions of the booming port. What a city! Stately avenues, elegant boulevards, towering stone buildings that would have graced Piccadilly or the Champs Elysées. No wonder it was called the Paris of the Orient. It was as if some grand European metropolis had erupted, fully formed, in the middle of Asia.

But Asia it was, no doubt about that. As we made our way on foot to the doctor, my eyes were drawn by a thousand wondrous sights. A purple pagoda in the shade of blossom trees. A fine Chinese lady with vermilion lips and black-lined eyes, wearing a traditional high-necked dress in pink satin. She surveyed the world like an empress from her gold sedan chair while her bearers puffed and sweated. Smoked ducks hanging in rows from their long necks. Sacks of rice piled high. Thousands of tiny bamboo cages, each one graced by a twittering songbird. An armless beggar rolled up in a doorway, his face grimed with sweat and dirt but wearing a once elegant silk tunic.

Isaac stopped in wonder before one stall that was selling hundreds of colourful tubes and boxes. The seller was toothless with a long pigtail hidden behind a broad-brimmed straw hat. A sign engraved with gold letters hung above him.

'You like?'

'What are they?'

'Fire,' the man explained. He pulled out a handful of something and threw it on the pavement. It exploded among us with deafening bangs and multicoloured sparks.

'Fireworks!' Isaac yelled with delight. 'You know that the Chinese invented gunpowder and fireworks hundreds of years ago.'

'Come on!' I tugged him along. 'No time to waste.'

'You go ahead. I'll catch up with you. I just want to talk to this man for a minute.'

'Hurry!'

Leaving Isaac, we went on. Our destination was a stately stone house, which could have been in Oxford. Though, I must confess, in my own town it would have been blackened by coal dust. While we kicked our heels in the waiting room I told my friends that we must be very clear about what we said. We couldn't confess to being poisoned. We must handle things more carefully. Isaac caught up with us just as we were ushered into Dr Sheldrake's room. The doctor himself, a bald man wearing wire-framed glasses, was sitting at a large ebony desk writing in a leather book. He barely looked up as we entered.

'One of us has been poisoned,' Waldo announced, as soon as we were in. 'We badly need your help.'

I groaned inwardly. He never could keep his mouth shut.

'Poisoned, you say?' the doctor looked up, interested.

'We believe so.'

'What was it. Chinese food? Infected water? Poor sanitation?' The doctor was peering at us over his half-moon spectacles. 'I must say, you all look the picture of health. How long have you been in Shanghai?'

'We arrived yesterday.'

'Hardly long enough to contract a bug.'

'No,' I explained patiently. 'We believe we were poisoned in England before we reached China.'

'How extraordinary. Which one of you?'

'That's just it,' I replied. 'We don't know.'

'How can you *know* one of you is poisoned if you don't know *who* it is?'

'Um . . . we were given reliable information,' I said, cutting off Rachel's explanation with a glare.

'A hopelessly muddled tale,' Dr Sheldrake said. 'Haven't you got things rather mixed up?' He was gazing at us as if we were soft in the head.

'We received a letter aboard ship that told us that one of us had definitely contracted food poisoning. Rather hard to explain, but definitely bona fide.'

The doctor was looking us over, a searching examination. I wondered how we seemed to him, Waldo, blond and blue-eyed, Rachel and Isaac with their glossy dark curls and nut-brown eyes. And me, Kit Salter, with my wide boyish face, always a little tousled and sticky. We were sunburnt from our voyage but still clearly foreign. Did he wonder what we were doing here? As I went into my story the doctor seemed to grow less suspicious. I *think* I convinced him.

'I suppose I should take a blood test from each of you then.'

We rolled up our sleeves and the doctor took blood from each of us, his massive syringe filling up. My blood looked unnaturally dark. Well, at least to me it did.

Then Dr Sheldrake did something that dismayed me. He asked all of us to lie down. There wasn't enough space on his consulting trolley, so he asked us to lie down on the floor.

'Why?' I wondered.

'Your craniums are fascinating.'

Reluctantly we did as he requested. Then the doctor knelt by our heads and literally *felt* our heads. His hands were bony and probing and the whole thing was most uncomfortable. I could see Waldo's mouth twisting in discomfort and Isaac frowning. At last his examination was over, although what it had to do with poisoning was a mystery.

'Very interesting protuberances on your head, Miss Salter,' Dr Sheldrake said to me as we rose. He added to Isaac. 'Your skull has definite possibilities, Mr Ani.'

'How so?' Isaac asked suspiciously.

'The marked development of your pre-frontal cortex makes me believe you to be highly mechanically competent with a developed rational streak. On the other hand, Miss Salter, your lobes, to use layman's terms, are less prominent. I believe you to be impulsive and reckless, with a marked distaste for reason.'

'Are you saying Kit is a bit silly?' Waldo enquired.

'That's not a medical term. But essentially yes.' Dr Sheldrake nodded. 'The young lady puts passion before reason.'

'You've hit the nail on the head, Doctor.' Waldo grinned.

'That's outrageous –' I began, then stopped. 'Look, we're not here for this. When will we get the blood samples back and find out about the poisoning? We're really worried.' I glanced at Isaac, who was tugging my sleeve. 'Stop it!'

'A few days.'

'We're in a hurry,' Waldo said. 'That's far too long.'

'I see. As a special favour I'll try to rush them through by tomorrow. Can't promise, mind. Where should I contact you?'

I was about to tell him the name of our boarding house when Isaac replied, giving him a false name. He was practically pulling me out of the door. Suddenly he seemed in a mad rush to be elsewhere. We said goodbye and tumbled out into the Shanghai street.

'Why did you give him a false address?' I asked Isaac in surprise.

'I didn't like that doctor,' he replied.

'Nor did I,' said Rachel. 'He was all wrong.'

'But it wasn't just a matter of not liking him. I think

107

he's positively sinister. You realise what he was?'

'No,' we chorused.

'Honestly, you lot are half asleep sometimes.' Isaac sighed. I let this comment go, even though Isaac is the most dreamy of us all. 'Doctor Sheldrake is another phrenologist. Didn't you see that bust in the corner? The phrenological head? He's a dangerous crank!'

Waldo gave a low whistle. 'There was a leaflet on his desk,' Isaac continued. 'I saw it out of the corner of my eye. It advertised the "Greatest Scientific Unveiling of the Mystery of the Human Mind Ever Seen". This meeting, whatever it is, is taking place at midday in somewhere called the Jade Dragon Theatre.'

I gasped. Things were clicking into place. I had an intuition, reasonable or not, that we *must* join the scientists at that meeting.

'Come on!' I said. 'We have got to go to Jade Dragon Theatre.'

Somehow Yin had sensed we must be there. Her enigmatic words were starting to make sense.

I'll meet you in the belly of the dragon.

☙ Chapter Fifteen ❧

We arrived late at the meeting, as the first cab driver that we hailed had taken us to the Jade Dragon temple. This ancient shrine was near the Dai Jin Tower, where the guardians of the city kept a lookout for Japanese pirates, near the stone wall that protected Shanghai from her enemies. It took us much confusion and explanation, in our pidgin Chinese English, to return us to the city centre. Luckily our second driver was more intelligent and took us to the Jade Dragon Theatre in Seven Lotus Lane. We had to bypass the watchful guards at the entrance to the theatre, creep up the stairs and into the meeting, which was already crowded when we arrived.

At first I thought I was back in Oxford, for it was the type of fusty, dusty gathering that my father frequents. Apart from a smattering of women and Chinese, most of those gathered here were elderly Europeans, with a scholarly air. Sitting here there was an artistic lady in fringed hat and beads, there a more robust type, perhaps a merchant. None of them, I was relieved to see, looked as if they would be much use in a fight.

If Yin turned up here, we might have to spirit her away by force.

I could see why the strange child had described this hall as the 'belly of the dragon'. It was painted in shades of red and pink and decorated with red silk banners inscribed with Chinese calligraphy. It did resemble the guts of an animal and I could imagine the fluttering silk as the pulsing of the beast's intestines.

Ah well, here I was being unreasonable again.

'Let's creep up to the front. Get a better view,' Waldo whispered.

We edged along the side of the chairs. Someone was striding onto the stage, a man dressed in a white coat. My heart nearly stopped when I saw it was the scientist from the *Mandalay*. The quack doctor who had kept Yin a prisoner. In his wake came two Chinese pushing a metal trolley covered with a sheet. It came to a stop near a green baize card table. There was a babble of talk now, a sort of hushed expectancy in the air, as the scientist held up his hands.

'Welcome to the Jade Dragon Theatre. I'm Doctor Richard Billings and I am going to present you with one of the most marvellous demonstrations of the human mind ever known to science.'

There was a smattering of applause. Then, more like a showman than a scientist, Dr Billings whipped the sheet off the trolley. I had already known what was underneath. Still, the sight of Yin's skeletal body, of her shaved, decorated head, shocked me. She was just a child, an innocent child, and here she was being offered up to these scholars like a performing monkey.

'Little Yin here is going to perform some remarkable feats,' Dr Billings boomed. 'I will give you a phrenological explanation of them. I guarantee today's demonstration is going to make waves across the seas, from Shanghai to London to New York!'

Yin had seemed to be in a coma but now, on cue, she rose and sat obediently on her trolley. The shaven skull covered with scrawls and the almost translucent white of her skin were chilling. She looked more than ever like a death's head. Her grey-green eyes were dull. Was I wrong to see a spark of recognition in them as they swept over me?

'Little Yin is the most phenomenal patient I've ever had,' Billings went on. 'She has a particularly enlarged perception cortex and, as you can see, her memory and time lobes are also very prominent. This means she has powers that would put any fortune-teller to shame. Now, do I have a couple of volunteers to come up on stage and test the girl's powers?'

A number of people put up their hands. Two gentlemen were chosen and ushered to the front. To my surprise, at the very last moment, Waldo barged in and took one of the men's places. When he saw Waldo walk on stage, along with a muscular man who carried a knobbly cane, Dr Billings paled a little. But he quickly carried on.

'Have you ever met this child?' he asked.

Waldo shook his head, as did the other gentleman.

'Very well. For her first amazing predictive effect I choose you, young man. Your name is . . . ?'

'Waldo Bell,' my friend said loudly.

'Mr Bell, prepare to be amazed!'

Billings indicated a pile of books which lay on the card table. 'Choose a book. Any book,' he ordered.

Waldo went over and picked out a book. I saw that it Mary Shelley's well-known work *Frankenstein*.

'*Frankenstein*. Aha,' Dr Billings said. 'Now, Mr Waldo Bell, I am going to ask you to flip through this book.'

Waldo took the book and flipped through it while the audience held their breath. Yin was watching him, or at least her eyes were directed towards him. What she saw, whether she saw, it was impossible to say.

'Waldo, I may call you Waldo, may I not?'

Waldo nodded.

'Pick a word, any word out of the hundreds, nay thousands, in this book.'

112

Waldo flicked through *Frankenstein* some more. Then shut it tight.

'Got a word?'

'Yes,' Waldo nodded.

'Remember the page.'

'Uh-huh.'

'Please write down the word on this piece of paper. Show no one what you've written.'

Waldo did as he was bid, folding the slip of paper and placing it face down on the table.

'Prepare to be astounded beyond your wildest dreams. For this child, this little girl with the amazing skull, will reveal the word Waldo Bell picked. Moreover she will tell you on which page the word resides. Yin –' the scientist turned to the Chinese girl – 'this is your moment!'

But Yin was gazing vacantly at Waldo and seemed scarcely to have heard Dr Billings.

'Yin!' Dr Billings snapped.

I was gripped by the drama unfolding on stage but Isaac was restless. 'I'm slipping out,' he said to me, and vanished down the side of the packed hall.

On stage the little Chinese girl seemed to have slipped into a waking trance and didn't respond to the doctor's promptings. Dr Billings was not having this. He walked over and hissed in her ear while around the hall a few restless shuffles and mutterings broke out. This was not the entertainment that these crusty old men had been promised. I believe I saw Dr Billings's hand slip to Yin's arm and give her a cruel pinch. The girl started and turned towards her master.

'Yin, you will enlighten these eminent ladies and gentlemen who have come here today to see your amazing psychic powers in action. You will tell them what word Waldo Bell picked out of *Frankenstein*, and from which page.'

I was sitting bolt upright, my back pressing hard against the bench. I was frightened for Yin. For some reason I wanted her to get the answer right and not be humiliated before this audience.

Yin shuffled round on her trolley and now she was facing Waldo, her prominent eyes bulging at him.

'This is no trick, ladies and gents,' said Dr Billings. 'Yin will now demonstrate genuine powers.'

'You pick "alchemists" on page 175,' Yin said to Waldo. Her voice was high and clear and rang out throughout the hall.

Waldo handed the slip of paper to the other volunteer, who read out, 'Alchemists, page 175.'

'How on earth did you know that?' gasped Waldo.

The hall had broken out into spontaneous applause and I myself was thunderstruck. How on earth had Yin known exactly which word on which page Waldo had chosen? She'd scarcely been awake.

Yin seemed indifferent to the applause, though Dr Billings was glowing with pride. She slumped back on her trolley, still apparently as drowsy as before. Now the scientist turned to the muscular volunteer and asked his name.

'Horatio Pyke,' the man answered in an oddly fluting voice for such a big man.

'Now, Mr Pyke, I will ask you to write down on these slips of paper the names of ten living men. And the name of one dead man. These men must not be famous. Just relatives or friends or suchlike.'

Mr Pyke did as he was bid, hurriedly scrawling names down on the slips that one of the assistants laid on the card table. When he had finished Dr Billings directed Yin over to the table.

'Now, for an even more stupendous feat of psychic perception,' Dr Billings announced, 'Yin will tell us, just from looking at the names, which of these men is dead.'

Yin slouched by the table looking at the slips of paper. She was frowning. She finished reading the names then walked over to the volunteer. She was looking, really *seeing*, for the first time. The voice that came out of her mouth was high and whining. It recalled the shrill moan that had haunted my sleep on the *Mandalay*.

'Something wrong,' she shrilled.

'What is the matter, Yin?' Dr Billings demanded.

'Dead man not on list. This is dead man.' She was standing right in front of Horatio Pyke.

'Pardon?' Mr Pyke spluttered.

'*You die today.*' Yin wailed. '*When the clock is two.*'

Dr Billings froze. This made no sense. Horatio Pyke was young and strong. Indignant voices began to hum. In the front row of the Jade Dragon Theatre a lady with golden hair began to scream. Then suddenly I was engulfed in something smooth and slithery and my vision turned blood red. I too began to scream.

'It's all right, Kit.' Isaac was lifting something away from my eyes. 'I've cut down the banner. Quick! We need to use the confusion to rescue Yin.'

I now saw that the banner that had hung over the roof of the hall had fallen like an ocean of silk over the crowd, engulfing them in swathes of bloody material. The three of us ran up to the stage, where we saw Waldo had gripped the volunteer, Horatio Pyke, in an armlock. They were struggling, the man kicking at my friend.

Dr Billings and Yin had vanished.

'Hurry!' Waldo grunted, pushing the man to the floor. 'The porters have taken Yin down there.'

We ran after Waldo, down into the footlights of the theatre. It was crowded with props and gaslights, all sorts of bric-a-brac. Of Yin there was no sign. The volunteer, convinced that we were villains, had come running after us. We ran down musty corridors and past foul-smelling chambers and then Isaac burst out into the street. There, right in front of us, we saw two coolies pushing Yin into a horse-drawn carriage. Dr Billings was already seated. The driver was holding the reins, ready to flick the two mares with his whip. There was no way we could catch her. But I put on a burst of speed and tried my utmost to reach the carriage door and the slight figure I saw at the window.

Waldo and I reached the kerb simultaneously, behind the volunteer, who was a fast runner. But the carriage had pulled away, the horses gaining on a cart filled with melons. We had failed. It had been a miracle to find Yin once in this noisy, crowded city. Now she was snatched away again.

We had failed. Failed.

As the horses cantered away I collapsed onto my knees in the middle of that busy road.

'Look sharp!' Isaac yelled, pulling me away from the road towards the safety of the pavement.

Just in time. Something was thundering towards me. A sleek black juggernaut, with screeching wheels. It was the carriage, which had somehow uncoupled from the horses. It rolled back at us, gaining speed as it came. But how had it broken loose?

'I did it, of course,' Isaac yelled, as I panted in his arms.

'Get Yin out!' I shouted to Isaac.

'I'm trying!'

Isaac and Waldo raced towards the carriage. The rudderless juggernaut rolled on, crashing into the pavement and overturning. There was the crash of breaking glass and splintering wood. Yin's head appeared at the window. She was bleeding from a cut above her eye. Isaac and Waldo frantically pulled her out till she lay in my friends' arms like a rag doll. Behind her was a moaning Dr Billings. I began to help him out of the window – not an easy task as there was jagged glass everywhere.

'Leave him!' Waldo hissed, pushing my hands away. 'Someone else will do it.'

It was true; already others had spilt out of the Jade Dragon Theatre. Hands were extended to Dr Billings, while Yin leaned against Rachel, limp and seemingly barely alive.

A figure was lying in the street beyond the wreck of wood and glass. Its hands were splayed out, its legs flung one on top of the other. It was the angle of the neck that told us everything. It was all wrong. There was no way that the volunteer, Horatio Pyke, could be alive. I turned away, bile rising in my throat. At the same instant I noticed the clock on the church opposite the theatre.

Its hands pointed to five minutes past two. Mr Pyke had died just as Yin had predicted. As the clock struck the hour. On the very second.

What kind of monster was Yin that she could foretell a strong young man's death?

I was in a daze, just standing there in the crowd, when Waldo caught me roughly by the arm.

'We've got to keep a hold of ourselves, Kit,' he growled. 'Isaac's found another carriage.'

Waldo pulled me through the throng and out again, into the carriage that waited beyond. There was such confusion, such scurrying, with stretchers arriving for the dead man, that no one seemed to notice us melt away. As I sat opposite Yin in the carriage, as I looked into her odd eyes, I could see only one thing.

The handsome bronze clock, its hands inching past the Roman numeral II.

We were all quiet because I think we realised for the first time what a truly strange person Yin was. The thought exploded shrill into my mind. Had she caused that man's death? In predicting Horatio Pyke's demise had she somehow hastened it? What kind of creature *was* she? Of course we all felt sorry for her – I believed she had been held prisoner in the Bakers' castle and experimented on like a caged animal on the ship. Who knows what manner of torture she had undergone?

And yet, yet . . . what did we really know of her? She was sitting between Rachel and Waldo, slumped against his shoulder. A ghastly thing, with her shaved skull and her shrunken little face. Her cheeks were so angular that I could see the bones poking up through her flesh. She was pitiful, yes. But not just that; she had power too. An odd sort of force of a kind I had never met before. Those eyes, those milky, mismatched eyes, so enormous they seemed to dwarf the rest of her face. What had they foreseen? What misery could they cause?

Yin seemed to feel my gaze on her because she looked up at me – and I felt something searing right through me. Not fear – but it was as if she had examined me thoroughly with that one glance. A child, a little girl. Yet she had wrung me inside out. I felt exposed, ashamed and at the same time an awful foreboding gripped me. *We had it the wrong way round*. We weren't some gallant knights riding to the rescue of Yin. She wasn't some helpless damsel in distress. There was a dark power emanating from her. She was an unknown force – volatile and deadly. Now she had us in her coils. Did she wish us harm?

Her presence among us was unsettling. Waldo and Rachel were almost competing to protect her. They were acting like they had rescued a stray kitten. And poor Isaac, staring out of the window, was pale, blinking nervously through his glasses. He bore a heavy load of guilt. He'd shown real initiative in spotting the doctor's carriage and sabotaging it so that we could rescue Yin. But now he believed he was the cause of a man's death.

I held Yin far more responsible for Horatio Pyke's death than Isaac.

Befuddlement gripped us all. None of us really understood what had just taken place at the Jade Dragon Theatre. It had all happened so fast. It was a blur of fantastical events. Perhaps it was exhaustion or the poisoning, the long steamship journey or the confusion of being in this steamy foreign land. Whatever it was, for a second I had lost my bearings completely when I saw Yin stand up and begin to dismount from the carriage.

'We must go,' Yin said, looking back at us.

'Where?' asked Waldo, who looked as bewildered as I felt. Outside was a wide boulevard, those circular Chinese straw hats, the scent of salt and fish. Nothing I recognised.

'Our boarding house. Bubbling Well Road,' Yin replied. Calmly she dismounted and waited for us on the pavement.

We stumbled after her, disconcerted, as if we had been rescued by Yin rather than the other way round. How did she know where we were staying? None of us had told her the address of our boarding house.

❧ Chapter Sixteen ❧

My mistrust of Yin deepened as we took her up to our room and changed her into fresh linen belonging to Rachel, who is smaller than me. The Chinese girl looked comical in these clothes; they were far too big for her. I sat by the pillow, unable to keep my eyes off her pinched face. Formless suspicions were growing in my mind. Unease, dark clouds billowing. I shook my head, trying to shake off my fears.

She's just a child, I told myself fiercely. But . . . I couldn't forget that dead man. Horatio Pyke. *What kind of child drives a man to his death?*

'Don't do that,' said Rachel, turning and noticing my stare. 'The poor mite's half dead. Do you want drink?' she asked, miming drinking from a glass. 'Oh, sweetheart. Look, she's trembling.'

It was true. Yin was shivering as if she had a high temperature. Thick on her lashes were crusty flakes. The numbered segments Dr Billings had drawn crawled over her scalp like black spiders. Rachel poured her a cool glass from the jug by the bed and tried to force it into her mouth. Yin's hand knocked against it, spilling the water. I don't know if she noticed the wet patch forming on the front of her dress.

I watched her coldly. There was something not quite human about her. Was this all an act to gain our sympathy? The child was as hard to know as a cat. Indeed there was something catlike, curving and sly, about her. Cats often had mismatched eyes.

'Maybe she's hungry?' Rachel suggested.

'We can get something from the kitchens, I suppose,' Waldo replied. 'Rachel, can you –'

'Of course,' she muttered, disappearing out of the door.

We clustered around my bed. Every minute Yin seemed to grow hotter.

'Yin,' I said, mastering my distaste to take her burning fingers, 'who are you?'

Abruptly the shaking stopped. She sat up. Looked around. Her hand reached for the glass and she took a few sips of water. Then she fell back in a daze, staring entranced at our kerosene light, which hung down low from a brass hook.

'Are you hot?'

Her eyes flickered to me for a moment and then back to the glowing lamp.

'Put a cold compress on her face,' Isaac suggested, as Rachel came back into the room with the news that there was no food available till dinner time. 'Rachel, have you a handkerchief?'

Rachel hurriedly soaked one of her handkerchiefs in cold water from the jug and placed it on the girl's forehead. She seemed barely aware of it, lost in a swoon.

'If she gets really ill . . .' Rachel murmured, staring at the girl's fever-racked form. 'Oh, I hope we did the right thing!'

'How could it be wrong?' Isaac hissed, suddenly angry. 'You saw how Dr Billings was making her do tricks, like a performing flea. That's not science, Rachel!'

'I know. Bu—'

'Don't talk then. Do something.'

I understood why Isaac was so angry, for if we had done the wrong thing in rescuing Yin, then the volunteer Horatio Pyke's death had indeed been for nothing.

The water seemed to be having some effect. Yin's eyes wandered, going round the room before settling on me.

'Yin!' I murmured, unable to keep the agitation out of my voice. 'Who are you?'

I approached her. 'Talk,' I demanded more roughly. 'We don't have much time.'

The girl's lips opened. 'Time,' she rasped.

Time.

That single word had unlocked a dam. Everything which we had been probing and looking for now came struggling out. It wasn't easy for her, even I could see that.

Yin had been raised in the far-off province of Henan. Her father was a scholar who did not regard the birth of a daughter as cause for dismay. Chinese parents commonly regarded their daughters as a burden. In fact thousands of girl babies were simply left out in the cold to die. Yin's father had even decided not to bind his daughter's feet. Many girls' feet are bound in layers of cotton from birth, their toes broken to keep their feet small – 'like lotus flowers'. Foot-binding blights this country. I had seen many Shanghai woman hobbling birdlike in tiny shoes, unable to walk properly. They are said to live in constant pain.

Luckily Yin was spared this torment and grew up happily with her brothers and sisters on the slopes of Mount Shong. Their lives passed in the shadow of the great Shaolin monastery. Then one day a wise woman from the monastery noticed her. Auspicious signs were said to hang around her. It was a great honour for her family. So Yin was given away. Aged about four or five she was taken to the monastery. It was a beautiful place, with bamboo glades, flower orchards, babbling brooks and herb gardens. All in a remote part of the mountains, sheltered by groves of ancient trees. The nuns brought her up and she was trained in all the disciplines of the Buddhist order. This included meditation or the ability to empty the mind of all thought, calligraphy, herbal lore and Kung Fu fighting.

When Yin was telling us this part of her life story I could not resist breaking out in wonder. 'You fought?'

She inclined her head.

'Goodness,' I said, for Yin could not be much of a fighter. My doubts about her story were growing. Was she a bare-faced liar? She was just skin and bones. It was plain to see that anybody, even Rachel, could break her in a fight.

'Stop interrupting,' Rachel hissed, and I subsided, letting the girl continue with her story.

The religious folk and other students were kind to her and she knew happiness. She wore the white sash of the student and her mentor was a nun, of great fighting ability, known as Grey Eyebrows. She was still small when she realised that the nuns had marked her out as someone special, someone of a particular ability. It was even said that one day she would be shown the rare honour of reading the Book of Bones.

'The Book of Bones?' I couldn't help interrupting again. 'The one the Bakers want?'

The others shushed me. But I persisted.

'What is it, Yin? This Book of Bones.'

Yin regarded me. 'It show how to do deep cleaning.'

'Sounds like a Chinese laundry.'

Isaac and Waldo tittered, but Rachel frowned and told me to keep quiet and the Chinese girl went on with her story.

Yin seemed to have an uncanny ability to foretell. To bend time. This was first noticed in small things, like when she knew, without being told, that there would be noodles for lunch. Soon she wore the black sash of a disciple and she was excused many of the student duties in the vegetable gardens, while Grey Eyebrows trained her in Kung Fu. She also learned other things: the English language, reading and writing. Her ability grew until it became unclear, as Yin disappeared into a trance, who was the trainer and who the apprentice.

Meanwhile these were unstable times in China. The foreign powers were pressing into the country and threatening the centuries-old rule of the decaying Manchu Empire. Opium flooded the land, fields went untended and famine followed. The court of the Manchu Emperor was corrupt and decadent. Warlords grew in strength. Many eyes turned to the monastery, coveting the wealth and knowledge of the holy fighters.

Then one day a violent warlord attacked the monastery – there was much fighting and plunder. Not that this Shaolin temple was easy to take – indeed the monks quickly drove off the marauders. Yin was unaware of what was happening, only later did she learn of these events. She was deep in meditation during the battle, sitting alone in the cherry orchard lost in wonders. In her trance-like state she did not even realise she had been captured and taken as a slave to a nearby town. There she was sold, along with many, many others, as a coolie. She was destined to be taken to the New World, where she would work from dawn to dusk building America's railroads.

What Yin was talking of was not news to me. For the sad truth is that although the slave trade has been outlawed – by the efforts of William Wilberforce among others – wicked merchants still trade in human flesh. These poor humans, be they Indians or Chinese, are called 'indentured labourers', but they are still caged and bought and sold like slaves. The pens in the *Mandalay* had been intended for such people.

Yin was traded in this way, bought and sold – she didn't recall how many times. Worse was to happen to her, for on the journey west an overseer noticed her strange trances. She was skinny, worthless as a worker. They were about to discard her, throw her overboard as human rubbish, when the overseer chanced on the mutterings of the other coolies.

The child was special. This child was different.

She didn't know how these mutterings caused her to wake up one day in a vast granite castle, with a sky the colour of lead bearing down upon her.

As she said these words Rachel, who had told me off for interrupting, broke in herself. 'That sounds like Hadden Castle – the Baker Brothers' home.'

Yin nodded. I could see she didn't want to dwell on the castle as she quickly went on with her story. She didn't know why the scientist – the 'Yellow Heart' she called him – shaved her head and scribbled on it. He hooked her up to machines which made her feel as if she was buried in a block of ice. Time passed – she was experimented on, prodded and poked and jabbed and hooked up to 'humming beasts'. In those days vivid images passed through her mind, of her mother and sisters and Grey Eyebrows.

Yin must have babbled. She was a shrewd girl and she tried to hold her tongue. She tried especially not to talk of the Shaolin temple, for that was sacred to her. But she believes the Bakers learned the secret of the Book of Bones' existence from her. The scientists and 'ghost men' were after her gift of prophesy, this she had guessed. All her life, her flickering ability to read time like you and I can skim through a book had marked her out as different.

But she claimed this ability was a broken gift.

Sometimes she could see clearly. More often, the future was as blank to her as to you or me. On some occasions she saw wrong, and what she beheld clear as glass did not come to pass.

Worst of all was when she saw disturbing things. Things that made her skin crawl and gripped her heart with horror. At such times she regarded her gift as a curse.

Then she was back on the ship and one day she woke up to see – us!

I must not give you the impression that Yin's story came out this clearly. I had to work hard, to guess and patch it up and tell it to you in proper English. I found as I listened that some of my suspicions of the child were melting away. Looking at the others I saw they believed her completely. She sounded so upset by her 'gift'. She was so young that it cannot have been easy to carry such a burden around. However, that lump of suspicion in my throat refused to go away. True she told her story well – but there were things that still did not make sense to me. I resolved to keep a close eye on her and not to take too much of her story on trust.

One thing I did believe completely about Yin's story was the bit about the Bakers. Men who could visit such cruelty on a child. They had put her through horror. Their souls were steeped in darkness.

I could see only one way out of the Bakers' trap. The doctor had not helped us – that visit had been more than useless. If this small child really had the 'gift' she claimed, only Yin could save us – and herself.

If she helped us, it would prove that she was not the dark force I imagined. It would also prove she was on our side.

'Yin,' I said, 'can you help us?'

She shifted her position on the bed uncertainly. 'What you want I do?'

'There *is* something you can do. Have you guessed?'

She stared back at me.

'One of us has been poisoned by the Baker Brothers. We don't know which one it is. All we know is that one of us will die if we don't stop it. Yin, you can see through time. Can you tell us which one of us is condemned?'

Yin shrank back against the headboard, her body rigid. Her eyes swivelled over Waldo, Rachel, Isaac and me.

'No! NO! I cannot *see* this.'

'Cannot or *will not*?' I asked, my doubts resurfacing.

'Please,' Rachel whispered.

'No. You never ask me this again!'

'So you refuse to help us,' I said.

'*I cannot see.*'

There was little more said that evening, as we bid goodnight to Waldo and Isaac and settled down in our cramped room. Rachel and I were sleeping on mattresses as it had been decided to let Yin have the big bed.

I had an unsettled night. In my dreams I saw a clock face, the hands swinging randomly forward and back. But both the minute and the second hand always halted on the Roman numeral two. There they stayed for a while, with an unnerving clack. Like a door repeatedly slamming shut.

❧ Chapter Seventeen ❧

I woke up at dawn, chilly despite the sun on my face. Something was watching me. Turning a little, I saw Yin. She was already dressed in the navy jacket and wide-legged trousers our landlady had brought for her – a small figure hunched on the windowsill. Her eyes, glinting green and grey, were fixed on my face. I shivered and pulled my blanket up to my chin. She was so peculiar, waiting for something, curled up like a cat in the sunshine.

Normally I talk *a lot*. I know I do because Rachel and Waldo are always keen to point it out to me. But that morning I was unusually quiet. Just as Yin had watched me, I watched her, searching for clues. As we trooped downstairs to meet the others for breakfast, I turned her story over and over in my mind. She could foretell the future, she claimed. Why then had she not foreseen the burning of her monastery and the Bakers' dark role? Why had she not stopped it? I know she claimed she could *see* only infrequently. So she saw what page of a book someone had been reading, but not important things like destruction. Was that plausible? Did anything about her really make sense?

Breakfast was served in the restaurant, an airy room with pillars, palms in pots and lotus flowers on the table. Sunlight slanted down on pale china, heaped with dumplings. Alongside were varnished sticks, lying in pairs by the plates.

'What on earth are these?' Waldo held up the twigs in wonder.

'Chopsticks!' exclaimed Yin, beaming. It was the first genuine smile I had ever seen on her face. Deftly Yin picked up a pair of 'chopsticks', holding them between finger and thumb, and placed one of the dumplings in her mouth.

Uncertainly I took hold of the chopsticks and tried to hoist one of the slimy dumplings into my mouth. It was devilishly hard.

'Bao Zi,' Yin said.

'Pardon?' I said.

'You know the Dim Sum?'

I hadn't the faintest idea what she was talking about. Why couldn't we have normal food? Yesterday we'd had porridge. We'd even had the luxury of spoons! Looking around I saw most of the other guests were Europeans, many in topis and cream linen suits, with sunburnt faces.

That handsome man over there, blond and blue-eyed, had a German air. That pale man looked like a Viking. In the corner, under the fan, was unmistakably a pair of Englishmen. Probably old China hands. In any case, they seemed to be stomaching the fare. As I pride myself on being adventurous when it comes to food, I took a bite. Waldo, Rachel and Isaac were watching suspiciously. It was horrible, some kind of sickly sweet bean mixture. I wanted to spit it out but there was such pride on Yin's face that I nodded vigorously.

'Mmm . . . delicious,' I said.

Waldo took a pair of the chopsticks and clumsily speared a dumpling. I watched, smiling, as he bit in. He was about to blurt out with a yuck. But in a rare burst of sensitivity, when he saw Yin's hopeful expression, he quickly turned it into a yum. So we ate the soggy things filled with sickly paste and made murmurs of delight while Yin looked on. We had washed her head clean of those disfiguring black lines and given her one of Rachel's bonnets to wear. Rest had improved her a little. I could imagine her after a few weeks of feeding, her face filled out a little and without the bones poking through her skin.

She'd look less like a walking skull. But there would still be *something* that set her apart.

'We should go back to Doctor Sheldrake's,' I said,

trying to shake off these thoughts. 'Find out about the blood tests.'

'He's horrible.' Rachel shivered. 'You'll have to drag me there kicking and screaming.'

'We've got to know the truth.'

'It won't do any good,' Isaac interrupted. 'The doctor is a waste of time.'

'Aren't you being a bit pessimistic?'

'While you weren't looking I saw Doctor Sheldrake throw our blood samples in the bin.'

'Why didn't you tell us?'

Isaac shrugged.

'That doctor's up to something, something sinister.' I went on.

'Or he never believed our story,' Isaac replied. 'Maybe he was taking the samples to humour us? Either way, there's no point going back to him.'

Waldo threw down his chopsticks on a lump of uneaten dumpling. 'I don't believe this!'

'What now?'

'It seemed like we were getting somewhere – with the doctor, I mean. Maybe he would have helped us. But he was a crank or a fraud – or something much more dangerous. And, well, we're stuck in Shanghai with a sick child.' He glanced at Yin. 'No offence.'

'I not offended.' Yin said.

'I mean, what the hell do we do now?'

I opened my mouth to speak. Then closed it again. Rapidly I ran over our problems. One of us was poisoned, we had to find this Book of Bones thing, we were stranded in a foreign land and we had Yin – spy or helper, angel or devil? Clearly an invalid, whatever else she was. How could we even search for this Book – assuming we knew how to get to Henan and the monastery – with Yin in her current state? She needed rest, care, soup – gallons of soup. Soup was meant to be good for sick souls, wasn't it?

We were in a right old mess.

'We're in a mess,' Waldo said, echoing my thoughts.

I glared at him. 'Talk about stating the obvious.'

'It never hurt did it? Telling the truth.'

'No!' a small voice piped up. 'We are not in mess.'

It was Yin. 'Today we go to tailors. We must buy Chinese clothes, more practical for our journey. Tomorrow we go Peking. We find help there for the Book of Bones.'

As one we stared at her, astonished. She came up to my chin, but here she was coolly making plans for us. The nerve of it. Waldo bristled a little and even Rachel looked dismayed.

'Keep quiet, Yin,' Waldo said, pushing away his plate of dumplings. 'This is serious talk.'

'Sorry,' the child looked down, flushing.

'Why on earth Peking?' I asked. 'The monastery we need to get to is in Henan.'

'Yin, you can't travel,' Rachel burst in over me. 'You're sick. You need days – no, weeks – of rest.'

'I am quite well,' Yin said. 'I say Peking, for Henan is difficult and dangerous place. I live there and I know – there are many warlords and bandits. We will go to Peking to get help – and from Peking we go to monastery in the mountain.'

'It's ludicrous to start taking orders from a little girl,' Waldo said.

This time Yin did not hang her head but stared back at Waldo. 'I am a girl, little. I agree with this. But I am Chinese. I know this country and have many friends who can help us. I know there is much danger. Please listen.'

I could see the sense of what Yin was saying – if she wasn't trying to lead us into a trap. We couldn't just wait in Shanghai for the poison to snuff out one of our lives, we had to act. Perhaps going to Peking was our best option. Besides, it made sense to buy comfortable Chinese clothes, because it would be easier for us to blend in with the natives.

'Trust me,' Yin said, looking in my eyes. 'Please.'

∞∞∞

138

'Your arm too long. Like monkey,' the tailor said to me, measuring from the tip of my fingers to my shoulder. He addressed Yin in rapid Mandarin. From the disgruntled tone of his voice I had the feeling that he was not exactly complimenting your friend Kit Salter. Yin answered him with a few soothing words, as if she was excusing me. Frankly, I didn't see what the tailor had to boast about. He was a sallow little fellow with a shaved forehead and a plait hanging down his back. His grey beard was almost as long as his plait, and he had hair growing out of his ears and nose. Altogether he looked as if he could have done with *several* haircuts.

This was the fifth tailor shop we had visited. We had started with the elegant emporiums near Bubbling Well Road, lined with bolts of turquoise and pink silks and richly embroidered tunics. Now we were in a dirty warren of streets near the Dongtai market. This was a glimpse of a different China from the grand European city: cages of songbirds, the click, clack of elderly mahjong players gambling their years of hard work away, and tattered clothes drying on bamboo poles. The problem was that Chinese clothes were not cut for our larger frames. Waldo, in particular, was almost a giant by local standards.

This shop, lined with clothes for dock labourers and river folk, was our last chance. To tell the truth, I was very keen to have a change of clothes. My serge travelling dress was stiff with sweat and the high-necked lace blouse I wore underneath was scratchy. The loose peasant trousers and jacket would make a welcome change. The others had at last found suitable garments so it was just me left.

In the tiny changing area I shrugged on the loose blue tunic that the shopkeeper handed to me. When I came out Waldo whistled sarcastically and Isaac gave me a funny look. In the mirror I could see that my arms stuck out from the sleeves. Never mind. I felt free in the loose, shapeless trousers and tunic. Chinese ladies might have their feet bound, but at least their clothes were comfortable.

We left the tailor's shop dressed like Chinese labourers, with our old garments parcelled up in newspaper. A small boy was sent to deliver them to our boarding house. I strode after Yin, relishing the spicy smells wafting down to us in the light breeze. We passed an old lady frying noodles in a great iron pan – they looked crisp and tasty.

'Want to try some?' I asked.

'Kit, you're mad,' Rachel protested. 'You'll get worms or, or . . .'

'I'm already poisoned, most like. Besides I'm famished.'

'The food is good,' Yin said. 'We must eat.'

She was right. The sun was setting and we hadn't eaten for hours. It was strange. As soon as Yin said it was all right, everyone queued for the noodles. When it was Kit's idea, it was another matter. I didn't really begrudge it. I had been watching her for the whole day, musing on her motives. Nothing new had struck me, though at one time I had wondered if she had some dark aim in dressing us like the natives.

Anyway, the bowl of noodles I gulped down just then was lovely. Long, slippery worms in a salty brown broth, served with steaming greens and prawns. Even Rachel, so unadventurous with food, was enjoying it. Perhaps I would have to add a Chinese restaurant to the Indian establishment I planned to open. The people of Great Britain would be in for a culinary treat.

My mood was lightening, my attitude to Yin melting. Perhaps it was simply the result of a full belly. I am notoriously easy to bribe with food. Maybe I had been too suspicious of the girl. Maybe the death of the volunteer had just been an unlucky accident. Perhaps we should follow the strange child to Peking. I was thinking thus, licking the last drops of sauce from my bowl, when Yin turned to us.

'We must hurry,' she said.

'Oh? Where?' I looked at the pink horizon. 'It's time to turn in for the night, I would say.'

'No,' she said, and muttered something under her breath.

'A nightclub?' Waldo and Isaac burst out in unison. 'Great idea.'

'Why on earth would we want to go—' I began, before Waldo and Isaac cut me off. A new foreboding gripped me. Where did the child want to take us at this time of night? Was it some seedy den? It felt suspiciously like a trap.

'I have the sense. There is no time to lose. Come now!'

With that the child disappeared into the crowd at the mouth of an alley, leaving us no option but to follow her.

❧ Chapter Eighteen ❧

My fears evaporated as Yin led us back into the European city. At night Shanghai was even more exotic, flaring with gaslight, humming with the strains of a thousand competing orchestras. Nightclubs spilled out revellers. Two lovely ladies dressed in silk ball gowns chattered in French to each other on the steps of the Astor House Hotel. A haughty young blonde in fox furs and a satin evening gown strode into a club where they were playing a Russian mazurka. Feet tapped, drums thrummed. Sweet, musky perfumes wafted in the breeze and the very air was intoxicating.

'Why don't we visit one of the tea dances?' I suggested, as we passed the Astor. This was one of the grandest of the stone buildings, with vast arched windows. A ball was in full swing, with enough jewels on display to light up the night skies. Liveried doormen guarded the entrance, but I was sure I could talk our way in.

'No.' Yin shook her head. 'Not.'

We passed the wide boulevards, the streets full of

bejewelled ladies and dashing men in bow ties. Instead of entering one of these bright places, we turned down streets that became progressively narrower and darker. Yin was leading us down the murkiest alleys, away from light and safety.

'Yin,' Rachel grabbed the striding girl, 'I don't like this.'

'We must go.'

'It's not safe.'

'You trust,' she replied, shaking her off.

Now we were in another alley, crowded, but with a certain grace. Wooden houses teetered together, their tiered roofs carved into the shapes of dragons and birds. Banners and flags were strung across the street. Red paper lanterns hung down from many houses and plangent music drifted through the air. Chinese ladies, their lips painted vermilion and cheeks rouged, lounged here and there, dressed in tight silk dresses. Many had bound feet, so tiny they tottered rather than walked. The streets were packed with Europeans as well as Chinese. There was something in the air that I didn't like.

'Yin.' My heart was pounding with fear that the girl was leading us into a trap. 'This isn't a good place.'

She darted forward. We were forced to follow even though Waldo and Isaac also looked scared. As we struggled through a knot of labourers carrying brightly coloured paper lanterns, Yin disappeared.

'Yin!' we called desperately. 'Where are you?'

From a doorway draped in crimson silk came a faint cry. We ducked through the hangings. The fug made my eyes sting. That sweet-sickly tang, which I'd noticed before in the streets of Shanghai, was in the air. Now it was so thick you could taste it in the back of your throat. Through the coils of smoke we made out our friend, flitting towards the back of the room.

Small cubicles, each containing a lone Chinaman, were dotted around the den. Most had their foreheads shaved and plucked till they were high and smooth, with their hair plaited at the back into a pigtail. They were lying about or smoking long clay pipes. The gloom was broken by oil lamps scattered on low tables beside each cubicle. Something was bubbling and crackling in the lamps. The stuff gave off that sickly tang. Mixed with the smell of sweat and grease it made me want to retch.

I recoiled, almost falling into the silk hangings. Smoke was in my nose, eyes, throat – so heavy I was gasping for breath.

Rachel's nails dug into my arm. 'What is this place?'

'Just a—'

'It's an opium den.' She cut me off.

Yin had darted to the back, where I could see bundles wrapped in rugs, scattered on a wooden platform.

'We'd better follow her.'

'No,' Rachel said. 'Absolutely no way in this world am I going in there.'

A man loomed over Waldo's shoulder, leering at Rachel with gluey eyes. 'Wantchee smoke? Wantchee eat?'

'Get away!' Rachel snapped, backing away.

'We've got to stay together.' Hurriedly I pulled her after me into the back of the den where Yin had vanished. I caught sight of her by the wooden platform, bending over a bundle, which I now realised was a human being wrapped in blankets. There were half a dozen poor beasts, lost to this world, slumped in their swoon. Some had spittle running out of their mouths, others' eyes lolled vacantly. It was an ugly scene. I wanted to get away as fast as I could. Trouble was, I felt sluggish. My legs were wobbly. I badly needed to rest, breathe properly.

'No worse than a gin palace,' Isaac said, his shaking voice contradicting his bold words. 'At least these poor wretches have gone to sleep rather than starting fights.'

'I feel odd,' Rachel said. Beads of sweat stood out on her face.

'Me too,' Isaac mumbled.

My vision was blurry, with lines forming and flowing towards me. Everything shimmered, glowing with its own power. I wanted to drop down onto that large soft bed. Why not? That sweet flute music. I was tired, so tired. Why not rest a little? Catch my breath. I saw the water, the cool blue of the river Cherwell. My Jesse, my good old mare Jesse, would want to rest awhile. My knees could only stand so much galloping over Port Meadow and through the woods . . .

'Kit!' From far away, I heard a voice.

'Who wants her?' I muttered.

'Enough of this.' Waldo's face was an inch from mine. He had a pimple at the corner of his nose. A huge red pimple.

'Listen to me now!' he pinched me hard on the check. Shocked, I jerked away.

'Get up.'

I realised I had sunk down on the platform. Shakily I tried to stand up but just swayed back and forth.

'It's the opium, you silly ninny,' Waldo grabbed my arm. 'It's gone to your head. You always were soft up there.'

Isaac and Rachel were staring at me through wide, shocked eyes. They looked very alike, dark, curly-haired, judging me. It was as if I had done something *wrong*.

Roughly Waldo heaved me up. I stood against him, panting a little, still feeling woozy.

'This is foul,' he said. 'We're leaving.'

'All right. No need to shout.'

Waldo was pushing me. I blinked, shaking off the clouds in my brain.

'I can manage, Waldo.'

Yin was prodding a bundle of rags. As I moved away, her hand reached out, clutching at me, though Waldo was pulling the other way.

'Come,' she pleaded. She was surprisingly strong.

'No.' I tried to shake her off.

'You come.' She pulled at my arm, tearing the fabric, while Waldo pulled on the other side. Yin's grip was stronger and I was forced back to the platform. The lumps of rags rolled over and I was shocked to see white skin and pale hair. I stood over the thing.

'Mrs Glee?' I said at last.

Lying on her back, Mrs Glee looked at me but didn't seem to see.

'It's not,' Waldo said to me. 'Can't be –'

'Shush.'

'That really you, Mrs Glee?' Waldo asked.

The woman's face was grey. She was unwashed and emaciated, in the grip of the drug. All her jewellery was gone, the gold wedding ring she always wore had vanished. She looked at us dumbly, her eyes dull. As we stood over her, urging her, something sparked. She realised for the first time who we were.

'We're taking you away,' Waldo said.

She shook her head.

'You're coming with us,' he insisted.

'It's no use.'

'We're leaving. Now.'

Together we pulled Mrs Glee up and hitched her between our shoulders. Limply, she allowed herself to be dragged away. We got to the exit without attracting much interest as everyone in the den was in their own poppy-tainted world. But at the door a broad Chinaman in padded trousers and maroon jacket barred our way. He had beady eyes and a pigtail tied with red satin.

He grunted something at us in his own language.

'We're taking this woman, like it or not,' Waldo growled, with Isaac scowling at his side.

'Wantchee 100 yuan for smoke.'

'Pay the man, Rachel.'

Rachel handed over the coins and we dragged our governess out onto the street. The air blew the last opium fumes out of my mind. Waldo's eyes were upon me as he lifted Mrs Glee through the dirt and spent fireworks. Flushing a little, I looked away. Not your finest hour, Kit, I told myself. I couldn't understand the dream state that had come over me in the den. All the others were gagging on the fumes, but they were not overcome.

I had no time to brood on my shortcomings as we had to flee this place as fast as we could. Somehow we found a cab and managed to heave ourselves in. The horse clopped its way through the throng of painted women and staggering opium addicts while I sat stiffly overcome with a mixture of pity and disgust. Mrs Glee was prone, seemingly unaware.

We journeyed out of the Chinese quarter back to the broad boulevards of the International Settlement. We had almost reached our destination on Bubbling Well Road when Mrs Glee woke up and looked at me.

'You can't do it,' she said to me.

I looked away.

'Do what?' Rachel and Waldo answered in unison.

'Get away from them.'

'From whom?' Rachel asked.

'The Brothers. I tried and tried. When Mr Glee died I thought I could do it. I ran and ran. I ran so far that I thought they would never find me. But they did. I was a housekeeper then. They found me and they gave me that stuff.'

'The Bakers *fed* you opium?' I broke in.

She nodded. 'They trapped me with that stuff. I need it more than life itself. It is the only reason I have to go on.'

'Well, your path is clear,' Rachel said slowly. 'You must give up the poppy and escape the Bakers.'

'I can't do it.'

'If you don't try, you'll never be free.'

'I *won't*. You can't make me. What's the point? There's nothing left for me any more.'

I bit back the retort that was on my lips, and as I did my eye fell on Yin. She was coiled in the corner of the carriage, a glint of light under her half-closed lashes. As always, remote from our agitation. Old doubts – and new questions – came crashing into my opium-dimmed mind. How had she known Mrs Glee was in that den? Were they in secret contact? It seemed Yin could sniff out misery just as a cat sniffs out vermin. This was another example of the feline way Yin prowled through life.

❧ Chapter Nineteen ❧

'I'm not sure I like her, and I definitely don't trust her,' I said.

'Shush,' Rachel whispered. 'She can hear us.'

Mrs Glee was asleep in the big bed beside Yin, who did not seem to mind the stale smell coming from her. The boys had gone to their room and Rachel and I talked in whispers as we lay on our hard mattresses.

I raised myself on an elbow and looked at the two of them: Yin was breathing regularly, her back to the odorous Mrs Glee.

'She's asleep.'

'Oh, Kit, how can you not like Yin? As for trusting her, she *saved* our governess.'

'Yes, but how did she know she was in that den?'

'She has these feelings. You know that, Kit. Why do you distrust her so?'

'Someone has to look out for us, make sure we're not walking blindly into a trap.'

'I'm tired,' she sighed. 'Give it a rest.'

Rachel shuffled over and soon was snoring gently. But my mind would not rest. I was anxious that we seemed to be following Yin's whims. Yet at the same time I had no better ideas. She had shown us that her instincts were moving towards something. She was still *odd*, and my doubts about her were like hard little lumps that would not go away. Yet, yet . . . If the rest of us were lost in a fog created by the Baker Brothers, she seemed to see a beacon shining somewhere. Some force was guiding her. Could we do better than follow it?

She was *different*, this slip of a girl. Not only for her culture, which was so strange to us, but because she lived much of the time in a sort of waking dream. We were learning that China is a society bound in many layers of manners. The Chinese like to keep the door firmly shut on foreigners. My other foreign friends, the Egyptian boy Ahmed and the Indian Maharajah, had odd beliefs too. But I'd never found another person as hard to understand as Yin.

The next morning, as we rose, some of my foreboding of the night before had evaporated. I decided to trust Yin, for now. We talked, or rather the others talked, while I watched the waters of the Woosung through our bay window. They told Yin the whole story, revealing details we had not mentioned before. How the Bakers had kidnapped us. How they had poisoned one of our number, thereby trapping all of us in their net. We told of the aches and pains that had beset each and every one of us on the boat, though less so since arriving in Shanghai. We had no idea who was sick. Who would die.

My friends also told her how the Bakers had found a strange elixir in the Himalayas, those snowy peaks that tower above the Indian plains. These waters had miraculously restored their youth to them and concealed their rotten souls in shining new flesh. Now they wanted to 'perfect their perfection' and believed the Book of Bones would help them do it. If we didn't bring this fabled Book back to them, one of us would die.

Yin knew the Book. She had grown up in its shadow. She'd already realised the Bakers wanted it, so in some ways our story was not new to her. Curled up on the window seat she listened to our story. By her side was an empty bowl. She had not been able to wait for breakfast so a waiter had brought her dumplings, which she had demolished in record time. It was rare, now, to see Yin without her mouth full of the sticky things. Still, they were at least starting to fatten her up a little.

The only thing about Yin I was beginning to understand was her love of dumplings. The rest of her was still a mystery.

'We must do what the Baker Brothers say,' she said. 'We find Book of Bones. I already say we go Peking. I know someone who help us.'

'You really think we should try to find this Book?'

'Yes.'

After breakfast, and more dumplings for Yin, we decided to set off to book our passage on a junk travelling up the Grand Canal to Peking. This is the oldest manmade waterway in the world and said to be much more splendid than the canal in Oxford, of which I am so fond. But before we set out, there was the matter of Mrs Glee to attend to. Our governess had slept like a goat. I'm not complaining, but my friend and I had passed an uncomfortable night.

'She can't come with us to Peking,' I hissed to Rachel. 'First sniff of opium and she would betray us.'

Even Rachel, good, soft-hearted Rachel, saw the foolishness of dragging our governess along. When we came to tell her our plan, Mrs Glee was tearful. I backed away and let my friend deal with her.

'I've made a mess of my life,' she told Rachel. 'I'm nothing but a burden to you.'

'How did you get away from the *Mandalay*?' Rachel asked. Mrs Glee was always looking for someone's shoulder to cry on now so it was wise not to give her too much of a chance.

Mrs Glee had merely shrugged. I was finding it hard to cope with my former governess. How could someone be so *weak*? I stood at some distance from the two of them and let Rachel do the talking. I knew my anger was unreasonable. At the same time this whole situation was unfair. Mrs Glee had been engaged as our governess. She was meant to look after us. Instead she had betrayed us and now we were looking after *her*.

I knew Mrs Glee had had a hard life – the snippets of her story that I'd heard showed that. Still, couldn't she just *try* a little bit harder? Luckily Rachel is kinder and more sympathetic than me.

'Will Mister . . . um . . . Lips . . . come looking for you?' Rachel asked gently. 'Vera, tell us. What are you going to do? How can we help you?'

In the end I left the room to see about getting our trunks. We only had one small one each to be taken by a porter down to the docks. When I returned, the matter was settled between Yin, Mrs Glee and Rachel.

Mrs Glee was to stay in the boarding house. We had paid for her board and food but left no money for opium. She would help the lady who ran the boarding house and try to get better and await our return. Guiltily, at the back of my mind, I wondered if we would come back. On the whole, though, this decision was a huge relief to me, for I found it hard to look our governess in the eye. The thought of dragging her through China as we ventured on our dangerous path had weighed on me.

It was mid-morning when we arrived at Soochow Creek to book passage on a boat north. A vast floating water-world greeted us. Hundreds – no, thousands – of sampans were roped together, hull to hull. They made a sort of giant, disjointed raft. The river folk, in their wide-legged trousers, some of them bare-chested, hopped from craft to craft. Many lived their lives on water, never venturing onto dry land.

There was a huge variety of craft on the river – elegant wooden junks with their hulls sitting low in the water, sails fluttering in the breeze, the river gay with multicoloured banners and pennants. Modern steamers puffed smoke from their red funnels. The Emperor's war junks were especially striking. The evil eye was carved on their prows to ward off ill luck and they bristled cannons with red-painted mouths. But though the cannon looked fierce, they were fixed and were armed with useless old-fashioned shot. Any reasonably swift British clipper could outrun their guns.

'Which of these boats will take us to Peking?' Isaac asked, looking around wonderingly.

Yin's tiny frame had already slipped through the throng. She had walked up to one of the junks and was on deck, talking to a sailor. She beckoned us to follow and we climbed up the ladder after her.

'This man want to see you. He is the captain of ship. He take us Peking,' she said.

But the sailor, a Chinaman with a high shaved forehead and pigtail hanging right down his back, was frowning. On his shoulder a monkey gibbered menacingly at us. I hated monkeys – ever since my experiences in India with a particularly savage one.

'No Bignose,' he said to Yin. 'No Red Barbarian!'

The monkey shrilled at us.

'Good big nose,' Yin replied, smiling winningly.

'Big nose?' I asked, outraged – for my nose if anything is rather trim and Rachel's is a beauty. Waldo pushed me and Yin aside and strode up to the captain, puffing out his chest.

'Looksee, Captain,' he said. 'We wantchee make sailee on shipee. You takee Peking, we payee muchee gold.'

'Why're you talking so strange?' I whispered to him.

'Shush,' he said in an aside. 'It's pidgin English. It's a mixture of Chinese and English, what all the Chinese speak here.'

'I spik English,' the captain said to Waldo coldly, overhearing his explanation. 'No need to speak pidgin.'

'My apologies,' Waldo said, colouring slightly. Then rallying, he went on. 'Why do you call us Red Barbarians? As an American, I must say I find it highly offensive.'

The captain looked at us icily, but Yin sighed. 'The

158

China person likes the old ways,' she explained. 'They suspecting foreigners. Say your skin red. Your nose big. You never wash your woollen clothes and you smell bad, of stinky meat.'

As Yin talked she had become quite animated, as if she agreed with these outrageous opinions. Indeed her eyes were shining with mischief.

'Our noses are not big. Mine, for example, is very well-formed,' Waldo said stiffly.

'How could this man insult us like this?' I burst out, a little childishly. 'He's one of the ugliest-looking—'

'Shush, no make trouble,' Yin interrupted. 'You smile and be good and I talk to captain.'

Reluctantly we did as requested while Yin went off and engaged the man in conversation. She won her way in the end, for we saw silver coins changing hands.

'You go down there,' the captain lofted a thumb at us.

Yin indicated to us that we should follow her, so we did, coolies bringing our luggage on board. We went down to the covered portion of the ship, where there were dozens of small compartments that looked strangely like the inside of a stem of bamboo. We were allocated one of these, a watertight cell really, with no window on the world.

'We're trusting ourselves to someone who hates us,' I whispered to my friends when Yin had disappeared.

'You can say that again. Captain Chen is a bigot,' Waldo agreed.

'The Chinese still think they're the best country in the world,' Isaac said. 'Even though their empire is falling apart, they're hooked on opium and all their best inventions were centuries ago. They believe England has nothing to teach them.'

A rushing sound, and much hollering outside, warned us that we were leaving so we rushed out on deck to take a look. We seemed to be part of a flotilla of craft, some proud and shining like our boat, others with pocked holes and dingy sails. The junks moved surprisingly fast, the wind billowing their sails and pushing them onward.

Yin was looking out at the water, her face shining. How she'd bloomed in the short days since we'd rescued her. A soft fuzz of new black hair was visible at the sides of her face, bristling beneath her new straw hat, and her eyes had lost that inward gaze.

'Best have company,' she smiled. 'There many pirates on the river.'

'Pirates?!' Waldo and Isaac exclaimed together.

'Not problem. Many boats together. If pirates chase, we fight!'

We were huddled together, gazing enchanted at the swirl of frothing water left in the junk's wake. The movement of this ship was very different to the stately progress of the steamer. You could feel the wind in the sails, the tip and tilt of waves. Unbeknownst to us the captain had crept up behind us and heard everything we had said.

'Pirate hate Foreign Devil.' He grinned, showing yellow broken teeth. 'I speak pidgin! Catchee, killee!'

❧ Chapter Twenty ❧

I toppled out of my bunk and crashed onto the floor, yanked out of my dream. The junk was lurching and Rachel and Yin were yelling. Shrieks came from the deck. Waldo appeared at our cabin door, his blond hair sticking straight up in the air.

'Quick,' he roared. 'Trouble!'

'What kind of trouble?'

'I'm not the fortune-teller!'

We rushed up on deck, where pandemonium reigned. Bare-chested sailors, shouting and cursing, rushed around in the fog rising from the inky waters. Other pig-tailed Chinese clambered up the rigging, sure-footed as cats. A lookout man in the prow cried out:

'Jeu-dow-li. Jeu-dow-li.'

'Pirate coming!' Yin translated in a fierce whisper.

We ran up to the prow. Downriver, stark against the silvery sky, I saw two dark sails. Pirate junks. Dimly I could see the graven eyes on their prows and the stout rope dangling between them just above the water line.

'This their trick,' Yin hissed. 'They trap this rope on our bows or our cable. When they catch us, they jump.'

A revolver had appeared in Waldo's fist. Most of our crew were armed, bristling with bamboo spears, cutlasses and pikes. A man handed something to Isaac, who instantly dropped it. It was a glove of stout leather with flails attached to the knuckles. An evil weapon – someone wearing this thing had enormously long fingers, with vicious ends to rip and slash his enemy.

'Fighting iron,' Yin explained. 'You young man, you must fight!' But Isaac was staring at the weapon, aghast.

'Er, NO . . . definitely no, thanks,' my friend muttered, backing away. 'Busy. Going back to the cabin.'

'Isaac hang on! We can't just leave Kit and Waldo,' Rachel yelled but she looked distinctly queasy. Brother and sister are the gentlest folk. Isaac in particular is terrified of violence. But he'd chosen the wrong moment to be a coward.

'Isaac, wait!' I yelled.

'Get back here at once,' Waldo hollered.

Too late. Our friend had vanished.

The fighting iron gleamed on the deck.

'I'll use it.' I darted forward and picked it up. I felt I had to apologise for my friend as I did not want the Chinese sailors to think Englishmen were cowards. The fighting iron was much too big for my hand, but I curled my fingers and kept it on. It was as heavy as a bag of lead. 'I want to help,' I puffed. 'I'll take Isaac's place.'

With a juddering jerk, the whole ship came to a stop. I fell face forward, just avoiding stabbing myself on the fighting iron. There was a splintering smash as the pirate junk rammed into our ship. Then in fast succession, from the other side of our vessel, another colossal crash.

The top of my head seemed to come off, my ears buzzed. The deck was raked by dozens of bangs, accompanied a second later by sparkling flashes. Sulphurous yellow light hung about the rigging. As I struggled to my feet something popped right under my nose, showering me with shards and enveloping me in gouts of flame. A minute later a rotten smell engulfed me.

'Urgh!' I gasped, struggling to hold down vomit. 'What is that?'

'Stinkpots!' Yin yelled.

I'd heard of stinkpots. Sulphur and rotten eggs in small clay pots, which the pirates let loose to stun the enemy before hacking them to pieces. But I had no time to reflect on this because now hundreds of men were swarming up the sides of our junk. They landed on deck, nimble and jangling with weapons. The battle was on!

To my relief Rachel and Isaac had disappeared. If

they weren't prepared to fight, then better to hide away altogether.

I swung viciously at the intruders and caught a pirate a blow against his chest. He went down with a thud but another was upon me. One sailor was doing battle armed with nothing more than a wooden belaying pin, which he was swinging about his body like a great club. There were grunts and shrieks and above it all the rat-a-tat-tat of guns. Then the deep boom of our cannon balls exploding on the pirate boats.

A spray of blood hit me in the eye. As I gasped, something punched me in the stomach and I went down.

In an instant Waldo was there, warding off attackers with his revolver. He was shooting in a masterful fashion, to disable rather than kill, aiming for the joints.

'Kit! Are you hurt?'

'No. I'm fine,' I lied, although it cost me all my strength. I heaved myself up clutching my stomach. My hands were wet with blood.

The Chinese crew and the captain were fighting gallantly. I saw that even the captain's monkey had joined the battle. It was perched on the rigging, armed with some sort of weapon which it was firing wildly on enemy *and* friend.

We were battling for our lives. But the enemy just kept coming, swarming like locusts upon us. Suddenly there was a massive rumble right in our midst and a six-foot-high flame flickered into life.

'What is *that*?' Waldo roared in alarm, backing against the sides of the junk.

The flame was as bright as the noonday sun and sizzled with an eerie greenish glow. Before our amazed eyes it snaked down the length of the deck and snickered past my feet with a hiss.

Along the ship, pirates and crew alike backed away in terror. Many sailors were so horrified that they dropped their weapons. The fighting had stopped, as we all froze, watching the flame roaring down the ship.

It wasn't random the way it was snickering this way and that. It formed a pattern and now we could see what it was – a giant eye.

'The evil eye. The evil eye,' the whisper ran down the ship.

It was too much for some of the pirates. Petrified they ran off the side of the deck into the sea. This touched off a frenzy with intruders running amok. Anything, anything to get away from the cursed eye! Pirates swarmed back down the ropes and ladders they'd thrown up, screaming, hollering in terror. Others took running jumps off the sides of the deck.

Within minutes the pirates had vanished. The battle was over.

The deck was slippery with blood – a few bodies were strewn among chunks of clothing and gristle. And all lit by the greenish glow of the evil eye. I could not bear to look at the bodies and turned away to watch the pirate junks. Their sails were vanishing across the black water as fast as they'd arrived. Yin and Waldo were at my shoulder, quiet too, for the aftermath of battle was sickening. Of Isaac and Rachel there was no sign.

I felt a tap on my shoulder and turned round, expecting my absent friends. I hoped they were ashamed of themselves. But it was the captain, with his monkey perched on his shoulder. His face was smeared with blood. I turned away, but he was talking in rapid excitement to Yin in Mandarin, a language I cannot understand.

Yin listened and then turned to me, her gaze troubled.

'The captain not know this weapon. It help us but he don't know where it come. Now he worry that ship is cursed.'

I shrugged, as I had no idea where the mysterious flames had come from either.

'If it was a curse, it's a helpful one,' Waldo said. 'We were pretty close to losing the ship.'

Suddenly Isaac and Rachel were in our midst. Isaac was grinning away.

'What are you so happy about?' I spat. 'Not very

manly, was it, Isaac? Running away as soon as things got a bit too hot.'

'I'm no soldier,' Isaac mumbled. 'Still, I expect you all to thank me, seeing as I saved your lives.'

'Thank you?' I snapped. 'For cowering in your cabin?'

But Yin was gazing at Isaac with admiration. 'So it you!' she gasped.

'What!' My brain was working agonisingly slowly. 'You mean that . . . that . . . flaming thing was *you*!'

Isaac shrugged modestly.

I stared at him in disbelief, half thinking he was making it up to cover his cowardice.

'Remember the firework seller?' Isaac asked. 'In Shanghai? Well, I bought some of his products and did a little tampering with them. Won't bother you with the chemistry, seeing as you wouldn't understand it, but yesterday, when I heard you all worrying about pirates, I thought I'd prepare a little trick. So I painted an evil eye on the deck with a phosphorus solution and well, tonight, when those rotters came aboard I lit the chemicals. Pretty spectacular, wasn't it?'

I was silent, staring at Isaac with something approaching awe. Never had I been so impressed by my clever friend. Waldo clapped him on the back, while Rachel glowed with pride. Even the captain cottoned on to the gist of what we were saying, for he was bowing to

Isaac. He muttered furiously to Yin then he turned to us.

'You clever bignoses. Good for ship,' he said, as his monkey jumped up and down with delight.

Isaac was looking at me, grinning mischievously. 'You don't have much time for brains, do you, Kit?'

'What?'

'You think being strong and brave is the most important thing, that's why you admire Waldo so much.'

'I don't admire—' I began heatedly.

'Sometimes a bit of brain gets better results than bare-knuckle fighting,' he muttered.

Tongue-tied for once, I blushed and looked down. Meanwhile a coolie had approached and was talking fast to the captain. He listened and then dismissed the man. When he turned to us he looked troubled.

'That man is telling that Foreign Devil on pirate ship. They see Red Barbarian woman on boat.' Then, although his English was as good as Yin's, he broke into Mandarin. She translated his words:

'The captain say that he know foreigners on pirate ship. It strange. Very strange.'

I stared at them silently. An image of Aunt Hilda had risen unbidden in my mind. My aunt aboard a Chinese pirate ship? My aunt attacking us? Surely this was nonsense. With all my willpower, I put the disturbing thought out of my mind.

❧ Chapter Twenty-two ❧

We entered Peking through a gate in the massive outer wall, jolting around on top of bags of rice. The driver of the horse and cart we had hired moved slowly, treating his mangy animal with care. So here we finally were, in the Celestial City, home of the Emperor of China. At first glance the place was hardly very heavenly – the narrow lanes paved with dung, the air filled with choking fumes. It was crowded with all manner of animals: mules, donkeys, camels, bullocks and yelling coolies.

Then we passed through another large stone gateway, elegantly carved, into the city itself and here the streets were wider. Flowering treetops exploded from secret courtyards. Carved roofs arched upward, many paved with yellow tiles that reflected the sun. Tiered pagodas and temples, brilliantly adorned with dragons and mythical beasts, glinted scarlet and gold. The streets were thrumming with life. Tea merchants resplendent in silk relaxed outside their shops, coolies pulled sedan chairs or were weighed down under sacks of grain. Up above hung banners and flags of all sizes, brilliant in turquoise, crimson and yellow. Silk lanterns fluttered in the breeze. Everything was flowery and elegant. Yin translated some of the signs written in gold Chinese letters: 'Garden of Eternal Spring' sold pickled vegetables. 'Brilliant Fountains' was a wine merchant.

She couldn't understand why we found 'Palace of Long Life', actually a coffin makers, so amusing.

'The Chinese would never call a spade a spade,' Waldo explained.

'What is spades?' she replied suspiciously.

I could sense they were about to argue when our cart was pushed back against the walls. Rachel almost fell head first into the street and was only saved by a helping hand from Waldo. Two burly men dragged split bamboos along the streets, making a splintering din. Behind them came two other men armed with whips. They shouted for people to get out of the way, flicking stragglers in the face with the lethal-looking leather thongs. Small boys ran behind wearing tall black hats, and among them was a towering bare-chested servant carrying a large red umbrella.

'Is it the Emperor?' Rachel gasped, for we could imagine no other person being given such royal treatment.

'Even Queen Victoria wouldn't make such a fuss at home,' I muttered, quietly.

Yin shook her head: 'Not Emperor. Mandarin. Very important government man.'

Finally, puffing round the bend, came three stick-thin coolies carrying a sedan chair. The man who had caused all the fuss was inside, fat as a toad. We glimpsed him through the silken hangings, dressed in a satin gown complete with a square badge adorned with two beautifully embroidered peacocks. His tall black hat was decorated with a peacock feather and topped by a large blue ball. The mandarin lay back against his cushions, perfectly content with the world.

'Mandarin of third rank. Peacock feather,' Yin whispered.

She obviously expected me to be impressed, but I found the mandarin's smug face repulsive. Sometimes Yin and I found it very difficult to understand each other.

Eventually the cart dropped us off and we followed Yin as she turned and twisted through lanes with a couple of coolies carrying our baggage. She stopped before a door of a *hutong*, which looked much like any other and knocked on the door.

'This important mandarin house. My sister Mr Chao's fourth wife,' she explained.

Rachel mumbled something and I saw Waldo and Isaac grinning in amusement, but Yin seemed unaware.

'Imagine being a fat mandarin's fourth wife,' Waldo

whispered to me as we were shown into the courtyard. But I didn't find the whole thing so very amusing. I thought Yin had said her father's views were modern, he hadn't forced his daughters to bind their feet, yet he had married off her sister to some high official.

The courtyard was so beautiful that I forgot to be angry. It was wonderful, with water splashing in a fountain. Silvery and spotted fish flitted around in little ponds shaded by flowering blossom trees. The floors were polished smooth as mirrors, the pillars around the courtyard lacquered in red. Through a half-open door I glimpsed hundreds of songbirds in bamboo cages warbling away.

Waldo whistled in amazement while the rest of us just gazed.

Then a golden sedan chair was carried into the court-yard and we saw the mandarin who was married to Yin's sister. A scholarly man, dressed in silk robes embroidered with a golden crane, his moustaches nearly as long as his pigtail. He peered at us short-sightedly, looking slightly dismayed at our tattered appearance, but then he bowed to us politely and we followed him into a drawing room, where he got out of his sedan and into a carved chair.

We collapsed into the remaining chairs. But Yin bowed down and knocked her head on the floor several times while we stared in surprise.

'You forget kowtow,' she hissed once seated. 'In China very important remember manners.'

I remembered vaguely now that one had to knock one's forehead onto the floor in China when greeting important people. This was called to 'kowtow'. Well, Yin might think it bad manners but I didn't intend to hurt my head, banging it like a slave. Englishwomen were free and bowed to no one. The moment had passed anyway, for now tea had arrived in delicate blue and white china cups. There were plates of unusual sweets.

Politely we sipped the chrysanthemum-petal tea and bit into the sweets. After a few minutes of this two small boys came in, dressed in yellow silk trousers and long embroidered coats. They knelt down before us and knocked their heads on the ground, humble as could be. Uneasily, I felt that maybe I had been ill-mannered. One had to try to adjust to the rules of the country. Maybe I should have kowtowed, though I hated the gesture. Having performed the ritual, the boys withdrew.

'Is your sister coming?' I whispered to Yin.

She shook her head. 'Only son meet guest.'

'She's your *sister*, Yin.'

'Girl not important. I see sister later.'

The mandarin, a Mr Chao, having finished his cup of tea and apologised to us in perfectly clear English for his lack of knowledge of our language, began talking animatedly to Yin. It seemed an age, us listening and smiling politely while Yin and the mandarin chattered in their fluting tongue, before we were dismissed.

The mandarin had invited us to stay. Rachel, Yin and I had been given a large and beautifully furnished chamber. The boys were put up elsewhere. Once we had all gathered together in the peace and secrecy of our room, I turned on Yin.

'What *are* we doing here?' I hissed.

Yin looked up from the plate of dumplings a servant had brought her and held up a small hand. 'Be patient.'

'Who is Mr Chao?'

'He a very good man. There is now battle in Imperial palace between reformers who say Chinee people must learn from West and others who say that China must go back to old ways and old days. But these old ways have become sick now. China must learn new things so she can be stronger. This is what Mr Chao say and he have ear of old dowager Empress. This Empress very powerful lady. They call her Little Orchid.'

We listened to all this, bewildered.

'What has this got to do with us?' I asked. 'I don't care two hoots for Empress Orchid or the old ways.'

Yin looked disturbed. 'Bad manners.'

'I know.' Rachel soothed her ruffled feathers. 'But you

must understand, Yin. One of us has been poisoned. *One of us is going to die.* Unless we do what the Bakers ask we're condemned, and time is running out.'

'True.' Yin sighed.

'So what are we doing here?' Waldo burst out.

'Looksee,' Yin burst into pidgin English for a moment. 'Mandarin Chao very kind man. He like foreigners. He not say you devils. He invite you his home. He kind.'

'We don't want to seem ungrateful,' Rachel said. 'We're just anxious about our mission.'

'This why I bring you here. When you tell me in Shanghai about poison, I not *see* anything. The future is fog. I think there is only one man in whole China can help you. This is a very great doctor. He is Empress's own doctor and he can cure you. This why I come to Mr Chao's house because he is friend of this doctor.'

'I'm sorry,' Rachel gasped, and we all added our apologies.

'Be patient,' Yin advised.

There was a knock on the door and a servant appeared, his arms full of rich silks. He handed the bundle over to Yin and disappeared with much bowing.

'Hurry!' Yin said. 'We invite to feast. Must change into proper China clothes.'

෴

I suppressed a giggle when Isaac walked into the dining room in his Chinese robe – he looked so very uncomfortable. Waldo wore his turquoise silk gown, embroidered with elaborate flowers, with a certain swagger. Like Rachel, who looked radiant in a loose red silk with broad red trousers, he does love dressing up.

There were already a number of people in the room, sitting at small square tables. I was pleased to discover ladies as well as men had been invited to the feast, which must mean our host was modern indeed.

Yin glowed when she saw the ladies and quietly pointed out her sister, sitting with a group of the mandarin's other wives. She was a tiny, slender girl – surely not more than thirteen or fourteen years old – with Yin's high cheekbones and slanting eyes. Like the other wives, some of whom were old enough to be her mother, she was dressed in an elaborate gown with her hair done up on top of her head in the shape of a teapot and studded with flowers and jewels. Still, her stiff clothes could not disguise the bloom of youth, which lay fresh on her cheeks.

Yin's sister saw us and gave us a small smile. She moved rigidly, her pink lips hardly opening. Her eyes were blank, puppet-like. This was the first time the sisters had seen each other after many years of separation. I expected the two of them, reunited after so much tragedy, to embrace. At the very least! But no. Once again I had misunderstood the formality of Chinese manners, for they barely acknowledged each other. Perhaps Yin didn't much like her sister. The disturbing thought came to me that maybe Yin was too cold, too wrapped up in her strange gifts, to really care for anyone.

We were shown to the top table, where Mr Chao was already seated, discussing something with a person wearing a vivid crimson robe. Politely, our host stood up and insisted we be seated in the place of honour. Equally politely we refused, as Yin had instructed us. Finally after a little of this to-ing and fro-ing it was good manners for us to sit down. It was only when we were seated that I saw the face of the person in the red robe.

It was Aunt Hilda. Her pleasant pug-dog features were wreathed in smiles, her sandy hair hidden by a velvet hat. She was dressed as a Chinaman right down to the fake pigtail dangling down her back. At least I assumed it was fake.

I goggled at her, totally dumbstruck. My friends were also gaping – only Yin seemed unsurprised, but of course she did not know my aunt.

'Not pleased to see me?' Aunt Hilda murmured. 'I don't call that civil.'

'Where have you sprung from?' Waldo demanded.

'Aunt Hilda!' I finally managed to gurgle. Of course I

wanted to fling my arms around her stocky shoulders, but I knew that would never do in China. 'What? What the—'

'I'll tell you later,' she hissed. 'In the meantime, eat Mr Chao's lovely food, smile and play along.'

Dumbly we nodded. Waldo managed one last gurgle: 'Why are you dressed as a Chinaman?'

'I'm an honorary man here,' Aunt Hilda said smugly. 'Much better all round. Now eat.'

This wasn't hard, for my stomach was grumbling. I was starving! The feast looked wonderfully appetising. I was coming to adore Chinese food. Heaped on the table in front of us were masses of small plates, brimming with sweets, nuts and rice. Each of us had been given a plate, a porcelain spoon, a pair of chopsticks and a wine cup. What an array of food. Sweet pork, shark fins, bamboo sprouts. Greedily we heaped our plates, throwing caution to the wind.

I ate with pleasure, savouring the salty tang of soy, the rich and deep taste of plum sauce. It was delicious, though unusual to devour sweet tastes with savoury morsels. But I soon got used to it.

A servant walked around the room with a kettle of steaming wine. I took a small sip – it was sugary and rich with a gingery bite. But I didn't dare drink more than a few mouthfuls in case it was intoxicating.

Mr Chao was placing something in a small bowl before me.

'Eat well,' smiled Yin. 'This special delicious.' Yin had certainly followed her own advice, heaping her plate with yet more dumplings.

It was a strange sort of soup, gluey-looking with odd fronds floating in it. I took a large swallow with my spoon.

'Mmm, not bad. What is it?'

'I dare you to guess,' Aunt Hilda said.

'Fish or some sort of prawn?'

'Birds' nest soup,' Aunt Hilda answered with a big smile. 'A speciality here.'

'Ugh!' Waldo, who had gulped down a large mouthful, turned pale.

'It's a delicacy!' Aunt Hilda hissed with a sideways glance at the mandarin who was looking on. 'An honour to be served it. Act like you're enjoying it.'

'But is it really made of birds' nests?' I gurgled, for suddenly it tasted foul, and the seaweed felt glued to my throat.

'They use a special kind of swallow's nest, I believe,' Aunt Hilda replied, glugging a spoonful with gusto.

I pushed the bowl away. Whatever happened, I wasn't going to eat birds' nest soup. Besides I was full to the brim, stuffed with the tasty food we had been gorging ourselves on. Little did I know that worse was to come. With much excitement Yin leaned over to me and whispered, 'The eight mountain delicacies.'

'What are they?' I asked suspiciously.

Aunt Hilda was enjoying herself. As the mandarin looked on she said, 'Let's see which ones I can remember:'

'Camels' humps.

'Bears' paws.

'Apes' lips.

'Leopard fetuses . . .'

The dishes, in the finest porcelain and steaming copper dishes, were being set down by the servants with much ceremony. The mandarin was beaming, for he was obviously doing us a great honour.

'Stop!' I hissed to Aunt Hilda, but she carried on regardless.

'Rhinoceros tails.

'Deer tendons.

'Live monkeys' brains.'

I closed my eyes for a minute as the servants lifted the lids off the steaming salvers. I had to get my friend's pale faces out of my head and also think fast, for we must find a way out of this awful situation. To my horror, Aunt Hilda was heaping her bowl with bears' paws and camel humps, which she ate with every appearance of delight.

'Live and let live, Kit.' She grinned. 'What is the

problem? Americans boil lobsters alive. The French eat frogs and snails. Thais eat crickets and Indonesians eat dogs. Surely a little monkey brain is not going to put you off your food.'

I scowled at her and looked to Yin for inspiration. The girl was as serene as ever, and I noticed that her plate was heaped with rice, vegetables and, of course, her beloved dumplings. None of the special dishes. Indeed she seemed to have some other, particular, dishes in front of her.

'Why aren't you eating this stuff?' I hissed at her.

'I come from the monastery,' she replied. 'I am Buddhist nun so I eat only vegetables. This is duck made from tofu.'

'What is tofu?'

'Bean paste.'

For the second time on this voyage I made up my mind to be a vegetarian too. A member of the little-known Christian vegetarian society.

Just then I heard squealing behind me and much commotion. The monkey, being led into the dining hall for its execution. They would cut off its head, then I would be expected to scoop up its brains and feast while the poor beast was still kicking and screaming! I gathered all my strength. However unmannerly it was considered, I had to put a stop to this. I had to say, 'No, thank you.

We are English and we do not eat our food alive.'

''Kit,' Rachel whispered, her face the colour of ash, 'get me out of here. I think I'm going to be sick.'

I turned but it was only our host's small sons charging in and upsetting one of the servants carrying a salver. Our host turned to us wreathed in smiles.

'My naughty son like eat,' he beamed. A look of deep sadness flashed over his face and he folded his hands. Turning to Aunt Hilda he bowed. 'I must say my sorry, Mistah Salter. We not able to make for you live monkey brain.'

My own brain heaved with relief. Thank goodness, no live monkeys' brains! Then the penny dropped and I looked at my aunt in wonder. 'Mistah Salter'! So it wasn't a joke – the Chinese really believed my incredible, my outrageous, aunt was a man!

≈ Chapter Twenty-two ≈

'Why Mister Salter?' I asked my aunt. 'What's wrong with plain old Hilda Salter? After all, you're always telling us Hilda Salter is one of the most celebrated explorers in the world. Famous from the Limpopo to the Gobi desert.'

My aunt wrinkled her pug nose, looking just like a stubby bulldog. The feast was over and we had all retired to our room. The five of us were huddled around my aunt as she sat in state in the one armchair.

'You must have noticed,' she replied, 'the Chinese do not think very highly of women.'

'They're awful to them,' I blurted. Yin caught my eye and looked away. She is very patriotic and becomes defensive at any criticism of her country. 'All this foot binding and getting rid of girl babies,' I went on.

'It's barbarian,' Rachel agreed.

Yin coughed. She stood up and slipped to the door.

'Where are you off to?' I asked.

'I must go. I come back later.'

After she'd left the room there was a moment's uncomfortable silence. Rachel had reddened and was staring at the floor.

'Do you think we offended her?' I asked.

'We shouldn't have said that about foot binding,' Rachel murmured. 'I mean it is awful, but if Yin had said the English were barbarians—'

'Poppycock, Rebecca,' Aunt Hilda interrupted, glaring at Rachel. 'You all namby-pamby that child. She probably just had to answer the call of nature.'

'Pardon?'

'She had to use the commode. The lavatory, in plain English!' Aunt Hilda snapped. 'Anyway, that Chinese child very thoughtlessly interrupted me. I was talking of my adventures. As I said, I thought my mission had a better chance of success if I travelled as a man. I had a false pigtail of the very best human hair made in London. A few local costumes, and hey presto, meet Mister Salter.' Aunt Hilda looked very pleased with herself. 'I must say it's been terrific fun. They've been surprisingly easy to fool.'

'But does Mandarin Chao really think you're Chinese?'

'Course not. He thinks I am a high-born English gentlemen travelling as a Chinaman,' my aunt replied, as if that explained the whole muddle. She sat back and surveyed us. 'Well, I've told you my tale. What about you? You've got some explaining to do.'

We told my aunt the whole story of why we were here, down to the last details of the poisoning and how we'd rescued Yin. I'd hesitated a moment before doing this, for my aunt moves in mysterious ways, but we even told her about the Book of Bones. She'd been especially interested in how the Baker Brothers believed they could use the Book to make them even more perfect. The mere presence of my aunt had soothed me; she had reassured uy coms all, promising she would do everything to help find an antidote to the poison. But though we'd gabbled on, so far my aunt had skilfully avoided giving anything away.

'How do you really come to be here, Aunt Hilda?' I finally asked her.

'It's a long, long story,' she replied, sinking back into the armchair. 'Do you think I could have an extra cushion? My back's a little achy.'

Waldo handed her the cushion he was using to sit on the floor and then repeated my question. Sighing, Aunt Hilda said, 'Do you recall a costume party at the Bakers' castle about nine weeks ago?'

The memory rushed back to me – my aunt, her stout body looking totally absurd in a fringed leather dress, her face painted and daubed with feathers.

'You were a sort of squaw – Aunt Hilda, what were you thinking!' And then the thought hit me. 'How did you know *we* were at the castle during the party! I never mentioned the party! Hilda, you're not—'

'Pish and tush,' she interrupted. 'I knew you were there because we have spies in the Bakers' castle.'

'Who is *we*?' Waldo burst in. I noticed Isaac was watching Aunt Hilda intently, his gaze never straying from her face. 'Who are you working for, Miss Salter?'

'I'm not really free to reveal my—'

'You'll tell us!' Waldo snarled menacingly.

'And tell the truth,' Isaac's eyes were unwavering. 'I'm watching you.'

'Very well.' She sighed. 'My employers are the British Government. Her Majesty's Secret Service.'

I nodded. I could well believe this. Unknown to us at the time, Aunt Hilda had been a spy before, searching for gold in the snowy mountains of the Himalayas. This time I felt comforted by her mission, for she would have the might of the British Empire at her disposal. If it came to a fight with the Baker Brothers and unknown Chinese villains, it was comforting to have Her Majesty on your side.

'What exactly is your mission in China?' I asked.

'First off, I came to rescue you.' Her eyes dimmed. 'Kit, you're like a daughter to me. I couldn't let you –'

'I know,' I said awkwardly.

'When I heard from my spy in the Bakers' household
187

that you'd been brought to China, I knew I had to follow, you. By the way, Kit, as you've not asked, your father believes you're travelling with me. He is very angry that you left without permission!' She glanced at the others. 'Your mother thinks the same thing, Waldo, as does your guardian, Rebecca and Israel.'

'My name is Rachel,' my friend murmured. 'My brother is called Isaac . . . Thank you anyway.'

'Don't mention it, Rebecca,' my aunt steamed on. 'Anyway, rescuing you was my number-one priority.'

'And your number-two priority?' I persisted.

'My dears, the situation in China is very delicate. The conservative faction in the Imperial palace wants to kick out all foreigners. They want to go back to the good old days of the Manchu Empire. Death by a thousand cuts, disembowelling, all that sort of thing. They don't want our fancy clocks and engines and trains—'

'Or our opium,' Rachel interrupted.

'As a matter of fact they do want our opium. From courtiers to peasants they're mad for the poppy. But the more modern reforming nobles, like dear Mandarin Chao, want to learn from the world. These are matters of top-secret international intrigue, I don't expect you to understand them at all.'

'So you're here to promote the reformers. Is that right?' Isaac asked.

'Mr Chao is vital to my mission. I don't want pea-brained children getting in the way. You must be polite at all times,' my aunt added hurriedly. She looked at her delicate gold wristwatch. Too pretty for a man, I would've said. 'Nearly midnight. I don't know about you night owls, but I need my beauty sleep. We have a long day ahead of us tomorrow. I want to see about this poison, for a start.'

After my aunt and the boys had departed I too was visited by a 'call of nature'. I walked the corridors that stretched endlessly around the gorgeous courtyard, going over the day's events in my mind. Aunt Hilda played a deep game – I knew she would never harm me, but there was no guarantee she was telling us the truth. Door after carved door stretched in front of me, but not the one I needed. I was becoming convinced that I had lost my way when something stopped me in my tracks.

A child was crying.

An awful sound. It reminded me of the sobbing we had heard on the steamship. And once before that, in the Baker Brothers' fortress castle. Who could be crying like that here? Without thinking, I pushed open the nearest door.

A candle was burning by an immense bed that was carved, gilded and draped with silken hangings. It was a lovely room, decorated with gold and jade figurines.

But I had no eyes for the beauty of the room, only for the two girls sitting on the bed. One I recognised as Yin's sister. But the face paint, embroidered gowns and elaborate headdress were gone, taking with them the illusion of proud beauty. I saw she was really a child, her hair loose, tumbling thick and black down her shoulders. Her eyes were red from crying. She was heaving with dry sobs, her arms around the second girl's neck, who had her back to me.

I must have made some small noise for the other girl turned and I saw that it was Yin. She wasn't sobbing, but her cheeks were wet. I didn't know whether from her own or her sister's tears. Of course I was going to go to them. I would comfort them, find out what I could do.

Something forbidding in Yin's mismatched eyes held me back. Green and grey, they glinted a warning. Uncertainly I took a step out of the room. I wasn't wanted there. Yin didn't want me. I had blundered into a private moment. The door swung back, blocking the two girls from view.

I didn't know what had caused these tears to fall – but I did now understand that Yin was not cold. However odd she appeared to me, she did love her sister. And deeply.

☙ Chapter Twenty-three ☙

The 'Forbidden City' was a fortress in the heart of Peking, strictly out of bounds to foreigners. Surrounded by a towering stone wall, it was said to be full of marvels – palaces crafted from jade and silver, flying bridges, dragon boats floating on turquoise lakes. This place, the home of the Imperial family, was spoken of in whispers as the finest flower of China. In the middle of the most populated city on earth, it had remained a mystery for centuries. The morning after the feast at Mandarin Chao's, the six of us – for Aunt Hilda accompanied us – were about to sneak our way in.

Our plan was madness, of course, sheer madness. But we had to see the famous healer who never ventured out of the Forbidden City. A life, one of *our* lives, depended on it. Yin was certain that only this doctor would be able to help us. More and more now, the girl was our guide, our only true friend here. I had come to respect her, almost be in awe of her. Something in her air held me back from asking her about the scene with her sister that

I had witnessed last night. If she wanted to she would tell me, but I knew I didn't dare intrude. I scarcely recalled why I had been so wary of her, so fluidly had Yin taken charge. I wouldn't have let a mere snip of a child boss me in England. But we were in China, vast and bewildering, so I let it slide.

We were dressed as servants, in shabby blue trousers and jackets, complete with false pigtails. The disguise wasn't very convincing, for anyone on close examination might have seen that our eyes and noses were uncommonly large for Chinese.

As we approached the magnificent moat which surrounded the city wall I was knotted up with fear. Tricking the Empress was a very dangerous thing to attempt. Behind the moat is a thirty-five-foot-high red wall, tiled at the top with yellow and green tiles, the gate guarded at all times. I was sure we would be unmasked as imposters. However, as servants of Mandarin Chao, we were waved through without much scrutiny. In China, mere menials are often not really *seen*. It helped that Waldo and Isaac, who were most likely to give us away, were huffing and puffing under the sedan chair, carrying the weight of the Mandarin. The first thing we came to was a wonderful courtyard dotted with flowerbeds and pines trained to form bowers, from which hung many golden birdcages. I couldn't help thinking it a shame that the birds here couldn't fly free.

After some time in one of the waiting rooms around the courtyard we were allowed to walk through three more courtyards till we came to a building carved so heavily with beasts it looked as if it was writhing with life. Large horn lanterns hung from balconies covered with red silk and jade amulets. It was most wonderful – all of us were awestruck for we had never seen anything so exquisite in its man-made beauty before. I began to have an inkling of why the Chinese were so very proud of their ancient culture. These sights – gardens of frangipane and wisteria, golden pagodas, weeping willows trailing into brooks – were truly magnificent. To think that such wonders were created while us Britons were living in mud huts.

'Still, you've caught up recently,' Waldo whispered to me with a smile, almost as if he could read my mind. I think he was overjoyed to have been released from his job as a chair bearer. 'Give me one of the Great Brunel's steam engines any day!'

If China was one of the great civilisations of the past, no one could argue that my small island's inventions were the new wonders of the world.

While my eyes took in these splendid sights, my head was somewhere else altogether. Blood pounded before my eyes. We were lunatic to come here to the Imperial home, but even more terrifying was what we would learn.

Soon a sentence of death would be pronounced. If it was Rachel, or Waldo, what could I do or say? If it was any of my friends. Underneath was the pulse of sheer terror – what if I was dying? What if *I* was *dying*?

While Mandarin Chao and Aunt Hilda went away to await an audience with the Empress, we were shown by three eunuchs to yet another waiting room. Time, I could see, crawls in the Forbidden City. People think it a positive honour to be kept waiting for three or four hours for an audience with a great lord.

We were lucky today. After an hour, during which Waldo and Isaac became terribly fidgety, another of those half-men known as eunuchs came to show us the way to the herb doctor's rooms. The chamber was lined with shelves of glass jars, dried roots resembling strange contorted heads, mushrooms, herbs, stalks, mummified seahorses. Even stranger were those jars filled with viscous liquid, in which floated things indescribable. Those rubbery red slivers were perhaps tongues, over there dried crickets hung in yellow fluid. Remembering the extraordinary things on the menu at the feast – apes' lips, camels' humps – I shuddered. If the Chinese ate such things, the medicines they used were even odder – but perhaps no more strange than Dr Billings's phrenology.

The healer was sitting bolt upright in a beautiful carved jade chair, his eyes closed, apparently asleep. He was an elderly man, with the same style of long pigtail and moustache as mandarin Chao, his face seamed and pitted. As he heard our footsteps his eyes opened. Irises like walnuts gleamed at us through layers of wrinkles.

Instantly we all dropped down and banged our heads on the floor. We had been given the strictest instructions to kowtow when we met the healer. Even though it hurts and makes you a little dizzy, I had given up my objections to it and was not about to argue.

We listened silently as Yin told the healer of our dilemma. I didn't know if it was last night's feast or the effect of the Baker Brothers' poison that made me feel so terrible today – weak and slightly nauseous at the same time. My aches and pains had slightly subsided since we'd left the *Mandalay*, perhaps because we'd become entangled in so many adventures that I scarcely had time to feel my own heartbeat. Now, though, I could feel every inch of my flesh. Every tingle and itch had become magnified and dreadful.

I prayed that the healer could help. The man in Shanghai had been a fool and a charlatan. Would this traditional Chinese herbalist be any better?

You may notice that I am talking as if I am sure that it was me, Kit Salter, who was poisoned. Well, I was. I had this instinct. My aches had not been imaginary. Secretly, I think, all the others were the same. Each and every one of us convinced that he or she was the one doomed to fulfil the Bakers' mission – or die.

While Yin told the healer our story he puffed, letting out little popping noises. Then he selected Rachel. Accompanied by Yin, he took her behind a screen decorated with turquoise kingfishers and examined her. We listened to the noises coming from behind the screen – while we stared at the bottles and objects. One of the oddest was the life-size statue of a man, in dull bronze, which was impaled with hundreds of the thinnest needles. They made him look like a hedgehog.

'Urgh!' said Waldo, holding up a bottle of grey lumps floating in a yellowish liquid. 'What do you imagine this is?'

'Pig's liver macerated in urine,' Isaac replied, grinning. 'A very popular Chinese tonic.'

'You don't know that,' I replied uncertainly. 'Anyway, I'm not going to drink that. Not after that feast.'

'Apes' lips.' Waldo shuddered in sympathy.

'What if it's the antidote?' Isaac asked, and abruptly our chatter ceased. The poisoning hung over us like a balloon full of lead, weighing down our spirits. We could not bring ourselves to talk about it more than absolutely necessary.

After that I had to wait while Waldo and Isaac were examined, as I was to be last. Finally it was my turn to go behind the screen. The doctor stood up and through Yin asked me to stick out my tongue. While I did so, he circled, *sniffing* me. That's right, sniffing, like a dog. He paid particular attention to my armpits. When I recoiled in disgust, Yin gave me such a ferocious look that I stayed as still as a lamb afterwards.

Then the doctor looked at my eyes, palpated my abdomen, felt my pulse, examined my hair and so on. Every inch of my body was poked and prodded. Strange as it was, he was so thorough and had such a remote look on his face that I felt reassured. Yin, who had obviously told him we were foreigners, though he would anyway have known it at once, trusted this man. He was related to Mandarin Chao and bound to Yin's family by ties of blood and honour.

Finally, after what seemed like hours, the healer indicated a white cotton-covered bed and asked me to lie down.

'No,' I said, backing away in alarm. 'What for?'

'Lie down, Kit,' Yin soothed. 'Healer need make more test.'

Reluctantly I did as bid, though I kept my eyes trained on the man. He was selecting a number of the long, thin needles and it dawned on me what he intended to do.

'No!' I shrieked, trying to jump off the bed. 'Never.'

'Kit.' Yin held me down on the bed. Her face was calm, though her grip was amazingly firm. 'This needles not hurt you. Trust me.'

'I am not going to be stuck with needles. Like . . . like . . . like,' I cast around desperately for the words. 'Like a pig or a hedgehog.'

'This is medicine, Kit,' Yin murmured. 'This not hurt you.'

The healer was watching us, the hint of a smile on his lips. Reluctantly I lay down. I screamed when the first needle went in, but after that managed to hold my nerve. After a while it wasn't so very painful, more of a prick than a stab. The man seemed to stick them everywhere, on my arms, legs – even my face. Then after a time he removed them and indicated that I was free to rejoin the others.

'So?' I hissed.

Yin shook her head severely. 'Must not rush him.'

The others had heard my screams. Perhaps they feared the healer was actually doing away with me! When I came out Waldo rushed over, as if he was going to embrace me, before I pulled away. We all waited, fidgeting, for the man's verdict.

Finally the healer came through, having changed his robes. He began to talk, the solemn sound of his words

198

hanging in the air. After several sentences, Yin translated.

'Rachel first. He no see any poison in your body. He say your Qi, your life force, very strong, though you must take care good of your heart.'

My friend gasped as she heard this, her shoulders sagging with relief. I realised we were all sitting bolt upright, tense as strung wires, while we awaited our fate. As soon as Rachel relaxed, she looked over at me a little guiltily. I could tell what the look meant. She thought I was the sick one. Also, she felt guilty for being well.

'One down, three to go,' I whispered, and Isaac flashed me an odd look.

'Waldo, you have very strong Qi and strong Jing, or essence,' Yin went on. 'This essence comes from your father and runs hot in your blood. The healer say you have much of energy and determination – but your Shen, or your spirit, is sometime low. Anyway, you have no poison.'

'Don't know what all that nonsense meant!' Waldo muttered, but I could tell he too was relieved. Now it was only Isaac and me.

'Isaac,' Yin continued. I could tell by the way she spoke that single word, that Isaac was fine. I didn't take in what she said about Isaac. Something about very strong Shen – but then anyone could have told you that Isaac is a brain on legs. I waited, skin crawling, heart thumping.

I waited and waited and slowly, reluctantly, Yin came round to me.

There was a look about Yin, watery, wretched, that made me not want to hear her words. Still, I *needed* to hear them, if you know what I mean.

'Kit, the healer he say your Qi marvellous. He see such strength very rare and—'

'Yes, yes,' I interrupted rudely. I had no interest in my 'life force'. I knew I had plenty of spirit, thank you very much.

'But he say there is something blocking your Qi. This something a poison. It weigh on you, like small leech living in your tummy, sucking blood and food.'

'Lovely,' I said sarcastically. But my throat was so dry and hoarse I could barely utter the word.

'The healer he fear this poison it kill you. He very, very surprise, because he not know what it is. That is why he put those needle in you. He never see this poison before.'

'Can he cure me?'

Yin was silent for a moment, studying the dragons on the carpet. Then the healer, who had been so silent, intervened, talking passionately and gesticulating. He had produced a small bottle of murky liquid in his wrinkled hands. At the end of the outburst Yin spoke again.

'He say your Yin is too strong. Your Yin energy and

your Yang energy need to be balanced, but he never see such an explosion cold Yin energy. He give you this bottle of Five Poisons Wine. It contain the blood of five venomous creature: centipede, scorpion, spider, snake and toad. This will give you hot energy to help – but he say he never seen your illness before. He do not think this cure you.'

'What will cure me?' I asked.

'He not know what to do.'

'That's not good enough!' Waldo burst out furiously.

Yin hung her head. 'This man a very wise healer. He know thousands of poisons. But he say he never see this one before. He say keep trying Five Poisons Wine but he be very feared.'

'That's as likely to poison Kit again as cure her,' Waldo snarled.

'Yes.' Yin nodded.

'What?' Isaac exclaimed.

'Too much of Five Poisons Wine will kill her. But it also keep her alive for now. The healer say he can see Kit is becoming worse. She dying.'

Rachel had put her arm round my shoulder and for a moment I lay limp in her embrace. Her eyes were warm and sad. For a moment I caught a glimpse of the healer's wrinkled face, his eyes a mournful reflection of Rachel's.

So everyone felt sorry for me. From now on I was

an object of pity. I sat up straight, bolt upright. 'I'm not giving in. I'm going to beat this.'

Waldo had sagged, he looked shrunken, defeated. His hands twisted and turned but I could see he was at a loss. Never before had he shown so clearly that he cared.

'You see what this means, don't you?' Waldo sprung up and paced around. 'This is no trick. We have no choice. We have to follow the Bakers' orders and find that Book of Bones. Kit must have that antidote at all costs!'

There was a sudden crash. The healer had dropped the book he was holding. Yin picked it up and handed it back to him.

Waldo went on: 'If we don't bring it back to England in a few weeks, well . . .'

'You won't have the bother of my company,' I said. There was silence after my little outburst, as all my friends turned to me. But no one, it seemed, could look me in the eye. I couldn't really blame them. What was there to say?

'Don't bother to tell me how sad you are,' I said. 'There's no point.'

I know I sounded self-pitying, but you'll forgive me, I'm sure, for feeling a little sorry for myself.

❧ Chapter Twenty-four ❧

The weeping willow by the bridge, the glittering red pagoda, the monumental stone dragon bearing down on us – I scarcely noticed them as we were shown out of the healer's chambers by two more eunuchs. It had taken just a few hours for the beauty that had so thrilled me this morning to shrivel and go stale. Those awful pangs that I'd experienced on the *Mandalay* were back, redoubled. There was an ache in the pit of my stomach, tingling in my limbs. The pain had spread to my head, which felt as if it was loosening itself from my neck and would soon rise like a balloon into the sky.

'Pull yourself together, Kit!' I hissed to myself. My words were empty. I didn't have the strength.

The two eunuchs escorting us were young. They had bloated faces and high, chirruping voices. The one in front of us had a cringing air despite his gorgeous robes and crystal hat button, which showed he was of high rank. All the boys who served in the palace were eunuchs – from poor families – and had been spayed like cats to ensure they did not flirt with the Emperor's hundreds of wives and concubines.

We were passing a gorgeous palace with a tiled roof that seemed to be almost lifting off the walls when I heard a yahoo. My aunt trotted into view, accompanied by Mandarin Chao.

'How did the visit to the doctor go?' she asked. But no sooner had I begun to tell her when she shushed me. 'Look!' she commanded. 'There's a sight few Englishmen will ever see, the Empress Dowager.'

A great hubbub was coming our way – a huge procession in the middle of which was a bejewelled sedan chair. From inside the chair I heard laughter, brittle as the chime of bells. A lady was holding back silken curtains to peer out. She had a perfect oval face, pale as a bowl of milk, and black eyes burning under arched brows. A beauty, they whispered of the Empress, a tyrant. She had ruled China since the death of her husband nearly ten years ago, often over-ruling her weak nephew, the Emperor Kuang-hsu. Empress Orchid, as she was called, wore a fabulous yellow satin gown embroidered with vivid pink peonies. Her teapot headdress towered like a crown, studded with jade and emeralds and more pink peonies. Over the gown she'd flung a cape made of thousands upon thousands of magnificent pearls, each one as big as a bird's egg. The only other thing I had time

204

to notice were her hands, adorned with massive rings and gold fingernail protectors curving over the ends like witch's talons.

A great crowd of eunuchs ran before and after her sedan chair carrying everything the Empress might need: combs, pins, powder boxes, fans, mirrors, cigarettes, paper and ink – everything you could think of. There were also two old ladies in her train, plus servant girls. This procession made a great hullabaloo and everyone who saw them fell to the ground kowtowing. I banged my head on the ground enthusiastically, for something in the way the Empress had cast her black eyes over us made me shiver. She looked very shrewd. I did not want to give her too much opportunity to study us as I was sure she would not be fooled by our Chinese disguises and would quickly spot us as imposters.

No sooner had the Empress's procession swept by than Mandarin Chao hurried along. 'We see oldest son. He now finish Imperial examination.'

He led us past a vast palace sprouting fantastical roofs, the Hall of Heavenly Peace, our footsteps quick and light in our Chinese cloth shoes. Then we came to another vast building, guarded by a giant stone dragon.

'Palace of Preserving Harmony,' Mr Chao explained. 'Place of examination.'

Guards were stationed outside the palace. They were

fearsome Manchu Bannermen, Tartar warriors from the steppes of Mongolia, with high cheekbones and slanting black eyes. They bristled with swords and bows and arrows and looked as though they would as soon slice off your head as say hello. Only now did Aunt Hilda remember to ask about the healer. I did not want to tell her anything, so Rachel broke the news. For a moment I don't think she believed my friend. She blinked and asked her to repeat herself. When she did finally accept what had happened, she reacted as Waldo had. We would set off tomorrow, she said, to find the Book of Bones.

A terrific boom resounded through the palace. Guards broke the seals on the doors, and hundreds of youths streamed out, Mr Chao's son among them. He was a thin, scholarly-looking boy. I expected them to embrace, but had forgotten how reserved the Chinese can be. While we were passing out of the Palace of Preserving Harmony our host was questioning his son.

Like fathers all over the world he was probably asking him how he had done in his exams!

I did not know if the son had acquitted himself well, for the father wore a somewhat gloomy air. He had not long to worry about his son's success – or lack of it – for a servant ran up to him and began babbling in Chinese. It was obviously some bad news as Mr Chao turned pale and trembled.

'All is lost,' he hissed to my aunt.

'What are you talking about?' she replied.

Hundreds of students were milling around us in the great court outside the Palace of Preserving Harmony. Mr Chao and my aunt had to whisper fiercely to be heard.

'The Empress herself suspect you. She say spy in Forbidden City.'

'Pish and tush!'

'This very serious. Terrible for reform party. My enemy must be behind.'

'We'll brazen it out,' my aunt replied.

'No. If they find you, they hang you. Or maybe death by a thousand cuts.'

My aunt went very quiet at this, for the gruesome Chinese punishments were legendary. Death by a thousand cuts involved literally bleeding someone to death by making countless small cuts all over their body.

'They won't dare,' she said. 'I'm a subject of Queen Victoria. They would never insult the British like that. Why, the Royal Navy would blow up Shanghai like that!' She clicked her fingers. I could tell, for all her bravado, that Aunt Hilda was terribly frightened. When she is scared she becomes even more proud and defiant.

In the distance, in the direction of those Imperial gardens full of scented wisteria and willows, came a terrible commotion. I had a view of some Bannermen running and the rat-tat-tat of gunfire. So they were armed with more than just swords and arrows. Mr Chao was pulling at his pigtail while he thought. Then suddenly he said a few words to his son and, indicating to three of his servants to follow him, he darted away into the crowd of weary examinees. The last I saw of him, he seemed to be running.

The son, a short, sallow youth with Mr Chao's scholarly air, turned to us and bowed deeply. 'My father trust me honour of looking after you. They look for imposters in my father's servants. He ask me to smuggle you out of Forbidden City.'

We had little choice but to follow the younger Mr Chao as he strode away, his pigtail bobbing down his blue coat. We hurried to keep up with him. Despite Aunt Hilda's bluster, we knew we were in deep trouble if we were discovered in this place that was sacred to the Chinese Imperial family. We went past pagodas, gardens and lakes towards the gate where we had entered. No one stopped us – we were only poor servants in the employ of one of the numerous students. In the shade of palm and jasmine trees we came to a small pavilion and a cluster of five guards, who were on their break. They stood in the shade of the trees smoking their cigarettes and chattering.

Mr Chao Junior turned to Waldo and said, 'We are in

nasty place. I have plan to take us out of here, but you must trust me.'

'We do,' Waldo replied. 'What's your plan?'

'Surprise,' Chao said. Then he barked out something to Yin, her eyes grew distant and she murmured, 'Stand like a Pine, Sit like a Bell, Move like Lightning.'

I stared at her, alarmed. This was a fine time for Yin to have one of her funny spells.

'Soft as Cotton, Light as Swallow, Hard as Steel.'

'Yin, you're not making any sense,' Waldo said gently.

'Kung Fu,' said Yin. 'These are the rules of Kung Fu.'

I had heard of Kung Fu. It is a sort of acrobatic fighting. What did it have to do with us? But my attention was suddenly diverted by Waldo, who was gripping my hand. Mr Chao Junior had vanished, reappearing like magic in the group of guards. He was chatting to them, smiling. I blinked, and in that instant two of the guards were lying on the ground, their bodies twisted.

'What the . . . ?' I stuttered.

'He's fighting them. Three against one – he's got no chance,' Waldo hissed. 'I've –'

'No,' Yin held him back. 'The best way for you to help is stand in line, make sure no one sees this fighting.'

She managed to restrain Waldo, who squirmed under her grip. The rest of us fanned out into a line. The three remaining guards were shouting for help. Luckily this spot was set well back from the main thoroughfare and there was no one around. One man had managed to draw his sword. He was slashing savagely at Mr Chao.

Mr Chao jumped back and forth, deftly evading the blade. With a vicious grunt the guard hurled himself at the student. The side of the sword caught Mr Chao's leg, slashing his trousers and drawing a thin line of blood. He cursed and for a moment I thought it was all over. Then, with a lightning movement, Mr Chao flicked his other leg and kicked the sword out of his opponent's hand. It rose in a glittering arc, falling blade first towards the earth.

Mr Chao and the guard both rushed for it. Our friend caught it awkwardly in his left hand, blade against palm. I winced as a crimson drop fell from his hand. The sight jerked the other guards out of their stupor. Except for the swordsman, they were sluggish. I wondered if they had been smoking opium.

But now their hackles were raised. They came for the student, three of them in a snarling pack of rage. Waldo had managed to break away from Yin and with a few bounds was in the fight. But Mr Chao now had the upper hand and was wielding the sword like a pike. Throwing it from hand to wounded hand, he advanced on the three guards – who backed away nervously. Then he did something completely and utterly insane. He shocked us by throwing aside the sword and moving empty-handed on the guards.

They were just as surprised as we were. Their heads jerked to the side as they watched the sword fall under a jasmine tree. Mr Chao took advantage of their momentary inattention. With a swift upward movement he had landed a blow on one guard, on his solar plexus. The man crumpled silently in a heap. The second guard was caught with a series of kicks – but now the third guard, the man who had pulled the sword, had a knife glittering in his hand. He was more vicious and much more sneaky than the other two. While Mr Chao felled his comrade with a kick to the stomach the third guard sneaked behind the student, dagger drawn. His knife was an inch away from Mr Chao's back when Waldo waded in, punching him from the side on his cheek. It must have been a ferocious blow. The man slumped heavily, and the knife slithered out of his hands into the grass.

'Thank you,' Mr Chao said, swinging round to Waldo.

'Why did you throw away the sword?' I interrupted. 'It was madness.'

'If I had the sword I might have killed a man,' Mr Chao replied. 'I trusted in my Kung Fu. These men are just doing their work.'

'He would have killed you,' I said, gesturing to the swordsman.

'Nevertheless, I do not want a life on my conscience.'

We gaped at Mr Chao Junior as he calmly wiped a sweaty frond of hair away from his forehead. His wounded hand left a streak of blood. Yin went up to him and taking out a handkerchief wiped away the smear. He was so callow looking, with his spectacles and air of frowning scholarship. Like a Chinese Isaac. Yet he had dispatched four guards almost before the rest of us had time to react.

While the rest of us were still dazed by these events, Yin was moving swiftly. She knelt down by a fallen guard and began to strip him of his jacket.

'I don't understand,' Rachel said. 'You provoked that fight. The guards weren't harming you.'

'I needed something they have.'

'What?'

Chao Junior gestured to Yin, who had stripped one of the guards nearly naked. 'Their uniforms. The soldiers at the gate are looking for foreigners disguised as servants. Not look for guards. It is only way to escape from Forbidden Palace.'

'Quick!' Yin said, turning round. Help me.'

Swiftly we dragged the remaining guards behind the trees and stripped them of their uniforms, praying no one would see and raise the alarm. Mr Chao had chosen the spot for his attack well, an isolated place a little away from the throng of eunuchs and servants that bustle through the Forbidden City.

In a matter of minutes we were all dressed in the padded blue trousers and coats and yellow sashes of the Bannermen. Of course the uniforms were ill-fitting and ridiculous. Rachel and me, in particular, looked as if we were wearing clothes that belonged to our older brothers. But at least we were better off than the unfortunate guards. They sprawled higgledy-piggledy in their underclothes. They were nearly naked, poor things – as unaware of their fate as babes sleeping in the sun.

'Do you think this will work?' Rachel asked, looking at me dubiously.

'It has to,' I hissed fiercely. 'Stand tall. Look confident. We must get out of here.'

I rose to go, but Yin was frantically searching her pockets. 'We need tally,' she muttered.

'Tally?' I asked.

'A guard's identification tally has two halves. We must have matching half to one held by senior officer at gates. Otherwise we may not leave.'

Mr Chao Junior was holding something up and smiling. Something that glinted in the sun. He'd found the precious tally, the piece of twisted metal that would get us out of the Forbidden City. We trooped after him, joining a long queue that snaked up to the smallest gate.

Out of the corner of my eye I noticed that Mandarin Chao, in his sedan chair, was queuing at the larger gate, the one for grander folk. All sorts of humble people were in our queue – vendors of chicken and silks, servants, guards, eunuchs. To onlookers we were just another group of guards, pleased to be ending their shift. As we got closer to the gate my heart began to thud painfully in my chest. The soldiers at the gates had been tripled and everyone leaving the Forbidden City was being thoroughly searched. The soldiers only had to ask us one simple question in Chinese and we would be sunk! We queued silently behind a man carrying a couple of squawking geese. Then it was our turn to go through the gates, but five burly Manchu Bannermen, with their yellow sashes, were barring the way.

'Courage!' I mouthed to Rachel, but my hands were trembling.

One of the guards was talking to Mr Chao Junior, joking and smiling. Our saviour handed the stolen identification tally to the officer. I noticed that he held his wounded left hand to his side, not revealing it to the soldiers. The officer barely glanced at us as he clicked the two halves together – thank heavens they matched.

We were through. Free, at least for the time being.

❧ Chapter Twenty-five ❧

Free, it turned out, was the last thing we were. The day after our escape from the Forbidden City, Yin and I ventured out into Peking to buy some provisions for our journey to Henan. We had scarcely made it to the next street when I saw a pen-and-ink drawing stuck on the bronze door of a magnificent *hutong*.

It was a 'Wanted' poster.

The six of us stared out at the world, looking decidedly shifty. Waldo and Isaac looked mean, while Rachel was unfairly plain. Aunt Hilda and I were sketched snarling like bulldogs. All of us wore our Chinese disguises. None of us, except Yin who was also included, were very convincing as Orientals. To be honest, I didn't recognise the people in the Wanted poster at all. But the sketch was still frightening in the way it pointed straight at us. There couldn't be many foreigners disguised as natives wandering around Peking.

Underneath the sketches was a description of our crimes in both Mandarin and English. We learned that we had invaded the Forbidden City and threatened to assassinate her Imperial Majesty the Empress Yehonala. Yes, that's right, we had planned to kill Empress Orchid herself. Only the foresight of the Empress – who had spotted us as imposters – and the courage of her Manchu Bannerman had foiled our dastardly plans. Now we were hunted over the breadth of the Empire.

Public enemy number one.

We had already planned to journey to the legendary Shaolin temple in Henan. The poster hastened our departure. We left Peking immediately and began our trek to the Songshan mountains. This was where the Book was kept, guarded day and night by warrior monks. It would be very difficult to steal. But the clock was ticking on my illness. Besides, we would be safer in the wilds of China. Safer from the Imperial guards, those frightening Manchu Bannerman with their lethal sabres and bows.

Now that we were fugitives, fleeing from the might of the Chinese Empire, we had little choice.

The journey to Henan was dispiriting. We went past parched wheat fields, through decaying cotton plantations and along dusty roads dotted with shrivelled villages. The broad, slow-moving Yellow River had turned to ochre sludge. Everywhere the pitiless sun beat down on us. Everywhere there was hunger and neglect. We saw groups of wretched people sitting by the roadside, just sitting, not bothering to do anything at all. And we heard the whispers. Fields lying untended as their owners smoked the juice of the poppy. Cruel mandarins taxing the clothes off the peasants' backs. How famine had driven people to eat dogs and cats – and even the bark off trees.

Finally we arrived at a rather humble Chinese country inn, at the foot of the towering Songshan mountains. It was not particularly clean and was full of bad smells. Still, here, hundreds of miles from Peking, at last we'd be safe from the Imperial army. We supped on meagre fare: rice, dried fish and pickled cabbage. The feast at Mandarin Chao's was a faint memory.

I took five drops of Five Poisons Wine every morning. As I glugged it down I felt like a laudanum addict, like Mrs Glee herself. How was she faring, I wondered, as I sipped the foul-tasting liquid. It had taken several days to train myself not to vomit when I took it. But now I was starting to become used to the brew. I almost *liked* it. You would realise just how strange that was, if *you* had tasted the stuff.

Five Poisons Wine cleared some of the fog that rooted in my head. The others had treated me differently since the healer's diagnosis in the Forbidden City. When they remembered, which thankfully was not all the time, they tiptoed round me. Even Waldo was considerate of my feelings. I realised that they now saw me as an invalid. While I was touched that they *cared*, that they were scared of losing me, part of me was tetchy with this treatment.

I was still the same Kit Salter wasn't I? Hasty, sometimes arrogant, but deeply loyal to her friends – and good in a fight!

Except I wasn't. The healer's verdict had sped up the process that had begun on the *Mandalay*. At times I felt dizzy, at other times weak. But the most common feeling, a sense that haunted me all day – and sometimes when I woke covered with sweat in the night – was one of unreality. I felt I was dissolving, floating away from being Kit. I would look down on *that* girl and see her from a vast distance. I didn't like or dislike her, my feelings were not particularly strong. But I was curious. The floating thing would wonder, Why was Kit so angry, so burning with rage? What was wrong with her?

Then I would remember. *I* was Kit Salter.

Rachel had found me that morning. Sitting down on the bed next to me she had taken my hand in her soft palm.

'It will all come right,' she reassured me. 'We'll find the Book of Bones, take it back to the Bakers and you'll have your antidote.'

I nodded, not able to speak. Whatever happened, I did not imagine the happy future she'd sketched would come to pass.

'Come out with us. Your aunt is going to the market to buy provisions for our trip to the Shaolin temple. We need presents for the monks and food for the journey. You shouldn't just sit here brooding. *Come on*, Kit.'

'No, Rachel. I'll stay here.'

'Please. It will do you good.'

'I need a bit of time alone.'

Throwing me a pitying look, Rachel left and I sank back onto the bed. It was placed right next to the window so I could look out on the teeming street below and at the fruit seller and hat makers opposite. At the small boys playing their game of dice in the dust. Further off a group of elderly ladies played a game of mah-jong – I could hear the faint clack, clack of their tiles. I saw my friends assembling downstairs, armed with bags and baskets for their trip to the market. The mood of indifference was strong in me and after a minute of watching I sank back on the bed and just stared at the ceiling. There wasn't anything of interest up there but it didn't matter, I was in a living nightmare.

'Wake up, Kit!' Hilda's red face was about a millimetre from my nose, her strong breath made me want to gag. 'You need all your wits about you for this journey. *I'm* not going to treat you like an invalid.'

'That's very civil of you.' I managed to smile up at her.

'Never believed in namby-pambying people. No matter how ill they claim to be.'

'Quite.'

'You on your deathbed, girl?'

'No . . . I am as you see me.'

'So do the decent thing. Get up, I say.'

'Aunt Hilda, listen to me. I'm not going to be bullied by you. Not now. I am staying here.'

'Exasperating child!'

Aunt Hilda flashed me a look and removed herself from my face. As she rose I saw something soft in her expression, pity diluting her disapproval. Things had come to a pretty pass when *even* my aunt couldn't bring herself to properly bully me.

Time passed. Minutes, hours. I enjoyed the silence, the fact that for once I was alone and not cocooned in my friends' artificial gentleness. I was dozing when I was startled by a commotion downstairs. Loud banging. A deep growling voice and then the innkeeper's falsetto. Heaving myself up on my elbows I sneaked a look out of the window.

Down below I saw the conical felt hats of a brigade of Manchu Bannerman. A multitude of red banners, sabres and feathery arrows bristling out of quivers. I could see the commander of the soldiers arguing with the innkeeper. The man was protesting, gesturing in the opposite direction to the market. As I watched, the commander slapped the innkeeper across the face. Pushing him out of the way he marched through the doors, a horde of soldiers in his wake.

With my heart thumping I stepped back from the window. I would have to disappear, quickly. But there was nothing in the room. Just four rickety beds and a red lacquer wardrobe. Where? My eyes flashed round the room for inspiration, while already I could hear boots clumping up the stairs. Luckily at the back of the room there was a casement window. It was a tiny opening, the drop to the alley, several storeys below, terrifying.

I had no choice. I had to reach the market before the soldiers did. Closing my eyes and holding my breath, I hunkered down on my knees and jumped.

❧ Chapter Twenty-six ❧

'We have to run,' I gasped.

'Eels,' Aunt Hilda said, ignoring me and plunging her hand into a vast bowl full of slimy wriggling things, 'are both tasty and nutritious.'

I had arrived at the market damp with sweat and out of breath to find my aunt transfixed by the live food stalls. Eels, crickets, snakes. The eels were particularly revolting, slithering around in a grey bundle.

I hadn't had much of an appetite for days, but these creatures were enough to put me off food altogether. Not so my aunt. In her love for the more outlandish Chinese food, she had gone native and barely gave me a glance.

'The soldiers will be upon us!' I hissed, tugging at her sleeve. 'Not a moment to lose.'

'Pretty succulent, these eels,' Aunt Hilda mused, shaking me off. 'Might need to take a cook with us. Can't say we'll be able to get much food in the Songshan mountains . . . Oh, hello, Kit, what's the matter?'

'The soldiers have been searching the inn. They'll be here any moment.'

'Why didn't you say so before?'

'I *did,* Aunt Hilda. Where are the others?' I was struggling for breath in my desperation. 'We've got to move – they'll kill us.'

'This way.' Now that I had her attention, Aunt Hilda was instantly alert.

Gathering her eels, she briskly led the way to the very edge of the market, where I found all the others bargaining with a horse dealer. The dealer was a Tartar, one of the fierce tribesmen from the north, wearing a colourful embroidered jacket and cap. Waldo, Isaac, Rachel and Yin were already seated on fine China ponies. We swiftly chose two more horses, one for my aunt and one for me, and hoisted ourselves up on them. My aunt threw a pouch of coins at the dealer and we rode away.

Our going was not unnoticed. Of course we had attracted attention in this small town. The usual whispers of 'Foreign Devil' and 'Red Bignose' had followed us. Now countless eyes clung to us, noted our passing. Already, at the other end of the market near the stall selling cotton bolts, there was uproar.

'This way!' Yin commanded, trotting down a dark alley on her pony.

Unquestioningly we followed her. Our saddlebags

carried the few possessions Aunt Hilda had purchased, the rest of our things were at the inn. But this wasn't what was troubling me. My heart was thudding painfully. The soldiers must have secured the road out of the town. We would be cut down easily as we tried to escape.

But Yin was not taking us towards the road but to a small lane with raw sewage running down the centre. Our horses galloped through sludge. At one stage a startled woman jumped out of the way, spilling mushrooms from her basket. We raced through the alley and out into rice fields shielded by papaya trees. There was no path, but Yin urged us onward and we followed her lead, our ponies stamping down the terraces between the slushy fields.

Villagers in straw hats were toiling in the fields. As we sped past they shouted at us for trampling their crops, but we ignored their calls. Out of the corner of my eye I saw Aunt Hilda scattering something in their direction, coins that flashed silver in the sun. The bribery was a wise move. These peasants were far removed from the capital, Peking, and their attitude to soldiers would be surly. When the soldiers came the peasants might be a little less willing to tell them about our flight.

The paddy fields shaded at the edges into bamboo groves that gave way to a vast forest murmuring with cypresses and pines. The trees grew upward, carpeting the slopes of the mountain. Past a row of golden maidenhair we were plunged into another world, cut off from the villagers' cries, the hustle of planting, and market day. The sun slanted down, dappling the ground. All around was dense vegetation. There was no path.

We rode hard through bracken and fern, swishing fronds that splattered us with mud and through soil carpeted with pine needles and decaying leaf mould. Everything was hushed in here, with only the screech of birds and the rustle of prowling animals. Here and there was the chirrup of frogs. We were climbing swiftly upward and very soon a mist came down that obscured the trees and made it essential for us to dismount from our ponies. Walking through the forest was bone aching, as we had to crouch and creep to avoid thistles and fallen branches. After many hours of this, Yin, who was leading our convoy, came to an abrupt halt. We were walking through a small clearing, which let light and air into the forest. All about was a carpet of mossy stuff, speckled with nodding flowers on delicate stems.

'We are tired,' Yin said, looking back at the parade of weary faces. 'We stop.'

Yin's transformation was such that no one thought to challenge her leadership of our expedition. Even Aunt Hilda had the sense to realise that Yin was our best guide through these mountains. Among the provisions in our saddlebags were the eels, but we had no cooking pot. How were we to cook then? I dreaded to think. I was not going to eat raw eels. I would starve rather than eat raw eels. Yin seemed to read my mind.

'Eel good.' She smiled at me.

'A rare treat,' grunted Aunt Hilda.

Waldo and Isaac went off to get firewood while the rest of us attended to the horses. Mine was a stubborn little thing, that I had named Orchid. She had something of the Empress Yehonala about her, with her queenly air. I fed her some leaves and gave her a glug of water. She was glad of a rest, as was I, for my thighs ached. Yin was hard at work. She grubbed under a tree trunk, pulling out a gnarled root, which she chopped into thin slices. By the time the boys had built a small fire, Yin had foraged several things, which she lay by the fire. A bunch of large green leaves, a handful of berries, even some sap. Curiously she had also collected a large lump of fresh mud.

'Do you have a plan?' Rachel asked, nodding towards the glistening eel heap.

'Yes.'

'Good. Because frankly, Yin, I'm already feeling a little sick.'

Smiling, Yin picked up a handful of the eels, wrapped some large leaves around them while they wriggled in her grasp and dropped in a few roots and berries. Then she moulded a thin layer of mud around the leaves and dried the package out in front of the fire. When it was dry and the eels had stopped squirming, she added another layer of mud, this time a thick one. She patted it firm and then dried it out by the fire, which by now had burned down to glowing embers. Then, using a stout stick, she created a hole in the ash and embers and buried the clay package.

Waldo and Isaac created another two other similar packages, while Aunt Hilda shouted out orders and encouragement. These two were also buried in the embers, along with the original package. We waited for the end result impatiently. I must say I was dubious. Muddy eel didn't sound much better than raw eel. After some time Yin removed the clay packages from the embers using her stick. They came out baked solid. She cracked the parcels open and there inside were the steaming eels. Amazingly, the eel's silvery skin had stuck to the baked mud, leaving the juicy pink innards for us.

I find it hard to admit this, but even in my sickness, the baked eel smelt good. Yin divided them up and we ate on large leaves – our only plates. It was tasty – delicious, even – pungent with the flavours of woodsmoke, juniper berries and forest.

'Mmm,' Rachel burst out, surprising me. 'This is the best meal I've ever had.'

Yin was beaming with pride, watching like a mother

lion as we were revived by the baked eel. It took several minutes for me to notice something. *She* wasn't eating.

'What's the matter with it?' Aunt Hilda barked at the girl, for she had caught my train of thought.

Yin, who was sitting very upright some distance from us, her back resting against a towering spruce tree, shook her head.

'Why don't you eat, child?' Aunt Hilda pressed.

For answer Yin took a bun out of her bag and began to slowly chew. Of course, more dumplings! Probably made of vegetarian tofu. Her face wore a distant look – and even Aunt Hilda knew not to badger her.

While the others were eating I wandered off into the forest to find a quiet spot. I was gone some time, returning through a screen of broad-leaved bushes. I caught my name and instinctively stilled my footsteps. Rachel had gone over to join Yin. They were talking about me. They couldn't see me, but I could see them clearly through the mist of leaves.

'You must be able to see *something*.' Rachel said. 'Anything? Is Kit going to be all right? Please.'

Yin didn't reply, but the look on her face made me choke. I leaned against a tree for an instant and then emerged out of the shrubs. They both jumped up – guiltily almost. But what had they to feel guilty about? It was not their fault.

It was time to move on. Yin insisted we stamp down the embers of our fire and cover it with dirt and leaves. She didn't want to leave any traces for possible pursuers, she explained. She expected the Bannermen to follow us here, up into the mountains.

We made good progress for the rest of the day. We strode, leading our horses by their reins, tramping ever upwards, the mountain peaks above us, always out of reach. As we went, the trees thinned out a little and the vegetation became more sparse. This was a vast forest and we were still surrounded on all sides by whispering trees.

Though bone weary and famished, our hearts beat a little more easily as the day ended. We had outrun the soldiers and our path through this dense and misty forest would be impossible to track. The crickets came out, their chirping accompanying our footfalls. Just as the sun was sinking behind the mountains and we were thinking about making camp for the night, Yin put her finger to her lips and hushed us. We all froze, dark blurs against tree and creeper.

'What is it?' Aunt Hilda demanded, glaring at Yin. 'Be precise, girl.'

But Yin was still. Then we all heard it.

Clinking.

Easy to overlook, but once you heard it, the sound

settled into a rhythm. It was definitely a man-made noise, distinct from the murmur of trees, the scurry of small animals, the squawk and screech of birds. It was a light clank of metal. The chink of bridle and stirrup. Was it my imagination or did I see a flash of yellow below us? Flickering down there through the trees. It must have been my mind, for in truth the mist was so dense we couldn't see trunks, let alone the Imperial soldiers.

Aunt Hilda spoke for us all.

'Drat it!' she swore. 'Bannermen!'

❧ Chapter Twenty-seven ❧

I gave thanks for the mountains. They were so thickly forested, so full of fog and creepers, that finding us would be impossible. It was as if they were on our side.

'We're going to be all right,' said Waldo, putting my thoughts into words. 'They won't catch us.'

Yin said nothing. Was very still.

'How can they find us?' I argued. 'These trees and fog and—'

'Listen,' she cut me off. 'The soldiers have tracker. You know what is this? Tracker?'

'You mean someone who finds things?' Waldo asked.

Yin nodded. 'This tracker, he can pick up a scent more quickly than a dog. He can read just by looking at the moss, who has gone and where. He will know people came this way, with horses. We cannot fool.'

Aunt Hilda squared her shoulders and drew out her pistol from the holster at her waist. She looked very plucky standing against these ancient trees, the battle-light in her eyes.

'To arms,' she declared. 'Always preferred to meet the enemy head on myself.'

She turned to me, gesturing with the butt of her gun. 'Kit, you go off into the woods there. Take Rachel, Isaac and Yin with you. Climb up a tree or something and keep your head down. Girls aren't much good in a fight and, well, I don't think Isaac has much stomach for the battle.'

'I'll keep a lookout,' Isaac stuttered.

'Provide strategic support,' Rachel interrupted, with a smile.

'Yup, that's it.'

Waldo had drawn out his pistol and taken his place next to my aunt. 'They only have old muskets and bows and arrows, anyway,' he declared. 'We can beat them.'

'I'll stay and fight,' I said quietly.

'Not on my life,' Waldo said.

'This is no time for heroics,' Aunt Hilda added, striking a ferocious pose with her pistol.

I stared at them both coldly. 'You can't stop me. If I have to die, I might as well go out with a bang.'

'Poppycock!' Aunt Hilda snapped. 'Cripples just get in the way on the battlefield.'

'Besides, you're not much of a fighter!' Waldo added. 'You've always been a bit deluded about that. Should have spent more time on—'

I was furious now. 'I'm staying,' I spat. 'You can't—'

'Wait!' Yin interrupted. Such was her authority that we all fell silent.

'Please, it is important you listen me now. No one is going to fight. It will not go well if fight now. Listen and we can trick these soldiers.'

Instantly everyone was listening, suddenly shamed by her soft voice into abandoning our petty differences.

'I know these mountains. I will take my horse down. I will distract the tracker and his party and make them follow me. Then I will lead them into a place where they will be trapped.'

'You'd be signing your own death sentence,' Rachel gasped.

'It's a suicidal plan,' Isaac agreed.

'Please. Listen to me. This is only way. The whole army will not follow me. Only tracker. We must save lives and also to protect our spirit for the way is hard.'

'How will you find us?' asked Aunt Hilda. 'I mean after you've dealt with the tracker. I trust you, Yin. I'm trusting you to do what you say.'

I flashed a look at Aunt Hilda. She was very quick to sacrifice someone else's life, I noticed. But Yin didn't seem to mind. She smiled, her face warm. It was rare to see her smile; it made you feel as if she meant it.

'Follow like you are going. Up, up and up. In one day of hard climbing, always with the peak of Songshan mountain before, you will come to a white rock. This is white dragon rock. There I will meet you.' Yin paused. 'There is two thing more.'

'What?' Aunt Hilda grunted.

'First, you must tread very light, always making sure to leave no track.'

'And?'

'You must let horses go.'

'How the hell do you expect me to carry all this,' Aunt Hilda gestured to the saddlebags of food and blankets. 'What's the point anyway?'

'We must let horses go,' Yin replied gently. 'We must send them down the mountain. It will confuse tracker.'

Waldo was already removing provisions from his mount, a stocky pony with sandy tail and mane. He hefted the bag over his shoulder and gave the pony a sharp prod. It didn't move, just moved closer to my friend and whinnied at him. It wanted food. Exasperated Waldo leaned down and picked up a stick. He gave the horse a gentle thwack on its flank, shooing it down the hill. Still the stubborn beast refused to go. Finally Waldo had to give it a sound whack before it went trotting down the hill, trampling the undergrowth as it went. I could see he felt forlorn as he watched the horse disappear into the mist – like me he had formed a bond with his doughty little steed.

'What will she eat?' Rachel asked as we watched the horse go.

'You must not worry,' Yin said. 'These horse live on the steppes in Mongolia. Very hard life. They know how find food.'

'But there may be wolves in these mountains. Bears . . .' Rachel persisted.

'Not worry.'

Isaac was already prodding his horse downhill and Aunt Hilda did the same. It was a sad goodbye. Finally Rachel let her horse go. I could see by her white face and the tears welling up in her eyes how painful she found it. But I held onto my reins. I wasn't about to let my horse go. I had another plan.

Yin was already turning off, plunging into a thicket of trees and creepers, spurring her reluctant pony ahead of her. Everyone was willing to let her go, everyone except me.

'I'm coming with you,' I said.

Yin stopped and looked over her shoulder at me. For a moment there was stunned silence as everyone took in my words.

Then Waldo burst out, 'Do you want to die?'

'No . . . it's just—' I began but he cut me off.

'You go sticking your head into every noose, you'll be dead any day now.'

'Don't even try to change my mind,' I said, clenching my teeth. 'I'm going with Yin. No one is going to stop me. No one!'

'I stopped trying to change your mind ages ago,' Waldo said, turning his back on me.

My friends knew me in this mood. They knew how hard I am to dislodge once my mind is set on something. It was even harder to change me with the poison running through my veins, distorting everything, making me reckless whether I lived or died. But I think they would still have tried to stop me, except for Yin.

Bowing her head, Yin murmured, 'Kit will come with me.'

My friends protested but the Chinese girl was unmoving. 'I need Kit's help,' she said.

'I'll help you, Yin.' Waldo walked up to me and tried to shove me off my horse. My Orchid reared back, lashing out with her front hooves.

'I must have Kit,' Yin replied.

Without another word, I pulled my pony forward and followed Yin into the grey mist. I felt a pang as I turned back and saw their faces, some furious, others bewildered and sad. Perhaps Waldo was right, perhaps I did want to die. Anyway, there was no point in dragging things out; this was the cleanest way to say goodbye.

❧ Chapter Twenty-eight ❧

We tramped on for several hours, climbing into the gloaming. Night fell, a darkness of hooting owls and scurrying creatures. The wolves were circling. Who knew what other predators would be drawn by our scent? It was chill up here. The lack of oxygen intensified my floating feeling and distanced me from the pain in my ankles and calves. I felt as if the top of my head was coming off. We moved very slowly, feeling our way, led by our horses' instincts. Once the moon came out, luminous and three-quarters full, it was easier to see. The stars were bright up here, the heavens close.

Yin's face was expressionless in the moonlight. Her wide eyes were empty. I couldn't tell what she was thinking. It was strange, the faith I placed in this tiny girl. My feelings for her had come full circle. She came up to my shoulder but I trusted her with everything, with my friends' lives and my own destiny.

Partly I think it was because she *knew*. This knowing wasn't a matter of seeing the future, more of sympathy.

Alone of my friends she understood the thing that had gripped me. How petty and pointless everything seemed to me. Yin knew. But unlike the others she didn't nag or try to talk me out of my despair. She simply let me be.

So I followed her into the night. Followed her wherever she chose to take me. If Yin let me down, I would be lost up here in this wild place. I did not think she would. Honour meant more to her than almost anything else. We had saved her from the cruel doctor; she owed us a debt of gratitude. A gulf of suspicion existed between the Chinese and the English. We saw Orientals as sly and inscrutable and made nasty remarks about their yellow skin (which was far from yellow, by the way). They saw us as red-faced, big-nosed barbarians who lacked refinement. Both sides held deeply unpleasant views about the other. Yin and I however had bridged the gap.

But deep down it was simpler than that. I liked her. She liked *me*.

We were friends.

I felt a cool hand grasping my own – Yin's tiny frozen fingers. I realised I had come to an abrupt halt and was staring at the moon.

'You need rest?' my friend asked.

'We'll go on.'

Yin smiled. She had smiled at least twice today, a record. 'The poison – it hurts your head?'

I shrugged. Somehow I didn't mind it when Yin talked of the poison, though I prickled when I saw my other friends' pity. Perhaps it was because she was so matter-of-fact about it.

'Very well. We will rest.'

'What about the tracker?' I asked. 'Will they follow us through the night?'

'I do not know,' Yin replied. 'It is harder to read the signs in the dark. But a very good tracker, he knows.'

'Then we should go on.'

'No. A few hours' sleep, then we will move.'

We tethered the horses to a stout tree and Yin unrolled two thin blankets from her saddlebag. I draped one around my shoulders. I wasn't really expecting food but Yin produced a couple of dumplings from her bags. We chewed in companionable silence. I could have been eating sawdust, so little did I notice the food. I gathered my courage to ask something that had been bothering me for days. There was a quality about this tiny girl that set her apart and made me reluctant to appear rash or foolish.

'Yin.'

'Yes?'

'How do you feel about the Book? The Book of Bones, I mean. I know you've said you'll help us steal it. But I wondered if it bothered you. You know, I understand that it's sacred to the temple and, well . . .' I came to a halt, stumbling over my words.

'I will do what I must,' Yin replied.

'What does that mean?' I asked, staring at her small, pinched face, which gave me no clues.

'It is simple, Kit. You are my friend. I must save you.'

I was silent for a moment, thinking over what she said. Then, 'I heard you . . . talking to Rachel. I'm going to die – aren't I?'

Yin looked at me. Part of me was desperate. I wanted her to jump up and down. To deny what I had said. Another part didn't really care. 'The future is not certain.'

'What does *that* mean?'

'I can see one path, Kit. One way through the future. But chance may offer others . . . There is always hope.'

I stared hard at her. 'I don't really mind, you know.'

'I understand this.'

'The way I figure it is that if I die – it'll give my friends a chance. Don't you see that, Yin? It'll release them from the Baker Brothers' trap. They won't have to find the Book of Bones. They'll be free to—'

'Quiet now. It is not time for thinking. Sleep. We have so little time for rest.' With that Yin closed her eyes, her whole body relaxing against the tree trunk. Within seconds she was asleep. I thought I wouldn't be able to sleep, I was so cold, so full of sickness and despair. You see, I understood what Yin had told me. She had foreseen my death. There was no way out from the poison creeping through my veins. I thought for a moment of the Bakers' dog. What was his name? Pippin, that was it. Just as there had been no reprieve for Pippin, there would be none for me.

But I must have been tired for within minutes I was slumbering. My sleep was full of dark shapes, which loomed all around me but meant nothing. They seemed like men but moved with a jerky, mechanical gait. There was menace in their thick limbs and round, featureless faces. When I woke up, Yin's eyes were boring into me and she was shaking me by the shoulder. Dawn was breaking over the trees, a pink flag unfurling in the dark sky.

'We must move, Kit. The soldiers are close.'

'How do you know?' I asked, scrambling up. I couldn't hear anything or see any signs of our pursuers.

'There are at least three men chasing,' she replied. 'It mean our trick worked.'

I saw that Yin had already fed and watered the horses and packed up all our belongings, except my bedding. I quickly rolled up my blanket and gave it to her and we set off. I followed the girl blindly, trusting that she had some plan. We galloped down, off the other side of the mountain and now I saw that we were coming to a sort of plateau. It was a small featureless plain dotted with greenery and low-lying shrubs. Yin dismounted and I did the same, following her lead. As we came out of the forest to the edge of the area I could hear the distant sounds of pursuit. Panting horses, trampling and whinnying. The tracker would be here within minutes.

'Shouldn't we be riding, Yin?' I called.

The girl ignored me, hurrying on, pulling her horse firmly by the reins.

Was she insane? In the forest we were shielded by trees, but out here in this flat stretch of land we would be sitting ducks. Our pursuers would be able to pick us off easily.

'Yin!'

She half turned – her face shining with confidence. 'You must follow very careful.' Yin called. 'This is a what you call it? Land of water?'

'Land of water?'

'Yes. Everywhere. You sink in mud.'

'A bog?' I gasped.

'Bog,' she agreed. 'One wrong step and you will sink. Horse will sink. Mud will suck you and you cannot come out. Come, follow me. But take care only go where I go.'

Swift and deft, Yin led the way. I hastened after her. She carefully directed her pony in front of her, herding it with a large staff she had picked up in the forest. With

242

no stick, I had more difficulty controlling my horse. We were about a quarter way across the bog when I heard calling and half turning saw three men emerging from the trees. They were dressed in the uniform of the Manchu Bannermen. A pigtailed young man with a long moustache was leading them. The men looked fearsome, festooned with bows and arrows, daggers and swords. They must have guns too, I thought, my heart beating.

'Don't look,' Yin hissed. 'Hurry!'

She was now scurrying in front of her horse, dragging it along. My moment's inattention had been fatal. My pony had stumbled off course and one of its legs was sinking, slowly being pulled into the mud.

'Yin!' I called in panic.

Already the mud was up to Orchid's knee. She was struggling wildly, whinnying as she tried to pull herself out. Her bulging white eyes were frantic with fear. Her whole flank was overbalancing towards the bog.

Yin turned around and with one look took the situation in. For a moment my courage failed as I feared she was going to tell me to leave my trapped animal. Thank goodness her heart prevailed. With two steps Yin was at my side and was pushing with all her might at Orchid's flank. Her help made all the difference. Her calm murmuring cooled down my pony and enabled us to lift her hoof out of the mud.

It was a close thing and we had lost valuable time, for I could now see that the soldiers were on the edge of the bog. I felt a pang of pity for the soldiers. They would fall in like Orchid. Being slowly drowned in mud was a foul death.

'Do not fear,' said Yin as we saw the soldiers hastening towards us. 'They will be trapped but not—'

Her words were cut off by an arrow that whistled over my shoulder, skimming the top of her hair.

'Quick!' She turned and was off. I followed as quickly as I could. More arrows were pelting towards us, then poor Orchid gave a howl of pain. A feathery shaft had sped by me and pierced her flank. Blood dripped down her hide, but we could not stop. Not for a second. Though it hurt me to do it, I slapped her ferociously, urging her onward. If we stopped they would cut us down.

As Orchid stumbled on I risked a fleeting glance at our enemy. They were flying towards us, skimming over the surface of the bog like dragonflies. The tracker led the way, yellow flags streaming from his fur hat. Blood pounded in my ears as I realised what this meant. Yin's plan was not working. The tracker knew the path through the bog.

'Yin,' I called, 'they know the way.'

My friend stopped and glanced backwards. The horror I saw in her eyes showed she had never expected this. She

244

had always told me that she couldn't accurately foresee the future. Her visions were mischievous and came to her only in brief, obscure flashes. Well, here was proof.

'Follow!' Yin growled, her eyes blazing and voice ferocious.

She veered to the left, making for a large boulder that stood in the middle of the marsh, fringed by feathery bushes. The path was even thinner here. At every step I felt the clutch of the mud, willing me to fall so it could suck me into the underworld. I held on, I think, more by luck than skill, Orchid just surviving too. The mist of last night had been burned away. The sun was straight overhead, lighting the scene without mercy. As we reached a spar of land about ten feet wide and surrounded by bog on all sides, Yin bounded ahead. She crouched in the shadow of the rock. I reached her a second later, knowing this was it. We had no chance. We would be cut down here, cut down and slaughtered.

Well, this was what I had volunteered for. Death approached in the shape of three Bannermen. It was time to be strong, for Waldo's sake, for the sake of all my friends. It wasn't time to indulge in regret. I could only hope it was swift – and that they took pity on Yin. I had to meet this with courage.

Yin glanced up, calm. 'We fight.'

'What?!'

'*I* fight,' she corrected herself.

'We have no weapons.'

Her eyes held mine steadily. 'We have me.'

'*You?!*'

'Yes, me.'

'But Yin –' I began, then, unable to go on, stopped. How deluded was Yin if she thought *she* could take on three trained Bannermen?

'If we can't run we must fight,' the mad girl said.

❧ Chapter Twenty-nine ❧

Seconds later the men came round the bend. The tracker, with the long pigtail and moustache, was ahead of his two men. He fingered his sabre and slowly looked us over. It was an odd moment of suspense. There was no shouting or firing of weapons, just a lazy appraisal of us – two girls crouching in the shadow of a rock. So calm was the atmosphere that our ponies were unaware of the tension as they chewed on the bushes.

Yin surprised me. She rose from the rock and very slowly bowed down before the soldiers, beating her head on the ground. What was she doing? Then I understood. This was Yin, I told myself. The Chinese were an oddly formal people. Even in the eye of death it was vital to maintain good manners.

Rising slowly from her bow, Yin spoke and the tracker replied. They exchanged several remarks in a language I didn't understand and the tracker began to smile in amusement. Behind him his two companions were chuckling. The two figures faced each other. Yin, no

more than four foot tall and the lithe, muscular tracker
– a grown man. A ferocious Tartar of six foot or more.
Unbelievably it looked as if they planned to do battle.

'Yin,' I hissed as my friend raised her left arm above
her face, 'what are you playing at?'

'Kung Fu,' she murmured, her eyes never leaving the
tracker's face. 'Stand like a Pine, Sit like a Bell, Move like
Lightning, Walk like the Wind.'

'Soft as Cotton, Light as Swallow, Hard as Steel,' the
tracker replied in Mandarin – at least I think these were
his words, for I remembered them vaguely from the
Forbidden City.

I sank back against the rock, my legs turning to jelly.
The tracker and Yin slowly began circling each other,
their steps formal. It was like the early stages of a waltz.

'You're no fighter,' I cried out, but even as the words
left my lips I doubted their truth.

Swift as lightning, the tracker broke the dance,
slashing at Yin with his right hand. Fast as the wind, she
parried the blow, raising her left hand to her face. The
next moves passed in a blur, with the tracker attacking
and Yin defending. Punch after punch, to abdomen, solar
plexus and throat. She hit back, swift and sure, moving
so fast I could scarcely follow her small figure. No doubt
she was getting the worst of it, because even though she
was fast she was small and frail.

Or was she?

Small for sure. But maybe Yin was not as frail as I feared. The tracker raised his hand in a claw-like movement that made me think of a crane rearing its head. Yin chose that moment to parry, charging at him with feet flying in the air. He caught her ankle and for a moment it looked over for my friend. But she pulled out her foot, back-flipped and then somersaulted right over the tracker, catching him in the back with all the force of her small body. And something more, some concentrated fire, for the tracker fell down heavily, landing on his face in the rocks. Yin advanced on the fallen man. His soldiers grew agitated and I saw one of them reach out for his sabre.

But the tracker was rising from the ground, the left side of his face heavily bruised. Rage was glittering in his eyes. He had been made to look a fool – and by a child. He gestured for his man to put away his sabre and pulled something from his belt – a cruel pike with a lethal pointed end.

'Hai!' the tracker bellowed, bearing down on Yin.

I didn't see her do it, but she must have picked up her staff because there it was in her hands. A piece of wood against a lethal weapon.

The tracker struck her with his pike and she retaliated with her staff, cutting it off. Crack, crack, crack, their sticks met mid-air, a dizzying blur of sounds and movements. A swipe of the tracker's pike at Yin's blue cotton jacket slashed it open from shoulder to elbow. My heart stopped. Blood dripped from a scratch on her skinny upper arm. 'Hai!' the tracker shouted in triumph. Yin hardly noticed the injury. She shrugged off the torn material and was grasping her staff again.

Pain makes me lose my head, makes my vision blur and anger rise up like mist before my eyes. I'd seen this happen to the tracker when he fell into the mud. Not so Yin. She shook off her wound and moved with the same cool deliberation as before. Flick, flick, flick went her staff, meeting her opponent's pike. But she was unlucky. The tracker feinted left, drawing Yin's eye. For an instant her attention was distracted and the tracker pounced. With a sudden stroke he disarmed her, sending the staff flying till it thumped down at my feet. Yin backed away and the tracker advanced, grinning.

I picked up the staff and sent it flying clumsily back to my friend. She caught it mid-air, moving like lightning. She thrust her staff behind his pike and flicked it away. In a second the tables had turned. His pike spiralled into the air, a shimmer of wood and steel. Yin dropped her staff. The tracker and the girl both rose to catch the pike. She hadn't a hope. He was taller than her. But while I was still thinking this, Yin soared up and grasped the pike as it fell downward. She held it firmly and pushed the tracker back, the spike held against his chest. His fellows were calling now, and one notched an arrow into his bow. Yin stabbed the tracker in the chest. He fell to the ground, screaming, blood splashed across his tunic. With a single movement, her pike snickering and flashing in the sunlight, Yin pushed the other men off the edge of the land and into the bog. The one who was trying to shoot his bow clutched at a rock, his hands scrabbling for purchase. She caught the bow and sent it whirling away into the bog. The other was looking at this small girl as if she was a demon, naked fear in his bulging eyes. He was clutching and clawing at his companion.

Yin was already spurring her pony away from the shrub, herding it back in the direction we had come from. I stood stock still, frozen in shock, staring at the grasping, wailing men with their piteous, contorted features begging me for mercy. I had come here to die – and instead this.

I realised now, with the smell of blood in my nostrils, that I didn't want to die. Not really. If, as Yin said, there was hope, I wanted to grasp it. But still less did I want to condemn others to a terrible end.

'We can't leave them. They'll be sucked down in the bog.'

'Follow quick,' Yin replied, over her shoulder. 'Now.'

'It's not right.'

'They will not die here. The mud in this rock is not deep enough. In an hour, maybe less, the rest of the army will save them.'

Without a second glance she was gone. I followed in her wake, hoping she was right. If Yin was wrong the fate that awaited the soldiers was horrible. Their screams followed us as we went down the narrow path through the bog. At the fork where we had taken the detour to the boulder, we turned left, walking away from the forest. I couldn't begin to understand Yin. Just as I couldn't understand China. I had never before encountered such calm, almost detached, ferocity.

It was a sop to my weak English soul that just as we were out of sight of the soldiers – traversing the plain – Yin suddenly froze.

'Have no fear, Kit,' she murmured. 'The soldiers are rescued. The army is here.'

I could see black dots moving through the landscape of sedge, bush and bog, coming from the direction of the forest. Was that a cry I heard magnified by the wind? I couldn't be sure, but relief lightened my step. Then I stiffened.

'That means they'll find us again.' I said. 'It was all for nothing.'

'Maybe,' Yin replied. 'We must ride fast to your aunt. I pray that without the tracker the army will be blind.'

It was too much for me. The soldiers, the bog, the savagery of the Kung Fu fight. I could smell the blood, hot in the marshy air. Bile rose in the back of my throat. I was going to be sick.

'I wish I'd never come,' the words were out of my mouth before I had time to bite them back.

Yin turned to look at me, surprised. 'If you were not here, I would be dead.'

'What do you mean?'

'You gave me back my stick. You saved my life.'

❧ Chapter Thirty ☙

China is full of wonderful surprises. Delicate bridges that seem to defy the laws of gravity, porcelain pagodas like lotuses in the sky. Here was another: a rock. This boulder, carved into a wonderful dragon shape, was so white it was almost translucent. We saw it from far off in the forest and my heart did a somersault. I understood now that I had never been ready to say goodbye. I had no desire to be a human sacrifice. Somehow we would *all* get through this. But as we neared our rendezvous, there was no sign of my friends. No grumpy, stocky aunt. No glowering Waldo, fatigued Rachel or irritated Isaac.

'They will come,' Yin dismounted from her pony and walking over to Orchid patted her flank. 'Take sleep while we wait.'

I was grateful for her advice. My head was light, spinning from the Kung Fu. Along with the nausea that dogged me night and day, there was the taste of blood in the back of my throat. I kept seeing the crimson spurt on the tracker's tunic.

I must have fallen into a deep sleep nestled against the hard shoulder of the dragon rock. When I woke up Aunt Hilda was glaring at me, red-faced.

'Sick or not, this is no time for forty winks,' she boomed as I opened bleary eyes. 'What with a whole regiment of the Chinese army on our tail.'

Waldo, Rachel and Isaac were clustered behind her, weighed down by saddlebags and baskets. They were dust-stained, their clothes ripped by thorns, but very much flesh and blood. As my aunt's hectoring voice went on and on I stood up and threw my arms around her, squeezing her ferociously. She hugged me back, her eyes looking suspiciously tearful.

'We should never have let you go,' she grunted.

'You didn't *let* me go.'

'Obviously she didn't need our permission,' Waldo muttered, as I tried to struggle out of my aunt's grip. She would not release me. 'Kit is bloody-minded enough to tackle the entire army.'

'We must put all our bags on horses,' Yin said, relieving Rachel of a cotton bag and loading it onto Orchid. 'Come. We must waste no time.'

I could see my friends looked gloomy. I didn't know if they had eaten or rested – it was after lunchtime. But somehow Yin was now in command and no one, not even my aunt, had the nerve to contradict her orders.

We trekked down the mountain and towards a plain. The countryside was wild, with a raging snow-melt river, which had fed the bog, and sedge, bracken and fern dotted with stunted trees. Some distance from the mountain we saw black smoke rising into the sky and with a cry of alarm Yin urged us forward.

As we came closer we understood, wordlessly, the source of her distress. A graceful set of buildings with arched terracotta eaves nestled in the lap of the mountain. The buildings unfurled like many-petalled lotus flowers. Two mighty stone lions stood by a flight of stone steps leading to a brick gable and stone entrance. This was the famous Shaolin temple we had heard so much about. This was where Yin had been raised by nuns, where she had learned Kung Fu.

It took but one glance to see that something was dreadfully wrong. The thick ropes of grey smoke. The drunken gate, smashed and pulled off its hinges.

We entered the monastery, sick with apprehension. Yin led the way, swaying from side to side. As we emerged into the huge courtyard she cried out and fell. I just managed to catch her before her body hit the flagstones.

It was scene of utter devastation. In front of us were four rows of stelae, ancient stone tablets, wrought with fine inscriptions. Many were engraved with delicate calligraphy. I saw one tablet bearing the image of a fat monk in a flowing robe. I had heard of these treasures. Some were said to have been decorated by Ming and Tang emperors in centuries gone by. Many of the tablets had been toppled and smashed. Worse, the building itself had been set on fire. The magnificent wooden eaves had been destroyed and were now a smouldering heap.

Yin rose out of my arms, babbling in Mandarin, and walked in a trance. We came to a hall, room after room, with fabulous painted eaves. They were all smashed and burned with a savage indifference to their beauty. In one such hall there were statues of two monk warriors with snarling faces and bulging biceps. One of the statues had been so thoroughly destroyed that all I could see was a remnant of its blue cheeks. The other, bizarrely, had been left intact by the vandals.

There was no sense to the destruction. It was just savagery. We wandered through the temple – dining rooms, training halls, shrines. The kitchens had been thoroughly demolished, ovens battered, metal pots cracked, porcelain bowls smashed to smithereens. It was a ghostly place. Not a single monk, nun or warrior remained. In the kitchen I saw a foot poking out of the huge oven. For a moment I didn't understand. Then I realised that it was the body of a monk, perhaps one of the cooks who had stayed behind when the others fled. One of the invaders had stuffed him into the oven. I hurriedly urged Yin away from the sight. We emerged from the kitchens into the fresh air with huge relief. Bad enough was the destruction. Yin's anguish, shown only in her mute, strained face, was heartbreaking. This was her home. The Shaolin temple had meant more to her than anywhere else in the world.

'They'll rebuild it,' Aunt Hilda muttered, once we were out.

'At least the monks got away,' Waldo added.

'Most of them,' I said, before I could stop myself. Luckily no one seemed to hear.

We scurried after Yin. She strode through the grounds, avoiding our sympathy and our foolish talk. We followed her as she skirted the Pagoda Forest, with tiered stone tablets reaching to the sky. Some were elaborately carved, some simple – but all were graves. I knew that many of the monastery's abbots were buried here. We tramped after our friend, not really knowing what comfort we could offer. I couldn't rid myself of the nightmare sight of the monk's body thoughtlessly stuffed into the oven.

Out here in the gardens, soothed by birdsong, lulled by the backdrop of ice-tipped mountains, the violence seemed far away. The invaders had not destroyed trees, thank goodness. They had left the ancient sycamores, the sun-dappled willows, the regiments of pines marching straight-backed towards the hills. We passed a gate into the peony garden. An explosion of crimson, scarlet and orange with here and there the deepest velvety aquamarine. The flowers turned their petal-draped faces towards the sun, and I longed to sink to the ground among them, to forget that such destruction happened in this world for no good reason at all.

My friend was sitting on a stone bench staring at a bed of peonies. Her eyes were clouded again, wearing that look she had when we first rescued her from the Baker Brothers' doctor. Isaac, Waldo and my aunt were hovering about her. It was Rachel, with her gift for empathy, who sat down next to Yin and took her hand. It took some bravery to do this, as Yin looked so remote. But she didn't pull her hand away.

'Who did this?' Rachel asked.

Yin shrugged.

'How evil, in such a holy place,' Rachel murmured. 'I can't tell—'

'It is more than that,' Yin interrupted – looking up at us clustering around the bench. '*We* did this.'

Her words shocked us into silence. But of course they made sense. It seemed likely that the soldiers had ransacked the temple as they looked for us. Then I stopped. We had outwitted the soldiers, left them behind as we diverted the tracker. How had they got here before us?

'But,' I said, 'the soldiers are stuck halfway down the mountain.'

'The Empress has many soldiers. Another regiment came here. I think many days ago,' Yin said. 'They look for the Book of Bones.'

'The Book of Bones,' I echoed.

Aunt Hilda was rigid, suddenly very alert.

'Imperial family, soldiers, merchants, foreigners . . .' Yin shrugged. 'All seek the power in the Book. They think the Book will make them strong, powerful. They think with it they will rule the world.'

'Why now?' I burst out. 'I mean, the Book of Bones has been in the monastery for years.'

'This is what I say. I think it is from *us*,' Yin answered. 'Maybe the Empress find about Book from Mandarin Chao.'

'But he didn't know about it,' I replied. Then fell silent. Perhaps he had overheard our talk or one of his spies had. I felt guilty thinking of that gracious, hospitable nobleman. His brave son. They had saved our lives. I hoped that their reward had not been disgrace. Had he confessed our secrets under torture?

Musing on this, my eyes followed a hummingbird which hovered above Yin, tame as a pet canary. It was a tiny thing, no bigger than the span of my hand, wearing an iridescent purple jacket. For a moment I thought it was going to land on her arm, but then it swooped away, spinning above a patch of plants. We watched its beating wings, moving so fast they were a shimmering blur. It dived down, dipping its long beak into the flowers. When I lifted my eyes, a nun had materialised in front of us.

At least I think it was a woman. She was so old, so very, very old, that she was almost beyond the difference between man and woman. She was grey all over, from her spider-web robe to her hair. She was an apparition. She must be. The ghost of a nun which had appeared to us. Nothing about her looked quite real. The shining dome of skull, the cheeks covered with wrinkles as fine as calligraphy, the slender, stooping back. Marbled eyes peered through shaggy eyebrows. She could have been a thousand-year-old sculpture come to life. All things were possible in China, this ancient land with its history running back to the dawn of man.

Yin had leaped up and was kowtowing to the ground. She turned to us, her face alight.

'Grey Eyebrows,' she explained.

I fell to the ground, kowtowing. Memories of what Yin had told us about her mentor, Grey Eyebrows, flashed through my mind. She had looked after Yin when she was brought to the monastery. The others followed my example, all except Aunt Hilda, who bowed her neck rather stiffly.

'Grey Eyebrows taught me everything. Kung Fu, meditation, English,' Yin explained. I could not take my eyes off the nun. There was something uncanny about her – so thin, pale and insubstantial that she appeared to float several inches off the ground. She didn't even look like a Chinese ghost.

'You must be so proud of your pupil,' Waldo blurted out. 'Kit tells me she is a great fighter. She destroyed soldiers of the Imperial army without any sweat.'

I blushed at Waldo's remark. From what I knew of the Buddhist teachings they followed in this monastery, pride was not an emotion to be proud of – so to speak. The monks and nuns here strove to be humble. Fighting was also something to be avoided. Though the warrior monks practised Kung Fu till they were highly skilled at it, they were meant to use their only art in self-defence. Never to attack others, or use it for evil. I feared the nun, Grey Eyebrows, would give us a lecture, but she merely smiled. Then she turned and her eyes locked into mine. They bored into me, bright points of fire that scorched. The smile had disappeared. A high voice issued from her, though her mouth didn't move. Like a ventriloquist's dummy, as if someone else was speaking through her.

'I must speak the prophecy.'

'What prophecy?' Aunt Hilda butted in.

The voice continued, ignoring the interruption:

> 'The Black Snake slithers
> Around Yin and Yang,
> Man and Woman,
> Old and Young.
>
> Only one can cut the knot.
> One who rides the great sleep.
> In the land of white sun the Shaman awaits.
> Then can the fruit return to the tree.'

The shrill voice ceased abruptly, leaving us all silent. I was chilled by the tone and by the sound of the words, though I could make no sense of them. I could see the same fear on my aunt's face, all of us shocked and uncomprehending. I sneaked a look at Yin, but her eyes told me nothing. Abruptly the nun's head jerked and her eyes refocused.

The nun gestured to Yin to come with her and the two of them walked away. We watched until the two tiny figures disappeared into the bamboo grove. I think all of us were unsure how to react – and what the appearance of this nun meant for our mission.

'This is a pretty kettle of fish,' Aunt Hilda said once they'd vanished. 'What do you think all of that means?'

'Doesn't look very good for my chances, if nothing else,' I said.

'Oh, don't go getting all nervy again,' Aunt Hilda harrumphed. 'For heaven's sake. They've gone and left us. What are we supposed to do now?'

'Patience,' Waldo replied, surprisingly. 'We've got to learn patience.' He sat down on the bench and I slumped by his side. My feet were aching and my head felt woozy. 'Yin would never abandon us,' he continued. 'She said before she would meet us at the rock.'

'She kept her word that time. She will now,' Rachel agreed.

'But she never explained anything this time!' Aunt Hilda pointed out triumphantly. 'She's simply skedaddled without rhyme or reason.'

⁓⊙⁓

We waited. We collapsed on that bench and waited, till the sun began to sink in a glowing bundle. The birdsong was constant, a musical chatter. No one talked much, as we were all affected by the monastery's strange presence and the nun's enigmatic words. I thought of Shamans and white suns. At some stage Waldo and Isaac went to find our bags, which we had left tethered with the ponies at the entrance. They came back with steamed buns, which we ate washed down with warmish liquid from our water skins.

I would be lying if I didn't say we were anxious. All

of us, each in their own way, were weighed down by doubts.

When even I thought Yin had abandoned us for some mission of her own, our friend appeared. She had changed her blue cotton pyjamas for a nun's orange robe, which caught the last rays and made her appear as a blazing phantom, gliding towards us. Her head had been shaved, all the black fuzz that had so softened her features brutally cut off. The sight was a cruel reminder of the Yin we had first seen on the *Mandalay* but without those black lines scrawled all over her skull.

I rose to meet her, suppressing my dismay, but she gestured me to sit.

'We rest here tonight. Tomorrow we go.'

'But what if they come back?' Rachel shivered.

'They do not,' Yin replied with calm certainty. 'The soldiers have gone.'

'Where are we going?' I asked.

'Grey Eyebrows speaks to me. She knows why you are here. She tell me, tomorrow we go.'

This was cryptic, even for Yin. 'Go where?' Isaac asked.

'We go to real place. I have much sadness for the monastery, but Grey Eyebrows tell me that the monastery is not in the stones. It is in heart and soul of our people. So we go.'

'Where?' Aunt Hilda snapped.

'To the cave. This is where Book of Bones is hidden.'

Blood rushed to my head, pounding in my fevered brain. Tomorrow we would go. This was it. My opportunity to save myself from the Bakers' poison and the madness coursing through my own thoughts. I could feel the Book of Bones calling to me, its voice clear above the birdsong. What was this book? We knew so little about it. Yin had been reluctant to tell us more. But I felt its signal nonetheless, spreading golden warmth. It would heal me. I was sure it was a force for good. This was my last chance, and as I rose and clasped Yin's arm my hand was trembling.

'Thank you, Yin. Thank you.'

☙ Chapter Thirty-one ❧

I clung to Orchid's neck and stroked her mane, which hung down her flanks in rough hanks. She smelt of horse, smoky and moist. I would have liked nothing better than to groom her, to wash away the dirt and brush her tangled hair. Instead I had to say goodbye.

'At least you'll be safe here. Grey Eyebrows will look after you.'

I could not forget my last horse, Tara, cruelly murdered in the Himalaya mountains by agents of the Baker Brothers. Orchid nuzzled my face. Her big brown eyes looked dolefully into mine. She seemed to know we would never see each other again.

Grey Eyebrows stood on the mountain path, very calm and still. Her ash-coloured robes moved gently in the breeze. Her eyes locked with Yin's and she moved her head downward, saying goodbye. I could see no emotion, nothing that I could spot anyway, on either of their faces. But I knew they must feel this renewed parting very painfully. The older nun was the closest thing to a mother Yin had known in the monastery.

As you know, I have no mother myself. I had only dreamed of having a mother. Still, I could imagine how it felt to say goodbye after the briefest of reunions.

Taking the reins of the two China ponies, Grey Eyebrows moved off down the track leading back to the monastery. She had come halfway up the mountain, to the spot where the path split in two, to show us the way. She was going back to her wrecked home. Though the nun seemed hardly of this world, her presence had given me a sense of safety. Now she was gone.

Yin led the way up the mountainside. I followed her, silently concentrating on my feet. It was very cold this far up. There was not a single place to hide – no trees or bush on the rocky slopes. The wind howled, stinging hands and faces. Bending my head, I battled on. The further we went, the more the path dissolved. We moved slowly, finding ledges for our feet. One stumble would be fatal, for the mountainside fell cleanly to the plains, thousands of feet below. Aunt Hilda was finding it especially hard work. She is as tough as an old boot, my aunt, able to withstand desert and glacier. But she is stocky, even a little stout, and hauling all sixteen stone of herself up bare rocks is not something she found easy.

I did not want to let the others down, did not mean to be a burden even for a moment, but I was not myself. My legs were slow to obey my brain, my hands annoyingly jelly-like. My fingernails were scabbed and bleeding from scrabbling around on the rocks to find crevices to hang onto. The soles of my feet had cracked and blistered and the pain was excruciating. Worst of all was my mind. It was dizzy, floating. The lack of oxygen in the air intensified my feeling of weightlessness. The moment in the monastery garden when I had imagined I'd heard the Book of Bones calling me felt remote.

We had been climbing for several long hours before we stopped for lunch on a patch of earth, by a large red boulder. It was more steamed buns, white and gluey, along with dried fish. I had become used to the buns and scarcely noticed the taste of the dry meal. Waldo and Isaac gathered a few stunted twigs and made a brush fire so we could boil a little water. It was incredibly hard to get lit, for the wind was so strong it blew out the first flames. After much trial and error Isaac managed to get it going. I think Aunt Hilda was more of a nuisance to him than a help, for she bustled around, poking at the twigs and generally getting in the way.

Suddenly the fire exploded. A gout of red flame shot up into the sky and burst in a shower of sparks. The sparks left a trail of grey smoke in the air, directly above us. We all screamed and jumped back, not that there was much place to move in the shadow of that boulder.

'Isaac!' Rachel howled. 'This isn't the time for tricks.'

'What tricks?' Isaac yelped, his face white and shocked.

'Your mad science experiments.'

'I have no wish to attract the Bannermen!'

'Calm down,' I said quietly, and because I was ill they stopped. 'Isaac is telling the truth.'

'How do you know?' she retorted angrily.

'I just know.'

Isaac, his face grey, said, 'It must have been something in the wood.'

While the others bickered, Waldo actually did something practical, shovelling earth with his bare hands and throwing it on the glowing embers. We all followed his example and soon the fire was covered.

'We must go. Run,' Yin commanded. 'Very bad if someone sees smoke.' I knew she suspected a joke or a trick.

We hefted our bags and trudged upward, past bleak boulders and stunted scrub. My blistered feet were aching and my throat was parched. My brain followed its own circular trail of thoughts about the explosion. It could have been a piece of wood, yes, or some bizarre properties of the sand and gravel on this mountain. Or it could have been one of us. If not Isaac, then who? Aunt Hilda? She always played a deep game. I didn't really know what her motives were here in China. But why would she want the Imperial army to find us? As an English spy, she would suffer more than anyone else.

My brain was as sluggish as my body. Hardly surprising that I did not find answers.

As I trudged on, lagging behind the others on that bare mountainside, I felt as if my stuffing was leaking out. My thoughts were on the prophecy. The Black Snake. The land of the white sun. The sleeper and the fruit returning to the tree. I could make nothing of it. It sounded like gibberish. Yet I had a sense that it had meaning, some message especially for me. I rested for a moment on a ledge no bigger than a tea tray, my back pressed against the rock, my knees trembling with the pressure to keep still. Then I did it. I looked down.

'*Don't look!*' Yin had commanded at the start of our journey.

I'd scaled a cliff before. I knew the importance of keeping my energy coiled and my mind focused on the task of inching step by step upward. But here I was dawdling, gazing down.

A very strange thing happened. I didn't feel the world tilt. I didn't swoon. Instead, a gust of wind whooshed through my head, blowing away the dust. What a glorious sight – ravines tumbling, monastery and fields laid out like a patchwork quilt. I felt elated. I was a hawk soaring high over a world of mists and tiny human ink spots. I was free, with one flap of wing, I was wheeling high.

'Kit,' came the anxious cry from above, 'are you sick?'

I didn't respond for a moment, unable to place the voice.

'Do you need help?'

It was not Rachel, the worrier, but Waldo, backtracking perilously down the mountain to find out where I was.

'I'm coming,' I called back, but I do not know if my words were blown away.

He came for me, his handsome face flushed. 'Here, I'll give you a hand,' he said, grabbing my arm. I tried to brush him away but he insisted. I saw Isaac grinning away, several feet above us, and decided to submit. Sometimes it is more relaxing just to give in.

I found it much easier to scale rock and boulder. Perhaps it was Waldo's guiding hand. My fingers seemed to know where to grip, my feet where to stand. I moved up, forgetting my cracked feet. My dizziness had somehow evaporated when I looked down. I was freed by the knowledge of certain death if I fell. The sight had brushed away the self-pity that had coiled about my heart for weeks, suffocating my energy.

Within minutes Waldo and I had caught up with the others. A new sound buffeted us, adding to rushing wind. Water drumming, tumbling, falling, swishing all around us.

'We must go through Water Curtain Fall before coming to Echo Pavilion,' Yin murmured.

Turning the corner of the cliff, we had come to a magnificent waterfall, which pounded down the mountain for hundreds of yards. A fine spray whirled off the water, coating everything in mist. But a path had emerged, traversing the mountain sideways. Yin scrabbled up to it. We followed, thankful when we reached it. Though it was still treacherously slippery, it was a definite track. Other feet had trodden this way before ours.

Except that it seemed to be taking us into the heart of the waterfall. We followed Yin's darting orange form. She was like a flaming sprite, luring us on. Somehow we were passing *under* the water, which roared and pounded above us as we walked through. Suddenly we were in twilight. A wavering, aquatic world, the sunlight filtering through the falls in streaks and uncertain shafts. Yin was dappled with dark patches, striped like an orange tiger.

I had a feeling we were nearing the end of our journey.

Yin stopped and turned to us. 'We are going into the mountain,' she murmured.

'Into the mountain?'

'Yes.'

'This is where the monks are hiding?'

She didn't answer my question directly. 'It is the Shaolin way. We fight only when we have to. Other times we hide.'

'But inside the mountain?' Rachel said wonderingly.

'There are secret places here. Echo Pavilion. Wandering Nun Grotto. Tranquility Pool. Places to disappear.'

Behind Yin was an opening in the rock, a gash of raven darkness, deeper than the smoky rock all around. We would have to crouch to go into this hole, this passage to her secret world.

'Grey Eyebrows tell me the Book of Bones is hidden here,' she whispered, so low I was unsure of her words. 'But to find the Book we must go through the Wooden Men Lane.'

'The Wooden Men Lane?' I asked absent-mindedly. 'What is *that*?'

'They fight,' Yin replied, flashing me a dark look. 'The Wooden Men kill.'

I remembered that Yin had once told me about these strange creatures. The Wooden Men were larger than life-size marionettes. Blank-faced oaken puppets with giant bodies. Their fists were more powerful than sledgehammers, their feet more deadly than an elephant's. But for all their bulk, they moved with the grace and skill of Kung Fu masters. They were swift as lightning and programmed with all the thirty-six strategies of Shaolin Kung Fu.

To fight them was the ultimate test. To win, all but impossible.

✺ Chapter Thirty-two ✺

The caves were dark so we lit candles to find our way. By the flickering light, hunching a little, we trudged through a narrow tunnel. The air was close in here, with even less oxygen than on the mountainside. Water was everywhere in a constant drip, drip, drip. It seeped through the rock face like beads of perspiration on clammy skin, coating the rocks underfoot. When I touched the walls they were slimy, like dipping your hands in sheep guts. Very soon we were all panting for breath.

All except Yin. I had the feeling she didn't need the candlelight to see. She darted, bat-like, ahead of us – a dark scampering shape. She was so tiny that she didn't need to crouch, and she was fleet footed, sure of her ability to stay upright. She'd told us that she had never been to these caves before. But Yin seemed to *know* where we were going. Trusting her, we followed. We all felt this trust, even Aunt Hilda. On some level we knew it was a folly, for what was Yin but a child? She had told us she didn't know her age, but she could not have been more than eight or nine years old.

On another level she was older and wiser than any of us.

I had seen her fight. I had seen her kill the tracker. None of us would have been able to act with such calm, not even Waldo.

After some time edging through the narrowest section, the tunnel opened out into a high chamber. Not a cave, it was too large to be called a cave. The roof soared hundreds of feet above. This was a magnificent underground cathedral. A gust of wind came from nowhere and blew out our candles. We didn't need them because shafts of light came from holes high above and stippled the rocky floor with radiance. I caught my breath for there were thousands of stalactites, hanging down like rows of knives. Stalagmites poked up from the ground – these rocks were breathing. Water had dripped down through these caves for centuries; here were the results. Daggers of rock that trembled above our noses and stabbed at us through our boots. Isaac muttered something about 'carbonisation' and 'limestone formations', but his face was alight with wonder and I knew that underneath his grand words he felt as I did: these mountains were alive.

Waldo chose this moment, as we were trudging through the stalactites, to bring up my adventures in those other mountains, the Himalayas. I had never told him about my journey to Shambala, though he had poked and pried and picked up enough to know the outlines of the story. Now at last I related how I met the Baker Brothers there, and their servant, a wretched monkey-man called Jorge. The three of them had drunk from the fountain of eternal life and been reborn young and handsome. But they were cursed, their beauty destined to crumble in the world outside. Waldo was fascinated by the waters. He wanted to know why I had chosen not to drink from them and become beautiful. He was so insistent about this that I had to tell him I found his attitude offensive.

'Aren't I pretty enough for you?' I smiled, slightly menacingly.

'Don't take it that way.' He grinned. 'I'm just saying you could do with a little help.'

'Like what?'

'You know, softer cheeks, longer eyelashes, fuller mouth – a little bit more rosebud-shaped, like Emily. I must say she's got a fine pair of lips.'

'Emily?' I glared at him. 'Who or *what* is Emily?'

'Just a friend who happens to be rather good at dancing. Actually, Kit, the best improvement would be a little less anger about the eyes. Whoa! All I'm saying, Kit, is that you should have drunk those waters. You'd be close to perfect if you were just a little more feminine.'

'What about you?' I hissed. 'No, wait, I suppose you think you're already perfect?'

'You said it.'

I turned away disgusted. I didn't want to let him know that maybe some of that miraculous water had found its way into my body. My scar had vanished so quickly after all. As for all the rest of it, well, in this otherworldly place I didn't want to become distracted by petty quarrels.

While we bickered, Yin had walked ahead, picking her way through the chamber towards the pool in the centre. She stopped underneath a large stalactite and turned to us. 'Echo Pavilion,' she said.

She didn't need to repeat herself: 'Echo, Echo, Echo . . .' Her words were thrown back at her face.

Yin smiled. 'Before we go to Tranquility Pool for meet Abbot I need to tell you about Kung Fu.'

Her words were thrown back by the echoes.

'Kung Fu is an ancient system of martial arts practised in China for many centuries,' said know-it-all Isaac, interrupting the sound display.

Yin continued. 'There are two kinds of Kung Fu: internal and external. External is to about fighting, speed and power. Internal is different.' She came to a stop.

'Go on.'

'I do not know how to say this. My English.'

'Your English improves every day.'

'Speaking to you make it better.' She paused again. 'Internal Kung Fu is stillness in movement. One movement, perfect. It is about precision.'

'Precision?'

'Yes, in Shaolin Kung Fu we aim to pursue less – or even nothing.'

This was dizzying stuff. I couldn't really understand what she was saying, I'd found this before with the Buddhist monk in Tibet. Less is more. Stillness in movement. It sounded like riddles.

'In losing or not yielding one can overcome,' Yin continued. 'You must not just develop strength and power but mind/spirit. Meditation. Stillness. Gathering your "Shen". This is the true test of the Wooden Men Lane.'

I could tell that the others were as befuddled as I was. From what I did understand, Kung Fu wasn't just about strength – or about killing. More importantly it was about your internal energy. Perhaps about having a quiet soul. Buddhist monks, like the strange man we had met in the Himalayas, sit still for years on end. Their aims are the opposite of our normal striving lives: nothingness, stilling thought, getting rid of the sense of self. In a way, almost, *forgetting* who you are and the constant whirl of chatter in your head.

'Come. We meet Abbot.'

Delicately the girl picked her way to the pool. It was easy to follow her – she was an orange moth beckoning us onward. There was a figure sitting cross-legged by the waters. At first sight I had taken it for another stalagmite. A piece of whitish rock, weathered by the years and dripping waters. Motionless, permanent as this mountain. But it was a living monk. We could see his shaved skull, pale as ivory.

We came upon the figure in the wake of Yin and heard her gasp. As my eyes fell upon the monk's face, I gasped too. It was not a monk, but a nun.

Grey Eyebrows opened her eyes and looked at us, her pupils contracting until there was nothing, just honey-coloured light in flooded irises. I had the feeling that I was looking through the nun – to something beyond.

They talked, Yin and the nun. Then slowly, silently, Yin began to cry. A single fat tear fell down her cheek, splashing on her robe. I had never seen such hurting, not even when her beloved monastery was so destroyed. I kept silent, as did all the others, even Aunt Hilda. Eventually Yin looked at us and spoke.

'The Abbot is gone. Grey Eyebrows take his place. Oh, Kit, you never saw Abbot. They call him Shadowless because he move so fast the sun could not find his shadow.'

I took her cool hand. Of course I wanted to ask how

Grey Eyebrows had found her way here before us, as we had left her on the path, making her way back to the monastery. I didn't dare. It was a mystery. I was content that some mysteries I would never untangle.

'Grey Eyebrows tell me, you – yes, you, Kit – must come with me.'

'Where?' I asked.

'I tell no. But Grey Eyebrows insist it is only way.'

'Where are we going, Yin?'

Yin paused, I squeezed her hand in encouragement. 'Wooden Men Lane,' she replied at last.

Rachel screamed and Waldo stepped forward so he was standing between us, forcing me to drop Yin's hand. He towered above the Chinese girl and above me as well.

'I'll go in Kit's place,' he said, as Aunt Hilda hovered behind him. For a moment I had a weird sense that this had all happened before. Then I remembered. Waldo had wanted to accompany Yin to decoy the tracker. But this time I hadn't demanded to go with Yin.

'No. You can't come. It must be Kit alone. More people, more danger,' Yin replied calmly. 'She is the one who is poison.'

'Look at her.' His blue eyes were unusually fierce and his mouth was set in an obstinate line. 'She's half dead already. If she has to do this thing, she needs someone with her.'

'She has me.'

'No offence, Yin. But she needs someone *bigger* than you. Someone who can *fight*.'

I think, in the heat of the argument, Waldo had forgotten that Yin was a master of Shaolin Kung Fu. He hadn't seen her fight, that was why. No one who had seen Yin fight would ever forget it.

Yin stiffened, perhaps he had offended her, for she had a touchy sense of pride. I thought she was going to refuse again, to tell Waldo off. Instead her eyes flashed over to the new Abbotess, seeking advice. Grey Eyebrows didn't move, though perhaps imperceptibly her eyelids flickered. Yin bowed her head and turned to my stubborn friend.

'Waldo. Because you love Kit, yes. You come.'

Waldo blushed, colour washing over his face till he was red as a tomato. Even with all the different emotions churning around inside me, I couldn't help enjoying his embarrassment. 'Rubbish,' he muttered, looking away from Isaac's twinkling eyes. 'Kit's the most annoying person I know.'

'You true friend,' Yin talked over him, while he muttered about *putting safety first*. 'Tonight we take rest. Tomorrow we will enter the Wooden Men Lane.'

❧ Chapter Thirty-three ❧

Tomorrow we will enter the Wooden Men Lane. Those were the last words Kit was able to write.

Sadly, it has fallen to me, Waldo Bell, to take over her tale. I do so because there is no one else who can tell it. Yin is not willing. The others are too distressed. Also they were not there, in the Wooden Men Lane. As for Kit, of course she can no longer speak, or write, as you are about to discover.

Forgive me, I am jumping over myself. I'm getting ahead of the action. You do not know what befell Kit. I will have to collect my thoughts, try to calm myself so I can tell you what happened.

I'll be frank. I was nervous and a bit angry that fateful morning as we ate our steamed buns and drank sour water. I hadn't forgiven Kit for Yin's words. (By the way, I'd like to clear that matter up before we go any further. I am not in love with Kit. She is one of the most stubborn, headstrong and all-round aggravating people in this world.) Yet here I was charged with looking after her as we went into the dragon's cave, so to speak. It is all very well to say we had the little Chinese girl, Yin, with us, but she is a child. She scarce comes up to my neck and her arms are like twigs, one snap and she would break.

I know, I know. There *is* something uncanny about Yin. But appearances are sometimes deceptive. Chance can take on the illusion of fate, if you take my meaning. Kit had waxed lyrical about Yin's fighting prowess, how she had killed a tracker and disabled two other soldiers. But I was not there. The tracker was probably a spineless fellow who fell along with his men into the bog. It is much like dear Kit to embroider every tale. To give perfectly ordinary events wild and fanciful overtones.

I am much more sensible. Kit needs someone like me in her life, to keep her feet somewhere near the ground. Isaac – well, his head is in the clouds. Rachel is just a girl. As for her aunt, she is a tough nut. I've got time for Aunt Hilda. But at the end of the day I wonder if Hilda Salter really cares for anybody but Hilda Salter. Certainly her own interests always come first.

You may ask why I would take so much trouble over a *girl*? Well, I haven't really got time to go into emotional nonsense here (please wipe that smirk off your face – it isn't anything of *that* kind). You'll be wanting me to get on with the story. Suffice to say that there is *something* about Kit.

Yes, despite her pig-headedness, arrogance, inflexibility – and general ignorance of how a young lady *should* behave – there is something about Kit.

Anyway, after breakfasting, the Chinese child, Kit and I went down a passage that veered in a south-easterly direction from the large cave. These mountains were riddled with holes and tunnels, worse than Swiss cheese. I wouldn't fancy our chances of getting out of there, if we didn't have Yin to guide us. It was as dark and unpleasant as the way we had come in. Soon I noticed the girls were choking and struggling for breath. I am fitter, of course, so I could battle on a bit longer. I offered to carry Kit's water bottle and bag. I was amazed when she simply handed them over. This was highly unusual. Kit never accepts anyone's help. Seems to think acting like a *normal* girl is a sign of weakness.

That was the first warning.

After about fifteen minutes we came to the end of the tunnel. There was another of those caves with natural lighting, a small one with sunshine pouring in from the sides. Right in front of us were the sinister Wooden Men. Two massive lines of them, down the centre of the cave. There wasn't much room to wriggle round them. At first glance, frankly, I couldn't see quite what there was to get so excited about. They were big, sure, about seven or eight foot tall, massive-fisted and footed. Yes, there was something blank and unpleasant about their faces. Actually they had no faces, just empty spaces, as if they were waiting to be filled in with personalities.

Hang on a moment, I'm getting as carried away as Kit! Dear Kit. She looked very pale and was swaying, breathing scratchily. I took her arm to steady her a little. Trembling, she almost fell on me, her eyelashes fluttering. It felt good to be able to help her for once, to feel her depending on me.

Yin cast a troubled look at my friend. 'I'm going in.'

'Wait a moment, Yin. We'd better talk strategy.'

The infuriating child ignored me. I started after her, but Kit was slumping against me and I had to gently help her sit down. While I did this, Yin had already walked up to the hulking wooden figures and made a deep bow.

Something very extraordinary happened. With a great creaking and groaning, a whistling of wind like a typhoon blowing up, the Wooden Men bowed back. That's right, they bent their wooden stomachs and kowtowed, just like ordinary humans of flesh and blood.

I've seen it all, I thought. Wooden men who move like they're alive. Obviously they must be powered by some sort of engine, but *I* couldn't for the life of me see what it was. My throat seized up, the idea of having to defend Yin and Kit against those hulking monsters was appalling. Yin was so tiny, maybe she could slip under their fists. Kit was bound to get into trouble, and then what could I do?

'Waldo. You and Kit wait here. I will gesture to you like this when you can come,' Yin said over her shoulder, showing me a sign of her thumb and index finger forming a circle.

'NO!' I barked at once. 'I go first. When it's safe—'

'It must be me,' she interrupted. 'You don't know Kung Fu.'

'You'll be beaten to a pulp.'

'Stay. Do exactly as I say,' Yin gave me a look from those ill-matched eyes, then she was gone, gliding towards those monsters. I wanted to rush ahead and push her backwards, but something was working in me, forcing me back. It was as if my feet were rooted to the ground, I was *powerless* to move. I glanced at Kit, expecting her to back me, but she was hunched up, her legs crossed, almost toppling forward. More colour had drained from her face. Torn between concern for Yin and for Kit, my limbs chose that moment to seize up. Every bit of me was flooded with an odd weakness. It was as if I had just woken up from a nightmare and could not move. This has never happened to me before at a moment of crisis. So I did nothing – just watched as the Chinese girl advanced into the pit.

Yes, I, Waldo Bell, watched as a slip of a girl marched

into a den of monsters – watched and did nothing. It was my lowest point. Believe me, whatever my faults I am no coward. But at this supreme test, I was a bystander. My feet would not move. They were stuck, totally glued, by something other than fear.

As soon as Yin stepped among the Men they swung into action. I saw a blur of dark shapes, punching and kicking. They seemed to have all the space covered, thumping, crunching – their fists and legs like deadly wooden mallets.

Imagine it. A small child fighting mechanical beasts twice or even three times her size. She hunkered down, kicking, leaping, flying through the air. I don't want you to think they were mere machines – the Wooden Men could move sideways or up and down. They surprised me by the speed of their movements and their lethal attack. I don't know how Yin managed to stay alive for more than a minute. Yet she did. As I watched, my mouth hung open and sheer amazement flooded my whole being.

Her trick was having something special in her head – brains. I didn't understand how she defeated the first pair, or the second. But I saw her outwit the third. She swooped and grabbed one Man's legs, then she threw him at his opposite number. Unable to tell friend from foe, he began to batter his face. As they fought among themselves Yin flew like a swallow, swooping, diving, striking through the battery of arms and legs.

Once, she fell straight into the fists of a Wooden Man, but by back-flipping swiftly over his head and between his massive thighs she was able to evade his blow and turn her force onto him. Crunch went her fist, aimed at his knee joint; crack, and her leg gave a lightning strike at his elbow. With a massive creaking the Wooden Man began to shatter, right in the face of his opposite number, who had come flying at Yin. Too late – the girl was much swifter than him. She had already disappeared and the automaton turned his fists on his comrade instead.

I knew then that my strange paralysis at the start of this battle had not been cowardice. Yin had somehow arranged it, for I was not ready. I would have been battered to death by this blank-faced army.

Never had I seen a more dazzling display of mortal combat. This was half a fight, half a dance. You wouldn't think a fight could be beautiful, would you? But this was. Yin had told me that the men were programmed with all the thirty-six strategies of Shaolin Kung Fu. I could see now that there were a limited number of moves the men could make. The secret of Yin's success was in starting a move – then changing it halfway through to another position. She took the automatons' expectations and threw them back in their faces. I was watching a giant game of chess here, and Yin was the grandmaster.

She also knew how to attack their weak points – their joints, knees and elbows, where the different parts of these wooden puppets were attached.

Then Yin was at the end of the row of warriors. Behind her were two rows of wrecked puppets, lying in splinters and chunks of wood. Turning to me she made the O signal with her thumb and forefinger.

'Come on, Kit,' I said. 'She's calling us.'

At the end of the vanquished warriors, I spied a pedestal holding a glass casket. My heart hammered, for I was convinced that this, finally, was what we sought. The Book of Bones. We were agonisingly close to the thing that could give Kit back her life. *So close*. To get to it, all we had to do was climb over wooden guts.

'Time to go.'

Kit moaned but didn't move from her crouch.

'Don't give up on me now, Kit! We're nearly there.'

She peered at me, as if she didn't know who I was.

'Do you need my help?'

Without waiting for an answer, I took her by her shoulders and heaved. Her eyelashes were flickering, her pupils dilated. Beads of sweat bloomed on her skin, a row of them above her lips. She leaned on me and we walked through the bloodless battlefield. Kit became heavier and slower as we neared Yin. I was impatient with my friend. *Trust Kit! She would chose the very worst time to swoon on me*, I thought. Then the both of us were by the marble pedestal. Kit leaning on me, heavy as a horse.

Dust puffed from the casket as Yin opened it. I held my breath. Yin took something out. Not a precious leather-bound book, not even a faded old manuscript. They looked like a handful of old bones. The sort of animal bones you see scattered by the roadside in China, bleached by the sun.

'What is *that*?'

'The Book of Bones,' Yin replied.

'What? That's it? That's what we've been chasing all these weeks? It's not even a book, it's bones and—'

'A book, Waldo, is anything that you can read.'

'Are you trying to tell me you can read bones?'

'These aren't ordinary bones. They belong to Bodhidharma – the great mystic who founded the Shaolin temple. Look over there.' Yin pointed to the opposite wall of the cave. I could see a faint outline on the wall, like a dark shadow etched into the rock.

'That is the Bodhidharma's soul on the rocks. He sat for so many years, still as a statue in silent meditation just here, that his impression is graven on the rocks. It is a sacred place.'

I nodded, though I didn't understand how a man could sit still like that. I could see that this place had something far beyond my understanding.

'The fame of the Bodhidharma's bones has grown far and wide. Some monks can read their message.'

'So this is what they're all looking for. The Baker Brothers, the Imperial government . . . I'll be willing to bet that even Hilda Salter's spies want it!' I began to laugh. 'But it's all one great big con trick—!'

Kit gave a convulsive shudder, cutting off my laughter. I turned to look at her. She had jerked upright and was gazing at the bones in Yin's hand. I have never seen such a look on Kit's face. It was fascinated, almost greedy. Yes, that's it. She was staring at the bones as if she wanted to gobble them up.

'Can I?' she asked.

Yin nodded.

With stumbling steps Kit walked over to the casket and took something out. She held it up, where it was caught by a sunbeam from the ceiling of the cave. A skull. It was slightly broken at the apex, the eye sockets gaping. The thing seemed to glow. My alarm was growing. Kit was having some kind of fit. Bright spots stood out on her cheeks and the look in her eyes was positively lunatic.

'NO. No,' Kit whispered. She was talking to the skull. 'What can you see?'

She was silent a moment, the skull quivering in her hand. It was as if she were *listening*.

'Stop this at once,' I hissed to Yin, but she shushed me.

'You *know*. Why can't you tell me?' Kit moaned.

'Who knows?' I interrupted.

'The Shaman.'

'What Shaman? What does he know?'

'Everything,' Kit said, and turned back to the skull. 'I can't go on if I don't – please – no more! I can't—'

In the middle of her sentence, her lips stopped, her hands opened and she dropped the skull. Yin sprang to catch it, just as Kit collapsed. She lay in a heap by the base of the pedestal, all crumpled up. I crashed towards her and took her hand, gently pulling her up.

'Kit! This is no time to go all ladylike on me,' I said, trying to hide my terror.

Her hand was clammy. Her face chalky white. No pulse in her wrist. Kit was gone. Instead of Kit lay this corpse. I backed away in horror, blundering into the pedestal.

'She's dead –'

Yin was crouching over Kit, her lips closing over my friend's. Her hands worked away, pumping at Kit's chest. The kiss of life. I stood there helpless, praying she would revive my friend. If anyone could work miracles, it was Yin.

Kit's lips, when Yin came up for air, were bluish, not a flutter of breath under her nostrils.

'What happened? One moment—'

'Be still!' Yin said and moved back to Kit.

The moments ticked by, long moments.

'Yin?'

She didn't answer, but her face as she came up told me all I needed to know. Kit was gone. I sat down and sobbed. The pain in my chest was choking me.

Kit was gone. Kit was gone. Kit was gone and I had promised to look after her.

Yin was laying her flat, gently easing her limbs straight, folding her hands across her chest. She smoothed the damp hair back from her forehead. She was preparing her for her funeral. In China they hold funerals straight away to prevent the corpse from decomposing.

A shimmer of light fell on Kit's face. I looked up and there was Grey Eyebrows.

'You move her too soon,' Grey Eyebrows said to Yen. 'She walks among us still.'

Yin looked up, confused.

'Talk sense! Kit is not walking,' I choked. 'She's dead. Stone-cold dead.'

'Not dead. No. But not alive.'

'You're either one thing or the other,' I said. 'There's no such thing as in-between.'

'In-between the world of the living and the great beyond,' Grey Eyebrows replied. 'At this moment your friend listens to every word we speak, but she cannot speak herself.'

'What are you babbling on about?'

Yin smiled, the relief shining from her. 'You call it coma. This is your scientists' name for the half-life.'

Yin began to murmur in Mandarin as I considered what Grey Eyebrows had said. I did not ask why she believed Kit was still alive. The scientific part of me thought it was utter nonsense. Kit was dead. She had no pulse, no heartbeat, no breath, was cold to the touch. But I wanted to hope. She had offered me this much and I wanted to grab at it.

Grey Eyebrows retrieved the skull and returned it to the casket. She has put the genie back in the bottle, I thought, wondering if it was the skull that had harmed Kit. Grey Eyebrows placed her hand on my arm. It was burning hot.

'Your friend has a worm inside her. It lives on her, feeding on her desires. It is always hungry, this grub. It has a mouth the size of a needle's eye and a stomach the size of a mountain.'

I turned to stare at her, shaking off her hand. At this moment I did not want comfort. Besides, her words made no sense. At this awful time she was talking in riddles. 'What are you trying to say?'

'The grub always wants to eat *more* and *more*,' Grey Eyebrows replied. 'It has been bleeding your friend, sucking her energies ever since she entered the sacred place.'

'What place?'

'Shambala. It was there that the monster entered Kit's soul.'

'Shambala!' I murmured. 'But she never drank the water. She told me so!'

'Perhaps not. But just to stand there, to breathe in the magic of those waters, is enough for one so young.

'When she came close to this holy relic, the power of the bones struck at the grub. And the grub struck back. The bones sought to kill the worm. But – a fight so terrible, what mere human could survive? If she had drunk freely of the water she would be beyond anyone's help. Look, I will show you.'

The nun led the way behind the casket to the back of the cave. There, laid out on a jutting stone ledge, was a *thing*. I cannot call it a man, as it looked more like a shrivelled ape. The waxy skin surrounded by rotting wrinkles was loathsome. I looked upon the man with horror. I knew without being told that it was Jorge, the monkey-man who had entered Shambala as the Baker Brothers' servant. The ancient, grasping soul who Kit had talked of, just once, as a creature of horror.

Grey Eyebrows' voice washed over me. 'See him.'

'How did this happen?'

'He too entered Shambala, twice, to bathe in the waters of immortal life. He was warned. He knew that to desire too much – to want immortality before you are ready to give up desire – is a curse. But he was a magician and very arrogant. So he drank, and meanwhile the grub drank too. It grew fat in him, coiled like a giant slug around his heart.

'Eventually this man knew, and his masters knew too, that their immortality was a curse. He was rotting from the inside. He believed the Book of Bones would save him. Instead it destroyed him.'

'You're lying!' I shouted. 'What about the poison? The Baker Brothers poisoned Kit. They will give us the antidote as soon we give them what they want. You're only making this up to protect these mouldy old bones and to stop us from taking them back to England.'

The nun regarded me. 'You *know* this is not true.'

'But the poison. Kit was dying.'

'Those Brothers, they never poisoned Kit. It was a trick.'

'I don't understand.'

'Kit was never poisoned,' she repeated. 'The only poison inside her was the grub, the darkness from Shambala. The Bakers knew this; they used this to fool you.'

'Kit was never poisoned,' I repeated in a daze. If this was true, our whole journey to China had been a gigantic trick. The Baker Brothers had played a gruesome practical joke on us.

'I told you, the Brothers make up a story to trick you. Because these two men also drank the waters in Shambala. They too have the worm gnawing at them, making their breath decay and their skin rot. They know their time of beauty and youth is short. They think the Book of Bones can cure them! But they are scared to seek it themselves. So they send first this man, this Jorge. When he failed to steal the book, they send Kit.'

The silence hung in the air between the three of us, with Kit's slumped body behind us and the corpse of Jorge laid out on the ledge.

'So this is it, is it?' I said finally. 'This is what happens to Kit? She's left here on a ledge like . . . like that foul monkey thing . . . till her bones crumble to dust?'

'Of course not.' Grey Eyebrows frowned. 'You *must* save her.'

'How? How can I save her?' I asked. 'I'll do – anything. Anything.'

'I do not know. Just one thing – talk to her.'

'And say what?'

'What you feel.'

We reach the end of our story. We might have found it hard to make our voyage home, except for the appearance of a group of British soldiers through the ruins of the Wooden Men Lane. What were they doing there? you might wonder. The answer lies with that lady of mystery, Hilda Salter.

It was she who had set off the fireworks on the mountainside to signal to a 'Special Battalion of her Majesty's Secret Forces'. These men, with the leathery skin of the hardened traveller, were half spies and half soldiers. They came to find the Book of Bones – and as an American patriot I've never been so pleased to see English soldiers in all my life.

But as they appeared – just as suddenly did Grey Eyebrows vanish, taking the Bodhidharma's bones with her. I tell you, she vanished. One minute she was there in the dripping cave, surrounded by solid rock. The next minute both the bones *and* the nun were gone.

What an adventure, yet what disappointment at the last. There was no Book, just mouldering bones, albeit holy ones that some monks claimed to be able to read. No poison – instead a foul grub that was sucking Kit's life away. We had been cruelly tricked into pursuing a phantom goal. So our voyage to China ended in misery. We didn't even find anything of value to carry back home with us.

Hilda Salter hired a nurse to look after Kit on the steamer back to England, even though we all argued. Her aunt waved away our protests. So Mrs Dalrymple, an elderly Yorkshirewoman, plain of face and blunt of speech, came into our lives. This lady was friendly to Rachel. I think she welcomed someone to share her load. But she treated me with suspicion. It was as if she didn't believe a boy could be Kit's real friend. Often, at the beginning of the voyage, she would shoo me out of the sickroom when I came to say hello to Kit.

Remembering Grey Eyebrows' advice, I persevered.

Once I was sitting alone with Kit, having relieved Rachel of the task, when Mrs Dalrymple came in.

'What are you doing here?' she barked, peering at me through her wire-rimmed spectacles. 'It ain't right.'

'Oh, don't be so foolish,' I exploded. 'She's my friend.'

'She should have a chaperone. Alone with a boy any time of day or night!'

'It may have escaped your notice but she's unconscious. She's hardly going to start kissing me. Anyway, even when Kit was properly herself, we were hardly on kissing terms.'

'Should hope not.'

'She was more likely to give me a kick than make eyes at me.'

Mrs Dalrymple began to laugh. 'You are a funny

bunch and no mistake. I never met a queerer lot than you three.'

'You mean us *four*. There have always been four of us,' I said quietly. 'The three of us aren't much use without Kit.'

After this conversation things were easier and Mrs Dalrymple made no further objections to my presence in the sickroom. When I sat at Kit's bedside I would remember what Grey Eyebrows had said; I'd take her hand and talk to her. 'Who is this Shaman?' I would ask her, recalling her last words. 'What does he know?' Sometimes I would talk nonsense to her – the jumbled words of the prophecy continued to haunt me. What is the Black Snake? . . . Where is the land of the white sun? . . . White suns, black snakes, Yin and Yang. It was all gibberish – wasn't it? Only one thing rang true – the reference to the one 'who rides the great sleep'. Who else but Kit?

She never answered my broken questions, though she was breathing evenly now. I didn't mind. I would talk to her, tell her my plans and dreams. Things I hoped we would do together. Perhaps I wouldn't have dared to speak to the other Kit like this, she was always so sarcastic. But on that ship I opened my heart to her as I have never done to anyone before.

I thought back to that last time, our row in those

stalactite-studded tunnels. I had teased her about not being 'pretty enough' – and seen with pleasure how annoyed she had become. Now I wished I had been more honest. I had been childish to stoke her jealousy over Emily. What did I care for curls and eyelashes? What did I care for rosebud lips? There were a thousand pretty girls, but only one Kit. Why had I never told her this?

Mrs Dalrymple, Rachel and I were the main ones who looked after Kit. Aunt Hilda rarely found the time, even on a long ocean voyage she was occupied with mysterious activities. Isaac, I think, found it too distressing and would scurry away at the first opportunity. We would take it in turns to sit with her and feed her, forcing soup and pureed chicken livers down her throat. Her mouth would not open; one had to push the stuff down her gullet, where a swallowing reflex would take it to her stomach. The first few times I found this ritual hard, even revolting. But I grew used to it and took satisfaction in the fact that I was keeping her alive. Bathing Kit, dressing her, was of course undertaken by the nurse or Rachel.

Sometimes I would fancy Kit was becoming stronger, that a tinge of pink was returning to her cheeks. At other, dark moments, I saw a translucent cast to her flesh. Her skin, always delicate however much she denied it, was taking on a bluish, waxy tone.

I kept waiting for her to start to complain. 'Waldo,

you great sissy,' she'd say. 'Stop talking such rot!' Her voice would be gruff – too similar to her Aunt Hilda's for any man's comfort. But I wouldn't mind because Kit would be back and ordering me around again. There was nothing so much fun as simply refusing to fit in with her plans! We would have one of our blazing rows. She would end up telling me there was no one as pig-headed as me on the face of this earth.

She would sit up in her big brass bed. Sit up, glare at me as if I was a mere worm and call me the worst fool in the world for letting her go through that cursed Wooden Men Lane. But she never did. And so we steamed back to England.

Turn the page for an interview with Natasha Narayan, author of the Kit Salter Adventures

✑ An Interview with the Author ✑

Where do you get your ideas for Kit's adventures?
The oddest ideas pop into my head when I'm lying in
the bath or drifting off to sleep. Also from the jumble
of life: reading, chatting to friends, talking to my kids.
Everything can wind up in a story.

What's the most exciting place you've ever been to?
Ladakh, high up in the Himalayan mountains. It is
remote, thrilling, like visiting the moon. I had awful
altitude sickness on the three-day bus journey from
Kashmir, and felt even worse when I looked over the
edges of the cliffs and saw crashed cars and buses strewn
along the mountainside, looking like papier mâché
models. We were lucky to get to the capital of the tiny
country in one piece. After the rocky moonscapes on the
way, Leh was a delightful green oasis.

Have you ever found yourself in a dangerous situation like Kit?
When I was a war reporter in Georgia [near Russia] I was
once caught in an ambush. Along with two other young

journalists, I'd rented a taxi and travelled from a besieged town. We were just going over a bridge when gunmen opened fire on us. We crashed into a ditch by the side of the bridge. Bullets were whizzing around everywhere. A bad situation got even worse when the taxi driver pulled out a pistol and joined in the battle. I still don't know how we got out of there.

What did you want to be when you were a kid?
A cook, a horse-rider, or failing that a writer.

Do you know any secret martial-arts moves?
If I let you in on the secret, I'd have to eliminate you straight away. With my martial-arts moves.

What are your favourite children's books?
As a child I adored *A Wrinkle in Time* by Madeleine L'Engle and the *Children Who Lived in a Barn* by Eleanor Graham. More recently I enjoyed *The Wind Singer* by William Nicholson.

What do you enjoy most about being an author?
I love it when the writing flows easily. When it is going well, writing is a wonderful thing. I also enjoy going to schools and talking to kids.

Where do you write your books?
In my tiny study, which used to be a bathroom.

Have you ever seen a real tiger or Egyptian mummy?
I've seen real mummies in Egypt – and let me tell you there is something very exotic about descending into a pyramid and seeing a real mummy. I've also seen tiger prints in Karnataka in India. But though I rode on an elephant through the jungle, we didn't actually see a wild tiger.

Where next for Kit?
At the moment poor Kit is in a coma. If she survives it, no doubt she will soon be trapped in another scary adventure.

Kit and her friends discover the terrible power of
ancient Egypt . . .

Exciting adventures around the world!

Join Kit on an amazing journey to the lost city
of Shambala . . .

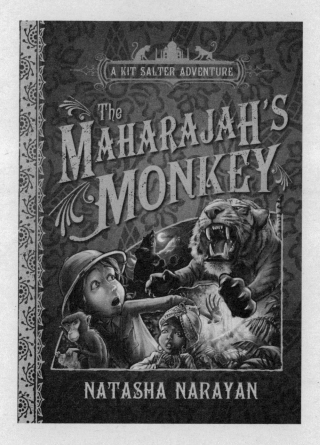

Exciting adventures around the world!

Kit Salter, adventurer extraordinaire!